SIDETRACKED

BRANDILYN COLLINS

SIDETRACKED

Sidetracked

Published by Challow Press in partnership with Christian Writers Guild Publishing

Author photo by E.A. Creative Photography
Author name logo by DogEared Design
Cover design by Dugan Design
Interior design by Katherine Lloyd, The DESK

ISBN: 0-578-13706-2
ISBN 13: 978-0-578-13706-3

PRAISE FOR SEATBELT SUSPENSE® NOVELS
BY BRANDILYN COLLINS

Dark Justice

"A nail-biting thrill ride from start to finish ... a frighteningly true-to-life scenario."
—*RT BookReviews*

Double Blind

"Collins keeps coming up with fascinating, unique plots ... Fantastic twists will keep readers guessing until the very end."

—*RT BookReviews*

Gone to Ground

"Moves along briskly. The popular novelist's talent continues to flower ... and sales will flourish."
—*Publishers Weekly*

Over the Edge

"A taut, heartbreaking thriller ... Collins is a fine writer who knows how to both horrify readers and keep them turning pages."
—*Publishers Weekly*

"Tense and dramatic ... a dense and compact narrative that holds its tension while following the protagonist in a withering battle."
—*New York Journal of Books*

Deceit

"... good storytelling and notable mystery ... an enticing read [that poses] tough questions about truth and lies, power and control, faith and forgiveness."
—*Publishers Weekly*

"Solidly constructed ... a strong and immediately likable protagonist. One of the Top 10 Inspirational Novels of 2010."
—*Booklist*

Exposure

"... a hefty dose of action and suspense with a superb conclusion."

—*RT Bookreviews*

Dark Pursuit

"Lean style and absorbing plot ... Brandilyn Collins is a master of suspense." —*CBA Retailers + Resources*

Amber Morn

"... a harrowing hostage drama ... essential reading." —*Library Journal*

Crimson Eve

"One of the Best Books of 2007 ... Top Christian suspense of the year." — *Library Journal*, starred review

Coral Moon

"A chilling mystery. Not one to be read alone at night." —*RT BOOKclub*

Violet Dawn

"... fast-paced ... interesting details of police procedure and crime scene investigation ... beautifully developed [characters] ..." —*Publishers Weekly*

Web of Lies

"A master storyteller ... Collins deftly finesses the accelerator on this knuckle-chomping ride." —*RT BOOKclub*

Dead of Night

"Collins' polished plotting sparkles ... unique word twists on the psychotic serial killer mentality. Lock your doors, pull your shades—and read this book at noon." —*RT BOOKclub*, Top Pick

Stain of Guilt

"Collins keeps the reader gasping and guessing ... artistic prose paints vivid pictures ... High marks for original plotting and superb pacing." —*RT BOOKClub*

Brink of Death

"Collins' deft hand for suspense brings on the shivers." —*RT BOOKclub*

Dread Champion

"Compelling ... plenty of intrigue and false trails." —*Publisher's Weekly*

Eyes of Elisha

"Chilling ... a confusing, twisting trail that keeps pages turning." —*Publisher's Weekly*

OTHER NOVELS BY BRANDILYN COLLINS

Dearing Family Series

That Dog Won't Hunt

Pitchin' a Fit

Stand-Alone Suspense

Dark Justice

Double Blind

Gone to Ground

Over the Edge

Deceit

Exposure

Dark Pursuit

Rayne Tour YA Series

(co-written with Amberly Collins)

Always Watching

Last Breath

Final Touch

Kanner Lake Series

Violet Dawn

Coral Moon

Crimson Eve

Amber Morn

Hidden Faces Series

Brink of Death

Stain of Guilt

Dead of Night

Web of Lies

Chelsea Adams Series

Eyes of Elisha
Dread Champion

Bradleyville Series

Cast a Road Before Me
Color the Sidewalk for Me
Capture the Wind for Me

For Delanie,
beautiful inside and out

"You keep trusting in deceitful words
that cannot help."
—JEREMIAH 7:8

April 2013

CHAPTER 1

In the beginning comes the end.

April in Redbud, Kentucky brings to full bloom the trees that give our town its name. Pink blossoms against blue sky. Daffodils push up yellow and sassy. Lilies are still in stem but boast lush promise. Tulips splash the yards, multicolored and fragile. Spring days are warm without summer's humid oppression. The time of renewal.

Spring was my favorite season. Once.

In the dark just after nine-thirty I drove away from the town's Methodist church, a white wooden building with a tall steeple. I was the last to leave Clara Ann Crenshaw's wedding shower, having stayed around to clean up. After all, I was the one who'd thrown the party for Clara. She had left a few minutes before, her car chock full of presents. The rest she'd left behind to pick up the following day. I locked them up in the church.

Clara was twenty-two, vibrant and in love with life. In love with Jerald Allen, too, who would become her husband in June. The church hall had been full of her friends, young and old. The rip of wrapping paper, laughter, and clink of forks against cake plates vibrated in the air. A true celebration. Clara wore her signature bright blue to match her sparkling eyes. Rosy-cheeked, she hugged me hard before she left. "You're next, Delanie," she whispered in my ear. "Mrs. Andrew Bradshaw."

I smiled. Andy *had* carried that look in his eye lately. I hoped I was reading him right. I was thirty-four already and so wanted to be his wife. Build my own real family—even though it would mean breaking up the pseudo one I'd gathered around me. Folks in town just knew Andy and I would be married before the year was out.

When you live in a town of twenty-five hundred, everyone assumes your business is theirs.

I drove out of the church's parking lot and rolled down quiet Chester Avenue. Streetlights spilled over the tree-lined sidewalks. No one else in sight. Redbud always shuts itself up early. At Walton Street I went left, my house about a half mile away. One block over ran Main Street—the home of quaint shops and cafes. For a small town, Redbud had built quite a local reputation on its fancy-painted store fronts. Many from around the area came to browse through the town's shops and dine in its homey restaurants.

Brewer approached. I turned onto it—and saw a shadow on the street. Faint, fleeting. Until it materialized again and went still, as if trying not to be seen. Washed pale by the umbra of a streetlamp, it looked like a man's form, wearing a baseball cap, hands raised to his chest. Legs apart, as though ready to run.

A chill needled my bones.

I slowed the car. Slid my gaze left toward the source of the shadow. He stood by a front yard bush as tall as he, backlit by the house's front porch light. I couldn't see his eyes, but I *felt* them lock onto me.

A forever second ticked by.

He swiveled and ran toward the back of the house. Disappeared into the night.

I braked to a stop. Peered into the darkness, looking for him.

He was gone.

Was this a robber? We had so little crime in our town. But this man was too out of place, too … raw. I was well acquainted with sudden trauma. Knew the feel, the smell of it. And this wasn't right.

Lights were on in the house, a form moving behind closed blinds.

I didn't know who lived there. But maybe I should knock on their door, warn them—

My eye caught some ... *thing* lying on the sidewalk three houses up.

The chill inside me crackled to ice. For the longest moment I could only stare at the object. How frighteningly familiar it looked. A silent scream wracked my head. *No, no, no!*

But deep within I knew. Death had followed me.

Heart rattling, I surged my car up close to the form. The wash of my headlights confirmed the knowledge borne of my past. A body. Crumpled on its side, facing away from the street.

I veered to the curb and shoved my car into Park. Jumped out and threw myself on my knees beside the body—and recognized the bright blue shirt. My legs went weak.

Some say memory blurs when you're shocked beyond belief. Not mine. I still remember every detail of that moment. The roughness of the sidewalk against my palms, the spill of Clara's blonde hair, the way the fingers on her one hand curled inward. A cry formed in the back of my throat but couldn't pass my clenched teeth.

The world started to go black. I fought the dizziness. Wrenched myself into a strength I didn't feel.

With reluctant hands I pushed Clara onto her back, knowing I was too late. Her eyes were open, stunned. Unmoving. I grunted out her name, laid the backs of my fingers on both sides of her neck, seeking a pulse.

Nothing.

From the light of a street lamp I could see bruises on the front of her throat.

I threw back my head, sick to the core, the world again spinning. Grief and rage surged through my veins, nearly tipping me over. I struggled to steady myself. To *think*.

Help her! Give CPR!

But it was too late for that. And I shouldn't stay here. A terrible and selfish thought, but there it was.

My wild eyes looked around and saw no one. But then I'd already seen the culprit, hadn't I? The man standing in that yard, fading into darkness.

I drew an arm across my forehead—and my gaze snagged on a car some distance up the street. *Clara's*. Sitting at the curb, driver's door hanging open, no headlights on. Why had she gotten out of it here, and in such a hurry? Her house was across town. Had she turned off the lights? Or had her attacker done that?

Vaguely, then, I heard the sound. The engine was still running.

On some other plane, my legs pushed me up. I stumbled to my car. Thrashed about in my purse, seeking my cell phone. Yanked it out. Twice my finger hit 922, and I had to erase.

Then my hand froze.

What was I *doing?* I couldn't call this in. No matter that I was innocent, had simply found Clara here. That everyone in town knew me as caring and loving.

I needed to drive away while there was still time. Let someone else find her.

My limbs shivered at the appalling idea. How dare I even think it? This was *Clara*. My good friend. So what if my carefully constructed world could come cracking apart? Wasn't it enough that I hadn't saved her? That I'd let her leave five minutes before me?

I could have stopped this.

Time staggered. Years of pain and fear and loneliness tumbled in my head. Still, despite all I'd lived through, no way could I run from this, leaving Clara here, silent and alone.

Tears came then, washing hot.

Trembling yet determined, my finger punched in the searing digits. Nine. One. One. Blurry-eyed and stricken, I clutched the phone to my ear.

As the number began to ring I prayed for Clara's family, then begged God to protect me in this. To save me.

But I'd prayed that before, years ago. Little good it had done.

CHAPTER 2

I slumped in a hard chair in an interrogation room at the Redbud Police Station, a rough green blanket over my shoulders. My body couldn't stop shivering. Bruce Melcher, Chief of Police, sat across the square table from me, recording my story and taking notes. The door to the room stood open. I had no idea what time it was. Hadn't the energy to check my watch. We must have spent at least an hour at the crime scene, Melcher and two of his officers, Hank Shire and Edna Rankle, showing up. Then the ambulance and the coroner. Not to mention people from up and down the street and blocks away as word spread. Yellow crime scene tape kept them back as Hank snapped pictures of Clara's body, the surrounding sidewalk, her car. Finally she was loaded up and carried away.

Shock set into me and numbed over my grief. Just like that a life—stopped. Everything on the brink for her now dead. All plans unraveled. My thoughts since then had been jumbled and random. Some ridiculously trite. How would Jerald Allen live through losing his fiancée? Who was the man I'd seen, and why had he done this? What would happen to the wedding shower presents?

What would happen to *me*?

I'd followed the Chief to the station in my car. By the time he sat me down I was shivering. I'd never been in the station before. Even in Redbud, where almost everyone was friendly, I avoided cops.

Especially Bruce Melcher. The man had a way about him. Macho and ego-ridden. As though the town belonged to him, and if you didn't believe it, he'd prove it to you. People in Redbud seemed to either love or hate their chief of police. Somehow he kept his position.

I needed Andy. Wanted his arms around me, his love-filled voice telling me it would be okay. He'd been in Frankfort that evening, working on one of his real estate deals. Someone was bound to call him—

"Anything else you can remember?" Melcher sat back, his round face still grim. Our chief of police was in his forties, his brown hair turning gray, hazel eyes small but keen. A stocky man with little humor. Had he ever worked a homicide before? The town hadn't seen one in over thirty years, so one of the other policemen told me. Redbud, Kentucky lay off Highway 60, eight miles northwest of Versailles and about twenty-one miles from Lexington—which saw a lot of crime. Our little town was a world apart from that city. Our townsfolk who worked in Lexington liked to come home to the quiet, the familiar sidewalks cracked from old oak trees. The safety.

They wouldn't feel safe anymore.

"Nothing else to tell." I'd related it all three times now. "Has someone called Jerald? And Clara's parents?"

"Hank went over to the Crenshaws soon as he could. Tried to beat someone else calling the family. He phoned Jerald first and asked him to be there."

I winced. What a task for Hank, such an empathetic man. As for Clara's family and fiancé, I knew the pain they would endure. The stone-cold nights and brittle days.

Up front in the station a phone rang for the dozenth time. Vaguely, I heard Edna's no-nonsense voice answer. A moment later she appeared at the threshold, receiver cupped in her hand. "It's Pete Baler, worried about Delanie. Says she's late coming home and isn't answering her cell phone, and what in tarnation is happening over on Brewer?"

Pete, my adopted grandfather. Doyen of the cobbled-together family who shared my house. I'd heard my cell ring numerous times in my purse. I should have known he'd be checking up on me. Probably had Nicole and Colleen gathered around him, just as worried.

Melcher sighed. "You want to talk to Pete?"

I shook my head. "Can you just tell him I'm here and safe? I'll be home soon." Somehow I'd have to find the energy to explain to him what happened. If he hadn't heard by then.

Edna nodded and turned away, pulling the phone back to her ear. I heard her arguing with Pete as she walked toward the front. No, she was too busy to fill in all the details for him now. No, I wasn't hurt …

I stared at the worn wooden table, wondering how I'd gotten here. Where this night might take me.

Nowhere, Delanie. This is different. You'll be fine.

The station door burst open. I heard the pound of feet, the familiar voice that made my heart surge. "Where is she?"

"Back there."

I struggled up straight, sudden tears biting my eyes. Andy's broad shoulders filled the doorway, his brown hair mussed and face blanched. He took one look at me and rushed forward, holding out his arms. I pushed up on weak legs and threw myself against his chest, the blanket falling to the floor. Sobs broke from me, deep and helpless, wetting the front of his starched shirt. I could do nothing but cling to Andy—for more reasons than he could possibly know.

"Thank God you're all right, Del. Thank God." His hand cradled the back of my head.

"Claraaaa."

"I know. I'm so sorry."

Melcher eased past us out of the room.

"Why, Andy, *why*?"

"I don't know. I'm just so sorry you're the one who found her."

So was I.

We pulled apart, Andy placing his palms on my cheeks. His deep brown eyes looked into mine, checking, assessing. Sometimes when he did that I'd think, *Surely he must see the lies there* …

He rubbed my face. "I heard you saw someone."

I nodded.

"Any idea who?"

"No."

Andy shut his eyes. "To think he got that close to you."

The station phone rang again. The front door opened and closed.

"Did he see you, Del? Enough to recognize you?"

The question froze me. Surely my car had kept me in shadow, even if I'd been near a streetlight. "Does it matter? By now the whole town's heard."

Andy looked away, his jaw moving back and forth—the expression that overtook him whenever he processed how to take care of a problem. The look mimicked his dad's in similar situations. The Bradshaws were the richest, most influential family in Redbud. They were used to fixing things.

"You should stay at my parents' house tonight." Andy squeezed my shoulder. "You'll be safe there."

"I want to go home." My relationship with Andy's parents was tenuous at best. I didn't fit their picture of the Kentucky belle their son and only child should marry. "Pete and Nicole and Colleen are waiting for me. They're worried."

"*I'm* worried." Our past discussions tinged the words. Andy never could understand my modern-day "boarding house," the eclectic trio I'd gathered around me. But then, Andy had always had family.

"I'll be fine. Besides, Pete has a gun."

"Pete's in his seventies."

"And knows how to shoot."

Melcher came back into the room, ending the conversation.

"Are you done here?" Andy's tone said he should be.

The Chief nodded. "For now. If we have more questions, Miss Miller, we'll let you know." He retrieved the green blanket from the floor and laid it on the table.

Andy picked up my purse and handed it to me. "You okay to drive?"

No. "Yes."

He turned to the Chief. "You need to find who did this *now*."

Melcher bristled. "We're working on it."

Andy stood a few inches taller than Melcher. He looked down and held the chief's gaze. "Nobody's safe until you do. Especially Delanie."

"I'm aware—"

"Especially if he thinks she can identify him."

The chief's mouth hardened. "I don't need you telling me how to do my job."

"I'm merely worried about Delanie."

"We'll do everything we can to keep her safe, Mr. Bradshaw. As well as the rest of the town."

Andy held the chief's gaze a moment longer, then nodded.

Melcher put his hands on his hips. The old cop swagger. "We're going to put the word out that she can't identify who she saw. It was a shadowed figure in the dark, that's all. Besides, that's the truth."

I managed a nod.

"Of course we still have the main issue. Whoever did this is still on the loose, and in that sense no one's safe." Melcher ran a hand across his forehead. "Mr. Bradshaw, see that she gets home. I've got a lot of other people to talk to. Won't be seeing my bed tonight."

The two men sized each other up. Andy embodied the town, all its citizens who would be pressing for a quick arrest. The chief clearly felt that stress already and wasn't about to look weak under it.

Andy slid a protective arm around me. "Let's go."

Once in our cars he waved for me to get on the road first. He would follow, watching my back.

I drove by rote, my spine not touching the seat. The night, so beautiful and full of promise a few hours ago, now hung heavy with portent. How many people lived without ever stumbling upon the body of a loved one? Now it had happened to me twice.

Was God punishing me?

Surely not this way, involving innocent Clara. But hadn't I always feared one day it would all catch up to me?

I needed to call Clara's parents. And Jerald. Tell them how sorry I was. How I wished I could have helped …

Fresh tears rolled down my face.

I turned onto my street, and soon my rambling brick house came into view. It had never looked so comforting. I pulled into the garage, Andy parking his BMW in the driveway. He followed me into the garage, making sure I closed the door. We'd barely stepped into the kitchen before Pete appeared. "She's home!" he yelled over his shoulder. Pete's voice was gravelly, his back stooped. He'd worked out West as a locomotive engineer most of his life, and his body bore the toll the stressful work had taken.

Pete hurried toward me with his hitched gait and slapped gnarled hands on my shoulders. "You all right, Del-Belle? I heard it all from Tucker, you know he lives three doors up from where you found Clara?" Pete's cheeks were red, at the least the part I could see around the unruly gray beard that spread down his neck. His small blue eyes glistened with concern. "We were so worried 'boutcha, started hearin' things 'bout somebody dead. Can't believe it's Clara, I just can't believe it."

Clara had been in our house many times.

Andy eased into the kitchen and shut the door to the garage. "Hi, Pete."

"Hi, Andy." Pete didn't take his eyes off me. "You okay, Del-Belle, are ya?"

My throat knotted. I raised my chin.

Colleen appeared, trailed by Nicole. In her mid-fifties, Colleen was big-chested and stout. Despite her odd ways she was the mother I wished I had. Always there for me, with a wise word and a soft touch. Colleen loved to run around the house in fuzzy multicolored socks that reminded me of Dr. Seuss. Her short brown hair was never quite in place, her hands always moving when she talked. At dinner she was known to take out a glass or two.

She hugged me hard. "I'm so sorry about Clara. Don't know what this world is coming to. In *our* little town."

I hugged Colleen back, even as I felt Andy's distance from the scene. He never knew quite how to fit into my "family." And they weren't quite sure what to think of him, either. Except that any future I built with Andy would mean the breaking up of our household.

Nicole was shaking as she stepped up to me. At twenty-one, she'd seen too much, lived too much. I knew what that was like. She'd lost her parents in her teens. They'd been abusive. She came to Redbud to live with her grandmother, who ended up needing Nicole's care when she became an invalid. The elderly woman died last year, leaving her house to Nicole. But Nicole needed a *home*. She needed love. I'd invited her to come live with us.

I wrapped my arms around her. "Shh, don't worry now. We'll get through this."

She shook her head. "I was *there*. I should have stayed and helped you clean up. Maybe if I'd left when Clara ..."

Faulting herself was something Nicole did well—in all circumstances. I attributed it to her difficult childhood. But Clara's murder would give her the perfect opportunity for self-blame. Hadn't I been doing the same thing?

"You couldn't have stopped this, Nicole. Any more than I could. It just ... happened."

The question was why.

Andy took charge, herding us all to sit down on the couch and chairs in our large "gathering" room. He talked with Pete about keeping his gun loaded and ready—a task Pete was more than eager to do. Andy tried to reassure Nicole, Colleen, and me, telling us to look out for each other.

"We do that already." Colleen waved a hand.

My heart pinged. Some things Andy just didn't understand. But then again—how could he?

"Well, do it more." Impatience tinged his voice. He pulled his head back, his tone lightening. "Sorry. I just ... I'm really worried."

Pete ran a hand down his beard, an old habit. "We all are."

Andy's cell phone rang. It was his mother, who'd heard what had happened. He said he was with me and would call her back. Apparently she wasn't too happy about being put off.

Phyllis and Doug Bradshaw lived on the outskirts of town in a huge Southern mansion. White pillars, long porch, and green shutters. Ancient oaks in the yard. They were of the country club set, born and bred. Phyllis stood tall and lithe, her Kentucky drawl as much a part of her as her perfectly groomed eyebrows. Her husband, a college football star, had founded a real estate company in Lexington years ago that now housed over one hundred realtors. Andy worked in that firm.

Andy slid the phone back into his pocket, shooting me a wry look. He loved his parents. He loved me. But the three of us were oil and water.

My own cell phone rang. I checked the ID, and when I saw it wasn't a policeman, didn't answer. Intermittently it went off again and again. This friend and that, surely wanting to know if I was all right. And no doubt seeking details. I didn't want to talk to any of them. At the fourth call I looked helplessly to Andy. I just wanted the world to go away.

"Babe," he said, "you don't have to feel guilty about not answering."

"I know but ... they're my friends."

"You've been through enough tonight." He took the phone from my hand and shut it down.

The five of us talked about Clara's death. Did she have any enemies? Who would want to do this? None of us could think of anyone. The Crenshaws were loved in Redbud. Townspeople had watched Clara grow up. She was one of their own.

I faded in and out of the conversation, my mind churning through pictures of death, recent and old. Ever since I came to Redbud almost five years ago, I'd met each day with a strange mix of freedom and entrapment. Both of them self-inflicted. I'd built my life here, created the family I lacked. Was on the verge of realizing my dream, if Andy asked me to marry him. Maybe then, I'd thought, I could really leave my past behind. Forever.

Now this.

I couldn't begin to sort it all out. What it meant. Why, on some cosmic level, I'd been chosen to lead a life stained with murder.

But how could I even be thinking of myself at a time like this? Clara was *dead*. Her parents and fiancé, devastated. The town, blistered and scared. Redbud was *my* town now. These were my people. Somehow I had to help them.

But a small voice inside me—a voice that sensed what was to come—whispered, *At what cost?*

CHAPTER 3

That night I slept fitfully, knotting my covers in scrabbling fists. Fear and grief warred for first place within me. I could not believe Clara was dead. I could not believe any of this.

In the morning I turned on my phone. It started ringing by six-thirty. I ignored all calls except Andy's. Told him I was okay. Which I wasn't. By the time I stumbled into the kitchen around seven, still clad in pajamas, Nicole was already seated at the table, eating her bagel and cream cheese. Breakfasts and lunches were do-it-yourself meals at our house. Dinner was a sit-down-together affair, made by me and whoever else was around to help. I knew Colleen would show up soon. Not Pete. He liked to sneak into the kitchen early, fill a mug with the strong coffee I made just for him—set the night before to go off automatically—and take it back to his room. He'd linger there until the "ladies" cleared out of the kitchen. Often he worked on his memoirs. Through his closed door I'd hear him recounting his rail-road stories into his little voice-activated tape recorder. After a few hours of that he'd head for the kitchen, where he could bang around making eggs and bacon with no one else in his way.

Nicole's eyes looked puffy. Probably no worse than mine. I gave her a somber smile. "How you doing?"

She lifted a shoulder, clearly in one of her I-don't-want-to-talk moods. Which didn't tend to be good for her.

I laid my cell phone on the counter and set about making more coffee. When I hit the power button the machine's loud bean grinder whirred on. I waited for the noise to die down. "This is Thursday. Which means you have a full load of classes, right?"

"Yeah."

Since Nicole came to live with me she'd returned to college, attending the University of Kentucky. She planned to major in business marketing.

"That's good. Gets you out of town and your mind on other things."

"But how can I think?" She put down her bagel. "How can I do anything?"

The ennui that comes after someone close to you dies. I remembered those days all too well. Now here they were again.

I pulled out a chair opposite Nicole and sat. "You do it because you have to."

Nicole looked out the kitchen window. She'd had plenty terrible days in her life. She should know how to push on. But she so easily fell into the victim mentality.

"Hey." I tapped her hand. "You know I'm not telling you to do anything I haven't done."

"I know."

Reservation coated her tone. From the stories I'd told of my past, she believed I'd lost my parents at a young age, as she had. An auto accident killed them both, I'd told her. Told everyone. But that's all Nicole knew about my hardships. In her mind, her abusive childhood loomed so much bigger, which meant I couldn't understand the extent of her pain. It was her excuse of choice when I nudged her to seize the world instead of letting it seize her.

If she only knew the truth of all I've lived through. But that was the irony of our relationship, of my relationships with everyone. Truth was everything to me. And truth was the one thing I could not give.

Still, Nicole clung to me as the mentor she longed for. And I wanted to help her all I could.

Colleen trundled in, wearing her hot pink robe, and headed straight for the coffee machine. Her bed-head hair stuck out all directions. Grief for Clara strained her face, but Colleen would not want to talk about it. "My phone's been ringing off the hook." She poured herself a cup of coffee, then headed for the refrigerator. "Everyone wanting to know what happened and how you are. Would you believe even my ex called? Like he has the right to ask me *anything*."

Colleen's jerk of a husband had divorced her six months ago, but not before tricking her into signing papers that gave him everything they owned. If I hadn't taken her in, asking for nothing more than money to cover her food, I don't know what she would have done. Now at least she had a job working at Granger's Gift Store on Main for seven hours every weekday.

"Did you talk to him?"

She snorted. "Not on your life." She pulled a box of cereal from the pantry and plopped it and the milk on the table. Fetched a bowl and spoon, and brought over her coffee. Colleen seated herself with a muffled *harrumph*. "Delanie." She pointed her spoon at me. "I think you should go shopping today. In Lexington."

"Shopping?"

"Hit fancy stores, buy yourself something nice."

"I don't even like shopping, you know that."

"What I know is, you need something to keep you occupied today. Otherwise you'll think and grieve too much. You can only clean this house so many hours a day."

"And do laundry," Nicole put in.

"And pull weeds in the garden." Colleen wagged her head.

"And go to the grocery store."

"And do all the other errands this household needs." Colleen sighed. "Okay, maybe you don't have time to go shopping. Do it anyway."

How odd, the way we talked about everyday things. While Clara was … where right now—in the morgue? I couldn't grasp it.

I looked at my hands. "Maybe I should get a job." We'd had this conversation before. With my inheritance, I didn't need to work. In fact that money had made it possible for me to pay cash for this house. I probably would be working if I didn't run the household for three people. But I didn't mind staying home, cooking for all of us and washing clothes. Made me feel useful. Not so alone. This was my family, and I wanted to take care of them.

Andy didn't understand this part of me at all. He wanted me to get out and work somewhere, learn something new. The very thought overwhelmed me. I didn't want to spend my time in some new environment. I was perfectly content in the one I'd created. Not to mention the huge problem inherent with applying for a job.

Sometimes I wondered what Andy saw in me.

My cell phone rang. I pushed up to check the ID. *Chief Melcher.* I steadied myself before picking up the phone. "Hi, this is Delanie."

"Hi." His voice sounded rough. In need of sleep. "I need you to come back down to the station."

"Now?"

"Soon as possible. I have some additional questions."

I didn't like his tone. Dread needled my gut. "I … need to get dressed."

"How soon can you get here?"

"Fifteen minutes."

"Make it ten."

The line clicked in my ear.

I hung up and tried to breathe. What had he seen in me, what had I done?

"Who's that? You're turning white." Colleen's spoon of cereal hung in mid-air.

"Chief Melcher. Gotta go down to the station." I tried to keep my voice light. Didn't work.

"Why?"

I pushed up from the table. "More questions."

"Maybe he's found something." Nicole raised her eyebrows.

Maybe he had.

Heart tripping, I threw on some clothes and minimal make-up. Combed my straight blonde hair. Tiredness clung to my face. Only thirty-four, but today I looked a lot older. In the mirror my green eyes looked back at me, full of fear. I couldn't let the chief see that. He'd wonder why.

Within half an hour of Chief Melcher's call, I was walking into the station, anxiety clawing at my chest. Why had he brought me back here so soon—I, who'd found the body? What piece of so-called evidence might already be working against me? I prayed my face wasn't giving me away, reflecting a guilt that shouldn't be there.

Melcher greeted me without preamble and led me to the small room where we'd been the previous night. "Have a seat." He gestured toward the table and took a chair on the other end. Melcher looked haggard. And weighted. Once again I sensed it—the pressure on him to solve this crime and return the town back to normal. Melcher wouldn't want to disappoint anyone. Least of all himself. He had his macho reputation to keep.

Well, let him have it. As long as he found who did this to Clara.

He rubbed his face. "You know Billy King?"

The name blazed through me, if only because the question focused on someone other than myself. "Sure." Billy went to our church. He was a tall young man in his early twenties, still living with his parents. Not quite mentally retarded, but somewhat slow. "He's a nice kid. Well, not a kid, but … Works at McDonald's."

Melcher nodded. "Afternoon to evening shift, one to nine."

In a flash I saw where this was going.

"You ever hear anything about Billy having a crush on Clara?"

I looked at the table. What if I refused to answer these questions? What if I just got up and left right now?

"Yes."

"Did he talk about it to you?"

"He talked about it to a lot of people. It was no secret."

"What did he say to you exactly?"

"Just that she's pretty." *Was* pretty. The thought hit me in the gut.

"Anything else?" Impatience tinged Melcher's voice.

"That he wanted to ask her out. I think he even did a couple times, but she gently told him no. That was before she starting dating Jerald. I think that kind of broke Billy's heart. After that he didn't talk anymore about her."

"Ever hear him make any kind of threats against her?"

"*Never.*" I looked Melcher in the eye. "He wouldn't do that. Billy doesn't have one bit of violence in him."

The chief surveyed me, as if wondering at my vehemence. He leaned back and sighed. "I need your help as the only one who possibly saw the suspect immediately following the murder."

"Okay." Fear for myself had morphed into fear for Billy.

"Billy King was seen running down Brewer Street about a block from where Clara was killed. According to the eyewitness it was right around nine-thirty, when you found her."

"I never saw Billy."

"You saw someone in the Graysons' front yard."

Grayson. So that was the name of the people who lived in that house. "It couldn't be him. He wouldn't do this."

Melcher raised his hand. "I wouldn't have thought anyone in town would do this. And maybe no one did. Maybe some tourist who came here to shop saw Clara and started stalking her. More likely it *was* someone from here. Someone who knew Clara. I have to sweep aside all preconceived notions. Just look at the facts."

"Why do you think the murderer knew Clara?"

"Because of how precisely the crime occurred. You told me Clara left only about five minutes before you did. It's almost as if someone targeted her. Knew she'd be driving up that street from her shower and waved her down."

I thought of Clara's car near the curb, still running, the driver's door open.

"Wouldn't he have a gun then, or a knife?" It took time to strangle someone. At least, from the marks on Clara's neck, that's how I assumed she had died.

"Not if he didn't expect to kill her."

"You said 'targeted'—"

"Not to kill her. Just to stop her car. Then something could have gone terribly wrong."

Terribly fast.

"You think Billy flagged down Clara's car?"

"He was seen on that street. At that time."

"I didn't see him." We'd been through this before.

"Delanie. You saw a man in the Graysons' yard. You were very clear that you couldn't see his face. But that he looked in your direction, then turned and ran."

"What was Billy wearing?"

"A dark hooded sweatshirt."

No. This couldn't be.

"If he was wearing that hood up, how did the person see his face?"

"The hood was down."

"Down." I worked to logic through that. "So he's running with the hood down, then in the middle of running, he stops to put it up?"

Melcher shrugged, as if the answer was obvious. "To hide his face."

"But this person who saw him—or saw somebody—they didn't see Clara? Her car?"

"They saw Billy a block away."

So the answer was no. "What block? Above—farther away from the church? Or below?" Neither made sense.

Melcher wiped his hand down his face. He was the one who was supposed to be asking questions.

"Because … look. I was coming up the street. If Billy was one block below Clara, I'd have seen him. If he was one block above, supposedly fleeing the scene, he would've had to turn around, run back toward Clara's body, pass her, then veer into that front yard. Why would he do that?"

"I think"—the chief's tone hardened—"you need to leave the investigating to me."

"Not if you're headed in this direction." The words slipped from me before I could stop them.

Chief Melcher raised his chin and looked down his nose at me. The air shifted. I saw nothing left of the man who'd felt empathy for me the previous night. This was the chief of police, suspicious and gunning to solve a homicide in his town. Fast.

I narrowed my eyes at Melcher, knowing defensiveness rolled off my shoulders. Clearly, he sensed the wall going up inside me. And right now he was wondering what I had to hide.

Tension coiled around the room.

"Billy is tall." I fought to push collaboration into my voice. "Maybe six-two. We can measure how tall the man was I saw. Because he stood by the bush in that yard. Remember, I told you the bush was the same height as he."

"I don't remember you saying that."

"Of course I did."

Melcher shook his head. "News to me. And I've gone over what you told me three or four times."

Heat surged up my limbs. Not again—a policeman pouncing because I'd neglected to tell him something. I *couldn't* have forgotten something this important. "Yes, I did. I remember thinking it at the time—the man was the same height as the bush."

The chief drew a breath. "I'll check my notes."

"We could go over there. You could stand beside the bush. You're what, six feet? We could at least get a feel for it."

"I'll take care of it. "

"But—"

"I'll take *care* of it."

He wasn't going to do it. Melcher didn't believe a word of this.

The chief and I eyed each other.

He tapped the table. "Why are you so strong on protecting Billy?"

"Not protecting him. Just … seeking the truth."

"You think I'm not?"

"I'm sure you are."

The air in the room grew heavier.

"How long have you known him?"

I swallowed. "About as long as I've lived here. I met him when I started going to the Methodist Church."

"Know him well?"

"Not really. I don't hang out with him or anything."

"But you volunteer at the church sometimes, and so does he."

"Yes."

"You've worked together on projects?" The chief was watching me carefully.

I shifted beneath his stare. "Sometimes. Simple things like folding programs."

"Did you talk during those times?"

"Sure. I guess."

"That when he talked to you about Clara?"

I thought a moment. "Probably."

The chief remained silent, waiting for me to say more.

"I can't remember exactly."

He absorbed the answer. "You know Billy's mother well?"

I squeezed my hands together beneath the table. This was feeling more and more like an interrogation. "Fairly. Cheryl goes to our church too. So did Lester. But he's gone now." Billy's father had died the year before from a heart attack.

"Didn't Lester King work with Andy?"

"You mean at the real estate firm? I don't think so."

Chief Melcher lifted a hand. "He was an inspector. I'm sure he inspected properties that Andy helped clients either buy or sell."

"Oh. Maybe." So what? In Redbud, everyone was tied to everyone in some way or another.

My cell phone went off in my purse. I made no move to answer it.

The chief thumped two fingers against the table. "Be right back."

He left the room, closing the door behind him.

I blew out air, my chest deflating. What did he think, that Billy and I planned Clara's death, and I was protecting him? That was insane. No one would believe that.

Oh, really?

After about five minutes Chief Melcher returned. Sat down at the table. "I checked my notes from last night. There's nothing in there about the height of the man you saw versus the bush." He seemed almost happy about it.

My insides froze. "There has to be. It's one of those details that stood out so clearly."

He shook his head.

"I just forgot it then. I was so upset."

"Before you left I asked you if there was anything else you could think of."

"I'm sorry I didn't at the time. But I'm telling you now."

He held my gaze. I could practically hear the cop gears in his head turning. *You only "remembered" after I asked you about Billy ...*

How little time it had taken. Not even twelve hours after the murder, and the Chief of Police looked at me with new eyes. This could not be happening. Again.

I steadied my breathing. "Anything else you need from me? I'd like to get back home."

Melcher gave me a long look. "Thank you for coming down, Miss Miller." He pushed back his chair and stood.

I was dismissed.

On the way home I drove a block farther south than needed so I could go up Brewer. In front of the house where I'd seen the Shadow Man I stopped. Gazed at the bush for quite some time.

It had to be shorter than Billy.

I drove on up the street. Crime scene tape still cordoned off the area where I'd found Clara. Four people stood beyond the tape, gazing at the empty sidewalk. I recognized Nancy Stillman and her husband, Frank; and Phil Tranke, who owned the town's drugstore. A few years ago Clara had worked in that store. Aaron Kater, a young man about Clara's age, stood next to Phil. Nancy was placing flowers on the sidewalk, beside other bunches of blooms. A makeshift place of mourning.

I passed the scene. Then on impulse I pulled over to the curb a few houses up. Walked back to join the group. Nancy faced me, her eyes teary.

"They said you found her." Nancy had left Clara's shower about half an hour before I did. An all too familiar emotion pinched her face—guilt. I could practically hear her thoughts. *If only I'd stayed longer. If only I'd done ... something.*

I nodded. My gaze fixed to the sidewalk where Clara had lain.

"And you saw a man?"

It wasn't Nancy's knowledge that struck me. In Redbud, gossip moved at the speed of light. It was the fervency in her tone, a near pleading. The need to find someone to blame roils all the more when people believe—rightly or not—that their inaction may have helped cause the disaster. The quicker a suspect is caught and brought to justice, the quicker self-blame can be soothed. Townspeople like Nancy—and I knew there would be many—would unwittingly put more pressure on the police for a fast arrest.

Everything within me wanted to deny what was coming. At the

moment I had no energy to deal with it. Wasn't grieving over Clara's death enough? But reality stared me in the face. The police would go after Billy King. Quiet, gentle Billy. No matter that their evidence was next to nothing. Evidence was a fluid word, manufactured in a suspicious cop's mind, packaged by a skillful attorney in court.

As Pete would put it, I had to sidetrack the train headed straight for Billy King.

"I saw a man in the shadows. Standing by a bush in that yard." I pointed down the street toward the two-story, white wood home.

"Did you see his face?" Frank asked.

"No." I sighed. "Chief Melcher said the Graysons live there. Anyone know them?"

Phil stuck his hands in his trouser pockets. "Jack and Beth. Both retired. Jack used to work in the bus transit system in Lexington."

Surely Chief Melcher or one of the other officers had talked to them by now.

"This should have been anybody but Clara." Aaron's face looked drawn.

Yes. "Did you know her well?"

Aaron gazed up the street. "We went to school together." His voice was low. "I've known her since second grade. We dated a few times. Back before she met Jerald."

Phil and I exchanged a glance. From the way Aaron spoke, it sounded like he still had feelings for Clara.

We stood there in silence for a few minutes.

I took a deep breath. "Need to see something." I walked into the street, around the crime scene tape, and down toward the Graysons' house.

"Where you going?" Nancy called.

"Just checking something out." I didn't look back. Last thing I needed was an entourage following me.

The Graysons' yard was well kept, flowers lining their front sidewalk. I focused on the section of yard where the man had run. Saw no footprints.

I went up the three stairs to the Graysons' porch and rang the bell. After some time I could hear footsteps approaching. The door opened to reveal a white-haired gentleman with piercing blue eyes.

"Hi." I could feel my cheeks flush. "I'm Delanie Miller. Last night—"

"I know who you are." Mr. Grayson stepped back. "Come in."

So the town gossip had reached them as well. Chief Melcher wouldn't have given them my name.

The house was old, with lots of character. Worn wooden floors and windows, a brick fireplace in the living room to the right.

Mr. Grayson closed the door behind us. He gestured toward a sitting room on our left. "Please, have a seat in here." He tipped his head back, facing the stairs. The skin on his neck was wrinkled and thin. "Beth!"

"Coming."

As I sat I heard Mrs. Grayson's footfalls on the steps. She entered the room with her husband, breathless. She was a short, plump woman, gray-haired and sweet-faced. "Sorry. Just doing some cleaning upstairs."

Mr. Grayson introduced us. They sat, Mrs. Grayson perching on the edge of a blue chair, ankles crossed.

"I'm sorry to bother you." My fingers laced and unlaced. "I guess the police have told you what I saw. I just wondered if you saw the man."

Jack Grayson shook his head. "Not at all. Wish we had."

"Scares me to death to think that man was in our yard." Mrs. Grayson raised both palms. "You can bet we're locking our doors tonight."

"He was in the shadows, standing by that big bush." I half turned, pointing over my shoulder. "Then he ran into your backyard."

Mrs. Grayson nodded. "The police looked all around back there.

I don't think they found much. There's no fence, so he could have run into a neighbor's yard, then who knows where."

I shifted in my seat, only then realizing I'd left my purse and keys in my car. A habit in "safe" Redbud. "One thing I noticed was that the man stood the same height as your bush. How tall is it, do you know?"

Mr. Grayson pushed out his bottom lip. "Don't know. Little shorter than me, I guess."

"Do you think we could measure it?"

He shrugged. "Sure." He pushed to his feet. "I'll get a tape."

"Hmm." Mrs. Grayson tilted her head. "The police didn't even mention that last night."

Had I really forgotten to tell Chief Melcher that? Or did he just not want to hear it?

Yellow tape measure in hand, Mr. Grayson and I went outside to check the height of the bush. I could only hope no one saw what we were doing—especially someone from the police department. I held the bottom of the tape to the ground while Mr. Grayson pulled it upward.

The bush stood five feet eight inches tall.

"Yup, like I said, a little shorter than me." Mr. Grayson rolled up the tape. "I'm six feet even."

Billy was even taller than that.

"So now at least we know the size of the man." Mr. Grayson ushered me back up the porch steps. "That's more than we knew last night."

"Yes. Five-eight. I know what I saw."

Anything to cement that fact in Mr. Grayson's mind. He'd probably tell others. By the time it got back to Chief Melcher—too late for him to deny. People would already have accepted it as fact.

Of course this was a gamble for me—going around the police in such a manner. What if I ended up paying for it? All Chief Melcher had to do was nose into my background, hoping to find something to discredit me. But I had to help Billy. And somehow in all this I'd

… rise above it. Five years of building relationships in town had to count for something.

Truth was, I couldn't bring myself to think of the alternative.

I chatted with the Graysons a few more minutes, then excused myself. Mr. Grayson escorted me to the door. "If you think of anything more, please let us know."

My lips managed to curve. These were nice people. "I will."

I turned to head back up the street—and spotted Billy King, standing alone near the yellow crime scene tape, staring at the place where Clara had fallen. The other mourners had gone. Their flowers now lay on the ground. Billy stood with his back to me, bent over and shoulders shaking. His lanky legs were spread apart as if to hold up a body that had no strength in it.

Even from where I stood I could feel his grief.

With a steadying breath, I walked up to join him. "Hi, Billy." I spoke quietly, taking hold of his elbow.

He jumped and turned toward me. His large brown eyes were red, his mouth trembling. "Delanie." My name sputtered out of him.

"I'm so sorry."

Billy lowered his head again, moving it back and forth in a slow shake. "It can't be true."

I squeezed his arm.

He swallowed hard, and his Adam's apple clicked. "They said you found her."

The scene rushed my memory. "Yes."

"Why'd this happen?"

"I don't know, Billy."

"Who would *do* this?" More tears fell, washing down his ruddy cheeks.

"Can't imagine."

We stood in silence, gazing at the infamous piece of sidewalk. Chief Melcher's words echoed in my head. *"Billy King was seen a block away on Brewer Street …"*

"Billy, were you in this area last night?"

He hesitated, then shook his head.

Oh, no. If he was lying ...

"Are you sure?"

He sniffed. "'Course I'm sure. I'd know where I was, wouldn't I?"

Defensiveness coated every word. I cringed. Chief Melcher would have a heyday with this.

"Oh. I was kind of hoping you were, Billy. Just because I ... hoped someone else saw something."

"I didn't see anything. I don't know anything about this." Billy wiped his face on his sleeve. "Maybe that's a good thing. If I knew who did this, I'd want to hurt him. Real bad."

The words pierced me. I'd never heard Billy say a threatening word about anyone. This could be another strike against him—that he'd utter any hint of violence.

"I understand." I struggled for what to say next. How to warn him without letting on I knew he was lying? "I had a long meeting with Chief Melcher, you know. I had to tell him everything I saw."

Billy's head snapped toward me. "What did you see?"

"Not much. Some man in the shadows of the Graysons' yard." I pointed around my shoulder. "Back that way."

Billy gave me a long look, then nodded.

"I don't why he would, but just in case Chief Melcher wanted to talk to you about last night, make sure to answer his questions with the full truth, okay? I had to be sure to do that. Talking to a policeman can be scary."

"Why would he want to talk to me?" Billy's voice sharpened.

I shrugged. "He'll probably want to talk to half the town. That's how investigations are done. In case someone saw something."

Billy looked back to the sidewalk. A car came down the street, slowing down as it passed us. I didn't bother to give it a glance.

"I should have brought her flowers." Billy gestured with his chin toward the blooms on the ground. "Need to go get some."

"I'm sure she would like that."

Billy's eyes probed my face. "Think so?"

"She was your friend, Billy."

He lowered his eyes, raw emotion creasing his forehead. "She was gonna be more than that. Susan told me."

Susan? "Who's that?" Someone who clearly had a mean enough streak to mislead Billy.

He lifted a shoulder. "A lady with blonde hair. She told me not to tell anyone. But now it doesn't matter. Everything's *too late*." A sob wrenched from him.

Billy's pain knifed me. I stood with him a few minutes longer, trying to think of something more to say. But nothing could stop his grief. Finally I took my leave, feeling so very helpless. As I walked away, my heart aching for him, he remained standing there, staring at The Spot.

I slid into the driver's seat of my car and lowered my head to the steering wheel. I prayed God would watch over our town. Protect Billy. Protect me. And see that justice for Clara came swiftly.

As I drove home I thought of my *"full truth"* words of caution to Billy. As if I had room to talk. And just now I'd had the audacity to pray. My conscience screamed at me, as it had done so many times since I came to Redbud. How could I ask God for anything? How could I claim to be a Christian when my very life was wrapped in deceit?

No answer for that, except to insist to myself I'd done what had to be done. Now it was far too late to unravel the lies. I'd trapped myself, no going back. The more I gained in this life I'd created, the more I stood to lose.

For the hundredth time I wondered: what would have happened if I hadn't chosen this road? If I'd simply trusted God to take care of me?

I turned onto my street, my beloved house coming into view. The very sight of it brought tears to my eyes. I loved my home and the people in it. I loved Redbud. I loved Andy and wanted to be his wife.

Yet I shivered to think of the even deeper deceit that would cost me.

I turned into my driveway, trying to pull my thoughts back to the present. I couldn't stay home long. I needed to gather my strength and visit Clara's parents. They needed my support.

It struck me then—this was April. How ironic. It had been April then too, those eighteen years ago when my world spun out of control. In my other life.

The life I'd vowed would never collide with this one ...

April 1995

CHAPTER 4

Laura Denton jumped off the bus at the end of her street in San Mateo, California, feeling the warmth of the sun on her shoulders. Her long-sleeved light blue T-shirt had felt good in the morning. Now the day was too warm for it. Her backpack was heavy with textbooks. She had two tests the next day, history and biology. And an English paper due the day after that, although the paper would be a cinch to write—they always were. Laura "had a way with words," as her teacher said. Still, really, what did school expect of a sixteen-year-old? There were so many other important things going on in her life. Like Matt Newton, the guy who sat in front of her in French class, and whether or not he'd ask her to the prom. He'd been hinting at it like only shy Matt could. Why didn't he just come out and say the words? Couldn't he tell she was *waiting*?

Only thing was, Dad would have to let Laura go to the prom. He'd said she couldn't date until she was sixteen-and-a-half. Crazy bit of math, if you asked her. Besides, that was a *world* away. She'd only had her birthday a month ago in March. (And gotten her drivers license a week later—yay!) Dad just didn't understand about dating. He was all wrapped up in his work at the mortgage company. Mom would give in since it was the prom, and she'd once been prom queen in high school and totally got it. Besides, she'd known Matt's mom for years.

Laura took off down the sidewalk, squinting in the sun. Her house was at the other end of the block, a beautiful home her parents had bought with cash last fall, after the inheritance from her grandmother came through. Her mom's parents had been worth a lot of money. Exactly how much Laura didn't know. Her grandfather had died three years ago. When her grandmother suffered a fatal heart attack, all the money came to Laura's mother, their only child. At that point Laura's parents sold their old house and moved into this one. Laura's dad bought a new red Porsche. Her mom bought a Mercedes. Laura was promised a new car this coming summer. Other than that, life had gone on as usual, both her parents working hard. And Laura still attended public school, where all her friends were. As for the rest of the money, it had been "socked away for early retirement," as her mother put it.

Laura's mom would be home by now, just off her six-to-two nursing shift. They had a ritual, she and Laura. That is, unless they were fighting. When Laura first came home from school they'd sit down over cookies or some snack and talk about each other's day. Kind of old fashioned, Laura thought, but she liked it okay. Some of her friends at school were actually jealous of her relationship with her mom. They hardly talked to theirs. Still, sometimes the "chats" felt more like her mother trying to get inside her head—know everything about her life. And that just wasn't going to happen. Some things you didn't talk about with your mom. If she pushed too hard, Laura might just storm off to her room. Then Dad would have to play peacemaker when he got home.

Laura and her mom had a fight like that just two days ago. Laura had been furious all the next school day. "You think my mom's so perfect," she'd told more than one friend, "you can have her." But by last night they'd made up. Laura had said she was sorry. Wouldn't do to have her mom all ticked off at her if she needed help to go to the prom.

Laura reached the short front sidewalk and went up the two

stairs to their front porch. If Matt would just get with it and call her today, she and her mom could talk to Dad about the prom tonight. She even had her dress picked out.

Impulsively Laura slid out of her backpack and opened a zippered pouch. She drew out a couple of dog-eared, folded catalogs of dresses she and her best friend, Kylie, had been looking at for days. Leaning against one of the porch pillars, Laura flipped through the pages now. Dreaming about the green dress, then the blue. No, maybe the pink. That color always looked great with her blonde hair.

Laura shut her eyes, imagining slow-dancing with Matt. How would it feel to be that close to him? Would he step on her toes?

Better than her stepping on his.

Oh, please, Matt, call! If he didn't ask her, if she had to stay home on prom night, she'd just *die*.

With a sigh, Laura slipped the catalogs into her backpack and turned toward the front door—

It stood open a couple of inches. Laura stared at it. Weird. How had she not noticed that? She reached out and touched the brass latch. Pushed the door open all the way and walked inside.

Silence.

"Mom?" Laura closed the door. She looked around, seeing the one step down into the living area on the right. Everything in place as usual. On her left was the kitchen, Mom's purse sitting on the long counter separating it from the entryway.

"Mom, I'm home!" Laura thumped her backpack onto the tile floor.

No answer.

Out of nowhere a chill blew over Laura. The house wasn't just still. It was … thick. She took a deep breath. Blew it out.

Well, this was dumb. Mom was probably in the bathroom.

Laura headed upstairs.

At the second floor she started to turn left toward her parents' room, but something on the beige carpet caught her eye. Her gaze swept downward. Footprints, leading from her Mom's bedroom into her own. In red.

Panic exploded in Laura's stomach and bubbled up her throat. Even before her mind could register what that red might be, on some unconscious level she *knew*.

No. No way.

She veered right toward her room, following the prints. Had her mom spilled something, stepped in it? But she was so careful about her house, her carpets—

Laura ran into her room. "Mom?" No one. The footprints abruptly stopped.

She whirled and sprinted back out of the room, across the wide hall and into her parents'. Her wild eyes looked left, right.

She saw a foot on the floor, sticking out from the side of the bed. "Mom!" Laura launched herself toward it, heart clattering. She rounded the bed—and spied her mother. Lying on her side, one leg up, the other extended. Arms curled toward her chest, hair over her face. Wet. Red. Blood. Splattered. Carpet-puddled. Still. Everything so *still*.

Laura's throat fisted shut. She launched herself on her knees before her mom, reaching for a shoulder. Reaching, pulling back, reaching, pulling back. Unable to touch. Afraid to *see*. Something outside herself clamped those hands on her mother, turned her over on her back. "Mm-mmo—" Hair fell away from her mother's face.

But not a face at all. Blood and tissue and gristle. All so red. Where was the nose? The eyes?

A raw scream writhed low in Laura's chest, got tangled in her ribs. Her mouth opened, jaw bulging, but only choking sounds came out. She ran shaking hands down to her mother's warm throat, seeking a pulse, finding none. More noises spilled from her. The sight before her glassed over, the blood and mess prism-cutting into a Picasso nightmare.

Laura pushed back on her heels. Brought her palms up. They

were covered in blood. More blood on her sleeves. For a moment she stepped outside herself, looking dully at her red hands, turning them over, seeing the red in her nails, in the creases between her fingers.

An unseen hand shoved Laura to her feet. She stumbled, fell. Her right shoulder knocked into her mother, smearing red on her upper sleeve. With a grunt, she forced herself upright again. Her legs were mush.

The phone. Where was the phone?

She staggered around the bed and grabbed for the telephone, knocking it to the floor between the nightstand and bed. Leaning over, eyes closed, she groped for it. Scrabbling fingers, spine at an odd angle, mind begging for this to not be *true*. She was some other place, some other girl, and any minute now she'd wake up, wake up, *wake up!*

Laura felt the hard plastic of the phone. Wrenched it up before her face. She stabbed in the fatal numbers.

"Nine-one-one, what is your emergency?"

The scream that wouldn't come now whipped itself from Laura's ribs and seared up her throat.

CHAPTER 5

In the moments after finding her mom dead, Laura's world cracked open, like baked ground in an earthquake. Laura fell down a chasm and couldn't climb out.

So many sirens. People were all over the house—*her* house—in no time. Police in countless cars, and the ambulance. Uniformed men and women she didn't know, questioning her, dragging her away from her mother's body. Outside on the lawn she shrieked at the sight of her own hands, red with her mother's blood. More blood on her light blue sleeves and on the front of her shirt. She dropped to her knees and tried to wipe the blood on the grass, but it was already drying. A female cop helped her up and tried to talk to her, but Laura didn't hear her words, *couldn't* hear. She saw neighbors slamming out of their houses, gathering on the sidewalk, whispering about what might be happening. Sirens wailed, and feet stomped, and yellow crime scene tape—what you're only supposed to see on TV and never, ever on your own house—was unrolled around the yard. Then two plainclothes men came, ducking under the tape and going inside.

"Where's my dad, where's my dad?" Laura cried, and finally he came, his new Porsche gouging out a parking place at the crowded curb. He flew from the car and sprinted toward her. Laura collapsed in his arms, taking in the warmth of him, his voice. But he smelled different, a smell of sweaty fear. "I didn't mean it, I didn't mean it," was all Laura could sob. Until just last night she'd been fighting with her mom, and now her mom was *dead*. How could Laura have been so uncaring? Now she could hardly remember what she'd been mad about. And her mom was gone forever.

"I'm sorry, so sorry." Her dad gripped the back of Laura's head. His hand shook, and his chest heaved, and once he even staggered while trying to hold her up.

He wanted to get into the house to see his wife. They wouldn't let him. Laura stood back, cringing, watching her father yell at the police, but they would not budge. For that she was glad. If he only knew, he wouldn't *want* to see her. Laura would spend the rest of her life trying to get that sight out of her mind.

Then a detective—one of the men in plainclothes—was taking them down to the station so they could "talk." He led them into a little depressing room with a wooden table and four chairs. A camera up in the corner. Only later would Laura learn he wanted to take her in there alone, but her dad insisted on being with her. The detective's name was Lester Standish, but Laura's fried brain stuck on the name Miles Standish because she'd just studied about him in history class. Detective Standish looked around her father's age, mid-forties. He had thinning dark hair and black eyes that looked right through her. One of those men whose beards you saw growing back by the end of the day. He was dressed in a gray suit and white shirt and really ugly black and gray tie. Like some funeral director. Like he some-how knew her mother would be dead today and had dressed the part. And for some reason that dumb thought made Laura so *mad* that she trembled and cried and told him to leave her alone, she didn't want to talk. Then her dad had to calm her down, and the detective went to get her a Coke. As if that would make it any better.

Laura slumped down at the table across from the detective, her dad on her right. Hands over her face.

"Laura, I know this is hard for you." The detective kept his voice soft, as if he really cared, which made her all the madder. He didn't know her, didn't know her mother. He was just doing a job. The anger rattled around inside her, looking for a way to get out. Then, as suddenly as it came, it melted away, and all Laura felt was a pain black and deep enough to swallow her whole.

"Come on, honey." Her dad's voice sounded weathered and old. "He's trying to help."

Laura's heart surged, feeling her father's grief. This wasn't fair. He didn't deserve this. She nodded. Took her hands away from her face.

Detective Standish leaned forward, elbows on the table. "Tell me what happened."

How could she talk about this? How could she put into words what she'd seen? Her throat was totally closed up. And once she could speak the words, they'd hang in the air, weight down the room. Echo back in her own ears.

Laura put her hands in her lap and squeezed them together, making them cramp. She forced all her emotion into those fingers until her throat had room to move. When words finally came out, they sounded flat in her ears.

Staring mindlessly at the table, she told them all she could think of. How she'd gotten off the bus and gone inside the house. How the door had been open. The footprints. The foot sticking out from the edge of the bed. The blood and ... *everything.* When she was done, she glanced up at her dad. His face was white, heavily tracked with tears. "I'm sorry," she whispered to him. He managed the smallest of nods.

The detective watched her intently.

He started asking questions then. What time did she get off the bus? What time did she walk through the door? As if she'd checked her watch during every move she'd made.

"I don't know. The bus usually drops me off around three-twenty. I walk up the block in a couple minutes."

Weird things started flitting through her mind. That she wouldn't be going to the prom. That now Matt wouldn't ask her, after he heard what happened. And how stupid a prom was anyway, and why had she ever cared? She'd miss a million proms to have her mother back.

"Laura." The detective laced his hands. "Do you have any idea who would want to do this?"

She shook her head. Her dad said the same thing. Nobody. Nobody would do this to Sally Denton. She was a nurse. She took care of people, and all the patients loved her.

"But you have to find out who it is." Laura gripped the edge of the table. "You have to find who did this to her!"

"We will. I promise you that."

As if it would do any good. As if it would bring her mother back. But this was the least Laura could do—see that her mother got justice.

Her dad stared across the room at nothing. "Was anything missing? Maybe it was a robbery …"

"We're looking at the possibility," Detective Standish said. "Did you notice anything missing, Laura?"

Yes. Breath from her mom. Blood—supposed to be in her veins, not on the carpet and everywhere.

Laura's stomach lurched. She did a slow lean to her left—and threw up. Right there on the floor. When she was done she stared at the mess through watery eyes as if it had come from someone else.

"I want to go *home*."

They had to move to a different ugly room while somebody cleaned up the first one.

By the time the detective was finally done with them, Aunt Nicky, Laura's dad's sister, was waiting to take them to her house. Her face looked red and splotchy. She hugged Laura and her dad hard, and they didn't want to let each other go. The detective gave Laura's dad his card and said he would be in touch with them.

"Please find who did this." Dad's voice was hoarse. "Please."

"I will, sir. I will."

Only hours later Laura would be back in that first interrogation room. The floor would be clean, the smell of vomit gone. And the detective wouldn't be so friendly.

CHAPTER 6

"You want something to drink, Laura?"

The detective was standing in the oppressive little police station room. Laura was sitting at the table in the same chair as before. This time her dad wasn't with her. Detective Standish had pressed hard to talk to her alone. Said it was best. Would be the most helpful. Laura's dad asked her if that would be okay. She'd nodded. What difference did any of this make?

"A Coke? Sprite?"

She hadn't touched the first one he brought her, earlier that day. Why would she want one now? In fact she hadn't eaten a thing for dinner, even though Aunt Nicky made broccoli and a salad, and Uncle Ted barbecued chicken. Her dad hadn't eaten either. How could they, ever again?

Laura shook her head. At the moment she couldn't feel the pain. Only the anger, rushing back out of nowhere. She wanted to hit something.

She clung to the anger. It was easier to feel than grief.

"Okay." Detective Standish sat down and leaned his arms on the table. He still wore the same dull clothes.

"That's a really ugly tie." The words bounced out of Laura's mouth before she could stop them. "My mom would dress you so much better."

She stifled a cringe. Why had she said that? Good thing her dad wasn't there. He'd have been really ticked. She'd never spoken like that to some adult she hardly knew.

Well, so what? She wasn't Laura Denton anymore. This wasn't her life. She was some other person filled with emotions that bubbled and flowed inside her like lava. Her veins felt so hot, her head so blazing, she was likely to say anything. How could anyone think when they felt like that? How could anyone be normal?

Maybe the anger wasn't so great after all. She wished she didn't feel anything. Better to be dead inside.

The detective didn't seem the least bit shocked at her words. He ran his left hand down his tie. Laura noticed he didn't wear a wedding ring. Maybe he was divorced. Maybe he didn't have a wife to dress him. "Your mom was good with colors?"

Laura nodded. He waited for her to say more. She just stared at the table, pictures of her mom on the floor, all bloodied, running through her head.

At least the blood was now cleaned off her own hands. She'd scrubbed at the area around her nails to get it off. As for the long-sleeved blue T-shirt she'd worn that morning, she'd thrown it away in Aunt Nicky's bathroom. But then the detective asked her dad to bring the shirt to the station, along with the jeans she had on. Dad had brought them in a plastic grocery bag. Now Laura's dad sat outside in the station, waiting for her. Wondering what was going on. His face had a grayness that wouldn't go away.

The detective cleared his throat. "All right. Let's talk about this afternoon. We checked with the bus driver about what time he let you off. He said it was 3:20, like you told us. He's sure about that. Said he happened to check his watch when you got off because he had a doctor's appointment at 4:30."

Laura kept her eyes on the table. It had a gouge in the wood. She ran a finger over it.

"But there's one thing that doesn't quite make sense to me, and I'm hoping you can explain it."

Like she could explain any of this.

"You said it takes you only two or three minutes to walk to your house. You went straight there. And you said you noticed the front door was open, and you felt something was wrong. You went upstairs and found your mom. Called 9-1-1 right away. How long would you say you were in the house before you made that call?"

Laura closed her eyes, reliving. "A couple minutes."

"You sure about that?"

She nodded.

The detective leaned back. Scratched the side of his neck. "Okay. Here's the problem Your 9-1-1 call came in at three-thirty-six. That's sixteen minutes after you got off the bus. If it takes you two to three minutes to get to your house, and it took another two to three minutes to make the call, that adds up to between four to six minutes."

Laura could barely follow his logic. Her brain refused to do the math.

"You understand?"

"Uh-huh."

"So, Laura. What happened to the other ten minutes?"

She looked up at him blankly. "I don't know."

"You don't know?"

She shook her head. Who cared about ten minutes anyway? Except that they were ten minutes in her old life. If she could just get them back now, relive them again. *Stay* in them ...

"Can you try to remember for me, please?"

Suddenly the answer came. "Oh. I didn't go in the house right away."

"Where were you?"

"On the porch."

"What were you doing?"

"Looking at catalogs of dresses."

"Catalogs? Where did you get them?"

"From my backpack."

"Why were you looking at them?"

Laura ran a hand over her face. She didn't want to answer because it would sound so stupid. He would never understand, this dark man in his ugly tie who didn't know her mom.

"Laura. This is important."

"Why?"

He spread his hands. "I need to understand every minute of what happened."

She sighed. "I was looking at pictures of prom dresses."

"For ten minutes?"

Had she taken that long? She shrugged. "I guess."

"How many pictures did you look at?"

How stupid was this? "I don't know."

"Why were you looking at them?"

No. Huh-uh. This man did not need to know about her private life. About Matt and the prom and her dreams and everything. How could he possibly understand? He couldn't even dress himself right.

"Laura. I need you to talk to me."

She shot him a hard look. "Kylie gave me the catalogs, okay?"

"Who's Kylie?"

"My best friend."

"What's her last name?"

"Russo."

"Spell it for me."

Laura spelled it.

"Do you have her phone number?"

Of course she had her phone number, what kind of dumb question was that?

"Would you give it to me, please?"

Laura gave him the number. "You going to call her?"

"I might."

"Why?"

"I may need to talk to her about giving you the catalogs."

"*Why?*"

He patted his fingers against the table. "Let's just talk about you, okay? Tell me about looking at the pictures of the prom dresses."

Laura's neck muscles felt like rocks. She stretched her neck to one side, then the other. "Fine." She told him about the dresses. He wanted to know more, pushing and pushing. He tried to sound nice, but it ticked her off all the same. Still, in the end she told him. She had to—he wouldn't let up. She talked about wanting to go to the prom with someone—she wouldn't say who. And how Kylie and she had talked about dresses and gathered pictures.

"So you stopped on your porch before going into the house, and you looked at these pictures?"

"Yeah."

"And you did that for ten minutes?"

Hadn't she already answered this? "I guess. I wasn't watching the time."

The detective nodded slowly. "You told me the front door was standing open. And when you saw that it seemed odd to you."

Laura's stomach felt so empty. A big cavern that could never be filled. Like the rest of her. "Yeah. Didn't look right. Mom never leaves the door hanging open."

Mom never leaves ... She'd said it like her mom was still alive. The thought froze her. How could she start talking in *past tense* about her mom?

"And you went in just after seeing the door standing open?"

"Yes."

"So ... the ten minutes you were on the porch, looking at the catalogs—all that time you didn't see that the door was open?"

Oh. Laura frowned. "I guess not."

"Your porch isn't very big. You must have been close to the door."

"Yeah. But I was leaning against one of the pillars. Not really facing the door."

"I see. Why didn't you tell me this the first time we talked?"

"I don't know. I didn't think about it."

"You said you told me everything that happened."

"Well, I just forgot, okay? My mind was a little full."

He nodded. A long moment of silence ticked by. "Another thing that bothers me, Laura. There was no sign of forced entry on that front door."

So? The door wouldn't have been locked. It never was when her mom expected her to come through it from school.

"What do you have to say about that?"

Laura only shrugged. The answer should be obvious.

The detective folded his arms. "Anything else you haven't told me?"

His voice had changed. Something a little … edgier. Laura eyed him. "No."

"You sure?"

"I don't think so."

He looked at her some more.

"Why? Is there something else you're thinking about?"

He gestured beneath the table. "The shoes you're wearing. Are they the same ones you wore to school today?"

Her *shoes?* They were just regular sneakers, one of three pairs she owned. These were blue. "Yeah."

"You sure about that?"

"Why would I change my shoes?"

"Okay."

"My dad brought you my shirt and jeans, like you wanted."

"Yes. Thanks for that."

Her mouth hardened. "You want my shoes too? And all the rest of my clothes?"

Not that she could get to them. They were in her house—the house she couldn't even go into.

"I will need your shoes."

"The ones I'm wearing?"

"Yes."

"You want to take the shoes I'm wearing off my feet?"

"I'm sorry, but yes."

"Will I get them right back?"

"I'm afraid I'll need to keep them."

What? Why was he doing this to her? Laura folded her arms. "And just what shoes am I supposed to wear? Since you won't let me in my house to get another pair."

"I'll go in and get you whatever pair you like."

"I like the ones I have on."

"I'm sorry, Laura. I know this is hard for you."

Laura shoved back her chair and thrust to her feet. "You don't know *anything!* You have *no idea* how I feel! I just lost my mom, and now you want to take my clothes and shoes? What's *wrong* with you?"

"I'm sorry." The detective spoke so calmly it made her want to slap him. "There are still things you and I need to talk about—"

"You're not even listening!"

The detective sat back and spread his hands. As if to say, go ahead, yell it out. So she did. She spewed it all out there, even though he'd heard it before. Finding her mother. The blood. The stunned *disbelief.* Wanting her dad. Her neighbors all looking at her. And people in the police station looking. Her aunt's phone had rung, rung, rung in the last few hours, all her friends somehow tracking her down, wanting to know what happened. Laura hadn't wanted to talk to any of them. She didn't know *how* to talk. She only knew how to say nothing and broil inside, or scream like she was doing now. There was no in between. There was no normal living. And she just wanted to go back to Aunt Nicky's and be *left alone!*

Laura's tirade ran out. She found herself leaning over the table, breathing hard, spittle on her chin. She swiped it off. The detective looked at her, waiting for more. But nothing would come. Only emptiness, and tears, and a dizzy wail in her head. Laura swayed, then slumped back down in her chair.

God, where are you? I'm dying here. She was a Christian, so was her mom. They'd tried to live right. How could He let this happen?

The detective stood. "I'm going to get you some water. Be right back."

She stared dully across the room. Wouldn't matter what he brought her, she wouldn't drink it.

But when he set a glass of water in front of her, she guzzled half of it down.

Detective Standish slipped back into his seat. "You ready to answer a few more questions now? It won't take long."

Laura closed her eyes, too tired to fight anymore. She nodded.

He asked her about her relationship with her mother. Did they ever argue? Laura hated to admit they did. How could she have ever treated her mom that way?

"Did you have an argument recently?"

"I don't want to talk about that."

"You need to talk about it."

There it was again. That edge in his tone.

"Fine. We had an argument two days ago. We made up last night."

Just imagine if they hadn't. If the last time she'd talked to her mom, they'd been *fighting.* Laura shivered.

"What were you arguing about?"

"Nothing important."

"I'd like to hear about it."

"It *wasn't important.*"

"Okay. What do you know about your mother's will?"

Laura screwed up her face at the sudden change in topic. "I don't know anything about her will."

"You know she inherited a lot of money from her own mother when she died last year?"

"Yeah."

"How much money?"

"I don't know."

"How much did your mother plan to leave to you in the event of her death?"

"I have no idea. Why would I even think about that?"

"Did she ever talk to you about her will?"

"No."

"Did you know she redid it a few months ago?"

"No."

"You had no idea."

"No."

"You told me you had a lot of talks with your mom."

"I did."

"But she never talked to you about her will?"

"I just *told* you—*no*."

Detective Standish flexed his shoulders. "Tell me about those footprints you saw. On the carpet."

Another topic change. Was he doing this to throw her off? Why? Wasn't he supposed to be *helping* her and her dad? "I already did. And you saw them—you were in the house."

"Where were they leading?"

Laura had to think about that. "They went into my bedroom. But then they stopped."

"Why do you think they stopped?"

"I don't know."

"And you're sure you haven't changed your shoes today. You wore the blue pair all day?"

Back to this again. Laura sighed. "Yes."

Detective Standish shifted in his chair. Rubbed his chin. "We found another pair of sneakers in your closet. These were green. They were hidden under a pile of dirty clothes."

Laura's back straightened. "What were you doing in my closet?"

"We needed to look all through the house—"

"But why *my* closet?" That was *her* stuff, her life. To think of this man and who knew who else going through *her* stuff.

"Are there things in there you wouldn't want us to see?"

Was this man a moron? "I don't want you going through my things!"

"Tell me about your green shoes."

Huh? "What about them?"

"When's the last time you wore them?"

"I don't know."

"Today? Yesterday?"

"I *told* you I didn't wear them today."

"Then when?"

"I *don't know*."

Detective Standish planted his arms on the table and leaned forward. His eyes lasered right through her. "Laura. We found blood on those shoes."

She stilled. "What?"

"You have any idea why that would be?"

"There's no blood on those shoes."

"How do you know?"

"Because they're *mine*. I'd know if I got blood on them. Besides, how would I do that?"

"You tell me."

"I wouldn't. I didn't."

The detective surveyed her. "So you have no idea how the blood got there?"

"*No.*"

He nodded. Gazed away for a moment. "You know we're going to test that blood."

"Test it for what?"

"To see if it matches your mother."

The words hit her deep in the gut. "What are you *talking* about?"

"You tell me, Laura. Do you think it will?"

What was happening here? "Why would it?"

"We'll have the results in a few days. You might want to go ahead and tell us now."

"Tell you what?"

"How the blood got on your shoes."

"I don't *know!*" She glared at him. "And I don't believe you anyway."

"Okay." He looked downward for a moment, as if processing. "I'll need those shoes now." He pointed to her feet.

"Right now?"

He nodded.

"What if I said you can't have 'em? You already took my other pair."

"I'm sorry, but I need them. Please take them off."

Laura felt her jaw go rock hard. She pushed back from the table and flung her upper body over to yank at her shoes. She sat up and slapped them down on the table. "There. Happy now?"

The detective's expression never changed. Just that same placid face, like she wasn't yelling at him, like she wasn't about to *strangle his neck*. He picked up one of the shoes and turned it over.

It had blood on the sole.

Laura jerked back. Her eyes filled with tears. Her mother's dried blood, on the bottom of her *shoes*. She brought a hand to her mouth, pressed her lips hard. The detective watched her cry, saying nothing.

She hiccupped inside, pulled herself together. "I … didn't know that was there. I guess I walked in it when …"

The picture came roaring back for the millionth time. The footprints. The blood. Her mother's body …

Laura gulped the rest of her water.

The detective leaned forward, gazing at the tops of her shoes. What was he looking at? He sat back. "So you say you got blood on the bottom of these shoes when you came inside the house today and found your mom."

She nodded. Her throat got all cloggy again. She didn't want to cry anymore.

Detective Standish rubbed his temple. "Here's the thing, Laura. You see the tops of these shoes? There's no tiny blood spots—at least that I can see right now—on the top of them. We call those tiny spots blood spatter. They happen when someone is hit with a heavy object. The blood sprays out in all directions—"

"I know what blood spatter is." Laura couldn't decide if her voice sounded hard … or dead. "I watch cop shows too."

He ignored the cutting remark. "Okay. Those other shoes we took from your closet—the green ones? They had blood on the soles, like these. They also had blood spatter across the tops."

Laura listed her head to one side. It felt so heavy. "So …"

"It tells us those shoes were present at the time your mother was attacked."

She frowned at him. "Somebody wore my shoes?"

"Looks like it."

"Why would they do that?"

"Would you like to tell me why?"

"I have no idea!"

He lifted his chin in a slow nod. "Another thing about those shoes. The pattern on the sole is a little different than these." He picked up one of the shoes from the table and turned it over. "See this, the way these spokes go out from the middle? Your other pair has more of a zigzag geometric pattern. That pattern matches the footprints on the carpet in your house. The prints leading away from your parents' bedroom into *your* room."

Laura could only stare at him. Her brain refused to put it all together.

"Why do you think the pattern on that pair of shoes matches the prints on the carpet, Laura?"

"I don't know."

"You must have an idea."

Some pathway in her soggy brain cleared. "Are you telling me that someone came into our house, put on my shoes, attacked my mom, then took off my shoes and put them back in the closet? That's *insane*. Why would anybody do that?"

Why would anybody kill her mom at all?

Detective Standish gave her a long, hard look. "No. I'm not saying that." He kept looking at her, until her skin felt all crawly. Until she wanted to slide right under the table, away from those eyes.

"There's something else we found in your closet, hidden underneath that pile of dirty clothes."

Laura stilled. She couldn't imagine what he was talking about, but the tone of his voice said it was bad.

"We found a hammer. Looks like it belongs to a set of tools from your garage."

Laura screwed up her face. A *hammer?* Underneath her clothes?

"Laura. That hammer has blood on it."

Slowly she leaned forward, her eyes never leaving his face. "Blood?" She could only whisper the word.

He nodded.

"My ... mom's?" Her whole body started to tingle.

"You tell me."

"I don't know. Why would it be?"

Why *wouldn't* it be? It wasn't her own.

"We'll test it. Like the blood on your shoes."

Laura swallowed, struggling to understand. She got it, really. Deep down. But it just didn't make any sense.

"Do you think somebody used that hammer to kill my mom?"

"Looks that way. She has marks on her face and skull fractures that match indentations that hammer would make."

Skull fractures. "You mean someone hit her in the *head* with it?"

The detective gave that slow nod of his. "Many times."

All the blood. That's where it had come from—her head? She'd been hit so hard her skull broke. Nausea rippled through Laura. "You have to find out who did this."

"I agree. I think it's time you told me about it, Laura."

Her mind wouldn't compute. Didn't *want* to compute. "Tell you what?"

"What really happened."

"I already told you what happened. Twice."

"I don't think you've been telling me the truth."

She stared at him, heart fluttering. "Why do you think that?"

He shifted in his chair. "You remember when your dad first got to the house? You were out on the lawn. You hugged him. Remember what you said over and over?"

She shook her head.

"You said, 'I didn't mean it.'"

Oh. Yeah.

"What were you talking about?"

Laura dropped her chin. "I was fighting with my mom the day before—I told you that. And after I ... saw her, I felt so bad about it."

"So when you said 'I didn't mean it'—what did *it* refer to exactly?"

"Everything I'd said when I was mad at her. The whole fight."

"I see." The detective scratched his cheek. "Why would you think of fighting with her after you'd just found her dead?"

Laura's heart wouldn't stop fluttering. "I don't want to talk to you anymore."

"You don't want to tell me what happened?"

"I've already told you what happened! What are you, stupid?"

He shot her a long look. "Laura, you haven't. I know you haven't. Because nothing you've told me lines up with the evidence."

"Well, it's the truth."

"There are fingerprints on that hammer."

"Good. Maybe that'll tell you who did this."

"We're going to test them against your fingerprints."

She raised a shoulder.

"Have you touched that hammer?"

"No."

"You've never touched that hammer. So we won't find your prints on it."

A memory flashed. "Oh, wait. Last week I used a hammer. I put up a picture in my bedroom."

"What picture?"

"Of me and Kylie. She took it with her camera, and it turned out really cool. She printed it out on a big piece of paper and gave it to me. I nailed it on my wall. Then I think I just left the hammer on my dresser. I didn't put it back in the garage."

"And this was what day?"

Who cared? "I don't remember."

"Would your dad know?"

"My dad never goes in my room."

Detective Standish sat back and sighed. "You know what, I'm getting tired of this. It's time you told me the truth."

Of all the— *"You're* getting tired of it? How about *me?"*

"Then tell me what really happened."

"I have told you!"

He pulled in a long breath, his voice softening. "Sometimes people make mistakes. I think *you* made a mistake. I don't think you walked in the door of your house planning on killing your mom. But things got out of control. And, Laura, now you need to do the right thing. You need to tell me the truth. It will go much better for you if you do. So please, help me help *you.*"

Laura stared at him. This guy was out of his mind.

A long minute ticked by. Detective Standish spread both hands, as if to say *come on.* Laura shook her head.

The detective sighed again. "Okay, then. Let me tell you how it went."

Fine. Since he knew so much.

"You got off the bus at 3:20. Went into your house two to three minutes later. Your mom was there. You got into an argument somewhere upstairs. Maybe you stormed into your room. Your mom followed. Like you just said, the hammer was still there from when you used it to hang the picture. You picked it up, threatened your mom—"

"Are you crazy?"

"She ran into her room. You followed. You started hitting her. And you just lost it. You hit her again. And again. Soon she went down by the side of her bed. And you kept on hitting."

Laura's breaths came hard, her chest rising and falling. This guy was *out of his mind.*

"Suddenly—it was over. Your mom wasn't moving. And you panicked. You hadn't meant to do this. Now you had to figure out what to do. You ran into your room, still holding the hammer. Looked down at your shoes and saw they had blood on them. You stopped and took them off. Hid them in your closet under a pile of clothes, along with the hammer. But you had to replace your shoes, so you put on the blue pair. Then you called 9-1-1."

Was the room moving? Or was it just her head? Laura tried to talk, but nothing came out.

"Isn't that what happened, Laura?"

She shook her head. Shook it and shook it until her teeth rattled. Who was this man to say such things? To even *think* them? She wanted to strangle him right here. Wanted to punch his teeth in. Her hands trembled. Her body felt like Jello. Somehow she got her legs under her, pushed back her chair. She stood, swaying. Planted her hands on the table. Laura leaned forward, looking the detective in the eye. "Don't. You. *Ever.* Say those things again. Don't. You. *Ever.* Talk to me again. Because I can *promise* you—I will never talk to you!"

She flung her chair aside and stomped to the door. Yanked it open, barged out, and slammed it behind her.

She couldn't breathe.

Laura threw wild looks up and down the hall. Which way? Where was her dad? She needed him *now.* Wait until she told him what the detective had said—

"Laura." Detective Standish appeared beside her. "I'm afraid you're not going anywhere."

"Get away from me." She veered down the hall.

"Laura, stop. Now."

She kept going. He caught her arm and whirled her around.

That's when she saw the cuffs in his hand.

April 2013

CHAPTER 7

The day after Clara Crenshaw's murder went from bad to worse. I'd returned home after talking to Jack and Beth Grayson, and seeing Billy King, intent on pulling myself together so I could head back out. I had to visit Clara's parents. Tell them how sorry I was. It would be a difficult visit, seeing their grief up close, feeling mine mingle with theirs. Was Dora Crenshaw fighting guilt of her own over her daughter's death? She'd left the wedding shower about fifteen minutes before Clara, too stricken by one of her headaches to help clean up.

Once inside my house I felt all energy slip away.

Nicole and Colleen were gone, Nicole to her college classes and Colleen to her job at Grangers Gift Store. Pete was in the kitchen, washing up his breakfast dishes. Nobody could get a kitchen messier cooking eggs and bacon than Pete Baler. He stopped his work when he saw me, a dripping cast iron pan in his hands. "Del-Belle." His blue eyes shone with concern. "How are ya?"

The comforting sight of him made me want to cry. All I could do was shake my head.

"You had any breakfast?"

I lifted a shoulder. "I'm not hungry."

"You need to eat."

"I … can't. Not now."

Pete put down the heavy pan and dried his hands on his battered jeans. "Come on over here, let's sit down." He beckoned me across the kitchen and into our gathering room. Pointed at the couch. I sat, and he settled beside me. "Where ya been?" His voice was gentle.

I looked at my lap. "Chief Melcher wanted to see me again. More questions." I told Pete about Billy King. Measuring the bush in the Graysons' yard. Seeing Billy at the site where Clara died. Pete leaned away from me as I talked, elbow on his thigh, watching my face. He had this way of hearing what I said—and what I didn't. He'd set himself as my protector long ago, as soon as he moved into the house. He loved me like a granddaughter and sometimes bossed me like one, too.

"Aw." Pete waved a hand when I fell silent. "Melcher'll come around. He can't hold it against you for long that you forgot to tell him somethin' last night. Just after you'd found your good friend dead? What's he expect of a gal?"

I wanted to believe that. But there were so many nuances of the encounter between the chief and me that I couldn't explain to Pete. The vibes that had quivered in the air. My hostility at his questions of Billy, and the chief's reaction.

"What if he doesn't 'come around,' Pete? I got the feeling my description of the man's height wouldn't be enough to turn the police from looking at Billy. He was seen in the area. Recognized. That means a lot."

Pete grunted. "Billy couldn't a killed Clara."

"I know."

"They'll see that soon enough."

"You don't *know* that, Pete!" A dust storm kicked up inside me. Whirled old dirt around. "People can be accused of crimes they didn't do, and their lives are never the same. Especially if the lead detective is under a lot of pressure to solve the case—like Melcher is. Or maybe the detective's just got an ego too big to fail. Melcher again."

Pete sat back, one finger pressed against his bearded chin. "Well, we just can't let that happen."

But how to stop it? I'd crossed a line with Melcher. He would not listen to me anymore. "Melcher is bound to question Billy soon. And I'm afraid Billy will lie, like he did to me."

"Maybe he's not lyin'. Maybe he wasn't on Brewer Street at all."

I pictured Billy's body language as he'd made his denial. Heard the defensive tone in his words. "He lied, Pete. It was obvious to me. And it'll be more than obvious to Melcher."

Pete ruminated on that a moment. Then shook his head. "What's happenin' is, the chief's gettin' sidetracked. And I'm here to tell ya, sidetrackin' a train's tricky business. Can cause some crazy accidents. Reminds me ..." He focused across the room, his eyes taking on that faraway look he got when gazing into his cherished past. I so envied him that.

"Back in '89, on a record cold day, one of our freight trains picked up three pusher locomotives in Helena, Montana for help gettin' over the Mullan Pass. Then the lead engine got some electrical problem. The crew parked the train at the Austin siding, east of the Pass. They uncoupled the engines from the cars—I think there were forty-eight of 'em—and set the air brakes, but not the hand brakes. 'Bout 5:30 in the mornin' the crazy cold temperature—I'm talkin' thirty-two degrees below zero—caused the air brakes to fail on those cars. They started rollin' backwards. Rollin' and rollin', pickin' up speed, headed back into Helena. Nobody was awake to see 'em comin', but even if they had ... There's just no stoppin' that kind of thing. The cars crashed into a parked work train at a crossin' in town, right near a college. Whole train caught fire and exploded. Amazin' no one was killed. But it did a lot of damage and knocked out power. That's pretty cold to be goin' without heat for days. People got real scared. That kinda freak accident happens to you once, and you suddenly realize life's full of random events that can rock you at anytime. Took the whole town years to come back from all the damage—physical and emotional."

For a moment we both sat in silence, picturing the scene.

Pete sighed. "It's too hard a thing, stoppin' a tragedy like that once it's done started. You got to keep it from ever gettin' goin'. Put on those hand brakes as a precaution, know what I mean?"

I nodded. "So what do we do?"

Pete pushed his lips together. His mouth nearly disappeared into his beard. "I'll think on it."

"Don't take too long. These things can move awful fast."

He gave me a long look, and I tried not to wince under his gaze.

My cell went off—Andy's ring tone. I pushed up from the couch to head for my phone in the kitchen. Pete wandered off toward his bedroom.

"Hi." Andy's voice was warm. Just hearing it made me want to cry. "How you doing?"

I wandered to the front kitchen window and gazed at the street. "Melcher called me back to the station. He's starting to look at Billy King."

"For the *murder?*"

"Someone said they saw Billy last night, near where it happened." Andy breathed over the line. "Why would Billy hurt Clara?"

"Who said he did?"

"You just said somebody saw him."

"Doesn't mean he's guilty, Andy. Just because he was nearby. Besides, he's too tall." I told Andy about the man I saw—and the bush. How I'd forgotten to tell Melcher that fact. "When I did tell him, he seemed to dismiss it. Almost as if he thought I was making it up just to save Billy."

"Melcher doubted your *word?*"

Andy's sharp tone stuck a knife in me. No one in this town—except our chief of police, apparently—would believe I'd tell a lie.

How fragile, the life I'd built.

"I'm calling Melcher right now."

"Andy, don't. You'll only make it worse for me."

"I can't let him treat you like that."

"This isn't about me. It's about finding who killed Clara."

Please, God, don't let it start to be about me.

"Yeah, but if Melcher starts ignoring key facts just to nab a suspect …"

I had no response for that.

"Look." I rubbed my forehead. "I need to go see Clara's parents. I should have gone over there first thing this morning."

"Okay. Keep me posted. And, Delanie, I want to take you out to dinner tonight. Away from town and all this. Somewhere in Lexington. I'll pick you up around 6:30."

I focused on a tree in my front yard. So green. So beautiful and full of promise in spring. I pictured someone taking an axe to it—and squeezed my eyes shut.

"Delanie?"

"I'm here."

Did I even want to go out tonight? Part of me said yes, anything to be away from this town and with Andy. How I needed to be with him. For the rest of my life.

But on this day I'd be such lousy company. So many things, so many fears I couldn't tell him. Now or ever.

"Six-thirty all right with you?"

"Yes. Thanks. I'm just …"

"I know." Andy's voice was gentle. "Call me anytime today if you need me, okay?"

"Okay."

"See you tonight. I love you, Delanie."

The words washed through me. "I love *you.*"

As I clicked off the call I spotted a police car coming up the street. It pulled to the curb in front of my house. Bruce Melcher got out, slammed the door, and strode with purpose up my front walk.

CHAPTER 8

The chief's hard pounding on the front door sent shock waves through me. I braced myself against the kitchen counter, my stomach queasy. He'd found me out, hadn't he. My cursed past. A little digging into my background—and suddenly Billy King didn't look like the best suspect anymore …

More pounding. I couldn't move.

Pete appeared from the hallway, a frown on his face. "All right, all ready, I'm comin'." He spotted me, my fingers digging dents in the counter tile—and raised his eyebrows.

"It's Melcher."

Pete stopped. Looked from me to the door. "Want me to answer?" he stage-whispered.

No. I gulped in oxygen. Being laid bare, my sins uncovered, would be bad enough. But to happen in front of Pete, who'd never doubted a word I said …

Melcher pounded again.

"Answer it." The words shot from my mouth. There was no running from this. Hadn't I always known this day would come?

Already I could feel myself shutting down, the old barriers coming up.

Lord, help me. Even if I don't deserve it.

Pete pulled back the door.

"Is Miss Miller here?"

"Yup." Pete didn't move from the doorway.

"I need to talk to her." Impatience tinged Melcher's words.

"I'm coming, Pete." Somehow my legs found the strength to move me into the gathering room.

Pete stepped back and let the chief inside. As he pushed the door closed, Pete shot me a look—*"I'm right here with you."*

Melcher and I faced off across the room. His jaw was set, hands on his hips and feet apart. I knew that police stance all too well.

"Somewhere we can talk in private, Miss Miller?"

Pete's gaze slid to me. A chill washed through my limbs. I couldn't dismiss my self-proclaimed protector without hurting his feelings—and leaving him to wonder why. "It's okay, Pete can stay."

Melcher shook his head. "This is police business. I can take you down to the station if you prefer—"

"No." I swallowed. "Come on into the kitchen. We can sit at the table."

Pete cast a suspicious look upon Redbud's chief of police. "I'll be in my room."

With the door open and both ears cocked, no doubt.

Pete shuffled off.

Melcher strode into the kitchen. I motioned to a chair, but he waved a hand at it. I sat down anyway. My legs wouldn't hold me. Pictures of all I had to lose flashed through my head. Andy. My friends. This house. My *life*.

The chief's small eyes narrowed. "I've just been over to the Graysons'. They told me you'd been there, had Jack measure that bush. Now I got *them* informing *me* how tall the suspect is."

I gaped at him, feeling the weight of my breaths.

"I *told* you the information about Billy King was confidential."

My brain could not reboot. This wasn't about my past?

"Miss Miller!"

"Yes. I … hear you."

"You had the unfortunate experience of discovering Clara Crenshaw's body. You've told me what you know. Now you need to keep out of the investigation."

"Okay."

My mind was beginning to kick in.

"I do not want you talking to anyone about Billy, you understand?"

"I haven't."

Chief Melcher gave me a look. "Then why did you go to the Graysons'?"

"To see for myself. I just wanted to see how tall that bush is. It's five feet, eight inches. Considerably shorter than Billy. So it couldn't be him."

Melcher stuck his tongue below his upper lip. "I'll decide who is a suspect and who isn't. Clear?"

"But it *couldn't* be Bil—"

"You don't know that."

"Yes, I do! I saw the man in the Graysons' yard, I told you that. He was the same height as that bush."

"I will not argue with you about this."

Oh, really? Because he knew everything? "How can you ignore an important piece of evidence?"

"I am not ignoring it."

"Apparently you are."

Chief Melcher drew back his head. He lowered his chin, lasering me with his eyes. "You listen to me. I'm in charge of this investigation. And *I* will solve it. I expect you to stay out of my way. *Is that clear?*"

I pushed to my feet, hands gripped at my waist. "Please don't drag Billy through this. He's such a gentle person."

Melcher tilted his head, looking at me as if I were an animal he'd never seen before. "Can you not hear?"

He really was going to do this. Ignore my pleas for justice. Real justice.

"Miss Miller!"

An arrest would devastate Billy. And turn the whole town against him.

I unlatched my hands. Pulled back my shoulders. "I hear just fine, Chief Melcher. I see just fine. And what I see is a policeman intent on nabbing a suspect in a hurry so he can stoke his own reputation. Who'll choose to ignore important evidence because it doesn't fit with his theory."

Bruce Melcher's cheeks turned crimson. He strode forward and stuck his forefinger in my face. "If you interfere anymore in this investigation, I will haul you off to jail! And that rich boyfriend of yours won't be able to help you."

I stood my ground, looking past Melcher's finger into his mean eyes, even as my heart rattled my ribs.

"I believe you've made your point, Chief Melcher. You can leave my house now."

He glared at me, moving his jaw from side to side. Then slowly he pulled back, drawing up to his full height. With a final scathing glance he turned on his heel and stomped for the door. On his way out he slammed it hard enough to shake the windows.

I leaned against the table, head drooping. Pete's footfalls sounded in the hall.

"Why, that no-good, puffed-up piece a flesh in a uniform." Pete huffed across the gathering room's wooden floor. "Who does he think he is?"

My eyes closed. "He's the chief of police, that's who."

Pete made a noise in his throat. "Some way to treat an eyewitness." He stopped before me. His voice dropped. "You okay?"

A part of me longed to confide in Pete right then and there. God knew I needed to talk to *someone*. If I were arrested, or if Melcher even decided to run a background check on Delanie Miller—what would he find? That was the great unknown. Why I'd never applied for a job anywhere. Yet to have been through what I had—and *not* help someone else facing a similar situation, someone as innocent as Billy King ...

My stomach turned over. Was I going to throw up?

I raised my head and tried to smile. Didn't work. My ankles trembled.

Pete clucked his tongue. "Come on now, Del-Belle, let's sit you down." He nudged me back into the kitchen chair. Took a seat on the other side of the table. Pete leaned forward on his elbows.

"You listen now." His words scratched. "You got to pull back on this. That man's not gonna listen to nobody. But I can run around town and do plenty behind his back. You leave it to me. I'll find out things. Somebody had to see somethin'. Maybe they're just afraid to say anything." Pete spread his hands. "But who am I? Just an old gee-zer who likes to gab. People'll talk to me. You'll see. I'll text or call you when I can, let you know what I'm up to."

Tears filled my eyes. Dear old Pete.

We talked for a few more minutes. Through sheer willpower and Pete's comforting words, I managed to pull myself together.

I pushed back from the table. "I need to go see Clara's parents. I'm embarrassed I haven't even talked to them yet."

Pete assessed me. "You sure you're ready to handle that now?"

Ready, no. But it needed to be done. I nodded.

"All right then. Just stay away from Melcher."

A bitter chuckle escaped me. "Don't worry."

"You should eat somethin' first."

The very thought of food ... "When I get back."

"You promise?"

I sighed. "Yes. Nag."

He wrinkled his nose at me.

I escaped to the bathroom and did what I could to fix my makeup. I felt one hundred years old.

Fifteen minutes later as I slid into my car in the garage, my cell phone rang. I checked the ID and saw the name Cheryl King. Billy's mother.

She'd never called me before.

I laid my head back against the seat rest. "Hi, Cheryl?"

"Delanie." Her voice pulsed with anger. "What did you tell Bruce Melcher about my son?"

Oh, no. "Why, would do you mean?"

"People have been calling, saying you saw Billy on Brewer Street last night around the time Clara was killed. And now the chief's come to our house and taken him down to the station!"

April - September 1995

CHAPTER 9

Less than six hours after discovering her mother's body, Laura was arrested for the murder. The detective put cuffs on her hands and chain cuffs on her ankles. She had to shuffle when she walked, like some mass murderer. To San Mateo County Juvenile Hall they took her, up a long hill to a wind-strewn bunch of buildings above freeway 280.

Arrested. For killing my mother.

They took her clothes and jewelry—stud earrings and the small ruby ring she'd gotten for Christmas. Gave her baggy cotton pants and a top to wear. Thick flip-flops for her feet. A woman took her through another door. The world just … stopped. Every door that closed behind her separated her more from where she should be. The walls of the building were dull gray concrete. Long hallways, rooms on either side, each with a door in the middle. In each door a small window, many of them with faces looking out. The faces looked dead, hopeless.

They put her in one of the tiny, windowless rooms with two hard cots. Her "roommate," a sixteen-year-old who had to weigh over two hundred pounds, with stringy brown hair and a face full of acne, tried to talk to her. Tricia said she was "in" for shooting another teen in a drug "transaction." Stated the fact like it was no big deal, happened all the time.

For people in here, it probably did.

Laura tuned Tricia out, and after some time the girl finally got the message and shut up. Tricia had some paperback books she could read. No pencils or pens, so no need for paper. Supposedly they could hurt themselves or someone else with a pencil point. When Tricia picked up a book, Laura lay down on her side and faced the grungy wall.

Soon after that came "lights out."

Laura welcomed the darkness. Not that she could sleep. She could barely feel her body. Her mind kept screaming this was a nightmare. Any minute she'd wake up and be *so* relieved. Was it possible just that morning she'd gotten up on a normal day, gone to school? That she'd been dreaming about going to the prom with Matt?

What would everyone at school say about her? She'd been arrested—for *killing her mother?* Surely no one would believe it. Especially not her friends. They'd come to her rescue, tell that stupid detective she couldn't have done it.

How long before he let her go? Before he realized he'd made a terrible mistake? As long as they thought she did this, they couldn't find the real murderer. Her mother deserved justice. Now!

Laura tried to pray to the God who'd always sustained her. But He didn't seem to hear. Why had He let her be dragged off to jail in the first place? *Why* had He let her mom be killed?

What was her dad doing right now? He'd lost his wife—and now his daughter had been dragged away. He'd just about come unglued when Detective Standish arrested her. He kept yelling they were wrong, how could they *do* this? That he'd never have let her be questioned by herself if he knew this was going to happen. Her dad had followed Laura as far as he could, until she'd been stuffed into some police car. He'd called to her that he'd get her out. To hang in there, he'd *fix* this!

Tomorrow he'd do it. Tomorrow she'd walk out of this horrible place.

The next day dragged by in inches. Most of the time was spent in her room. Except when they went out to eat, or when they were allowed some time in a lounge-type area. It smelled dusty, and the furniture was old and beat up. And she didn't want to talk to anyone. Worse, her dad didn't come to get her. What was he doing? What was happening out there in the real world? Laura went from crying to stone stillness and back to crying again.

Her roommate told her to stop hoping. That she'd thought the same thing at first. No one came to rescue her. Now she was in there for six years.

Six years. It was a lifetime.

On the second day Laura went to her detention hearing. Finally she'd get to tell someone she didn't do this!

They brought her into court, still wearing the scuzzy clothes and shoes. A bunch of other teens were there too. So was her dad. She was allowed to hug him. He looked gray, like he hadn't slept at all. Neither had she. "I'll get you a good lawyer," he told her. "The best I can find."

"Why do I need a lawyer? Why can't I go home?"

He just shook his head.

When she got in front of the judge, she'd convince him to let her go.

Court began. Some guy Laura hadn't seen before—a prosecutor or something—read the charges for each of the teens in front of her. Then he and some other people would talk to the judge about the case. Then the teen would be led away, back to his or her room in juvenile hall. When Laura's turn came she wanted to melt through the floor. In front of everyone they talked about how she'd killed her mother. How the evidence was strong. She'd been assigned some woman public defender, who argued halfheartedly for this and that. Laura tried to talk, but the judge told her to be quiet. Panic shot through her. Wasn't this supposed to be her chance? Why wouldn't anyone listen?

"I have to talk to him!" she insisted to her lawyer. But the woman only said, "I'll handle it." And the next thing she knew, she was being led away. Away from her dad and the windows that looked outside to blue sky.

She refused to eat the rest of that day.

The next day, and the next, and the next, and the next—no change. No rescue. Laura fell into a kind of stupor. When she ate, she didn't taste. When she talked it was in phrases. Sometimes she thought of her friends and school. What class she'd be in at any time of the day. Now English. Now she'd be in history. She'd have taken her tests days ago, and by now gotten back her grades. She'd have turned in her English paper. Mostly she thought about her mom. Remembered the good times. Christmases and other holidays. Their afternoon talks. The times they'd gone to movies together. And had tea parties when she was little. She pictured her home and her room. Imagined her own soft mattress beneath her, and her pillows. Her own clothes. How she longed for her own nice-smelling shampoo. And toothpaste—the kind they used in the hall tasted awful. All the things she'd so taken for granted, she'd give anything to have back now.

Her dad hired a lawyer. Devlon Brooks, supposedly the best of the best. He looked older than her father, maybe in his fifties. Graying hair and a smooth face. Unlike Detective Standish he dressed in nice suits and ties. He met with Laura numerous times in the glass-walled visiting rooms within straight eye-shot of the people working the desk. The first time they met her lawyer told Laura the "straight-out truth." She'd be in the hall until her trial—maybe six months away. He needed that long to prepare.

At that, Laura went cold.

They had a lot against her, Devlon said. (He insisted she call him by his first name.) The shoes hidden in her closet had her mom's blood on them. Rushed DNA analysis had proven that. And the blood on the tops was spatter, like Detective Standish had told her. The only way that could happen? Those shoes had to be at the scene when her mom was being beaten. They also had the murder weapon—the hammer—with her mom's blood on it, plus Laura's fingerprints. That, too, had been found in Laura's closet. Plus there was the ten minutes of extra time she couldn't account for. Not that she could prove, anyway. And then there was the inheritance, half of her mother's estate. That provided the motive.

"I didn't know anything about that inheritance," Laura said.

Devlon nodded.

"And of course my fingerprints are on the hammer. I'd used it just the week before."

"We'll make sure you get to say that in court."

"I *didn't* kill my mother. I didn't wear those shoes and hide them. I didn't hit her with a hammer. I didn't do *any* of that stuff."

"Who would have done this, Laura?"

She had no idea. Certainly not her dad. Besides, she'd learned Detective Standish had cleared him within hours of the murder. He'd been in his office at work. "Whoever it was made it *look* like I did it." Why would anyone want to do that?

Her father visited as often as he was allowed. At first they talked about nothing but her case. After awhile Laura started asking him about the neighborhood, his work. Had he talked to any of her friends? Kylie and a few others had called a couple of times, he told her. They knew she was innocent.

At least there was that. Something to cling to.

She asked him to tell them to write her. She could receive letters. How she wanted to hear firsthand from her friends. He said he would.

Laura lived for her father's visits. They were all she had. Until he began to change.

At first she told herself he just had a lot on his mind. Maybe problems at work. Or he was especially missing her mother. But his next visit was no better. And during the one after that he could hardly talk to her. Which ticked her off. She'd lost her mother too. And *she* was the one living in this pit.

"What's the matter with you?" She kicked the metal leg of her chair.

Her dad gave her a long, dark look. "There's a lot of evidence against you, Laura."

Like she didn't know that.

"That's what Devlon's for. To prove I didn't do it."

His gaze shifted to the floor. He sat there a long time, fear and dread and ... something else flicking across his face. "Did you?"

He said it so quietly, still focused on the floor, that at first she wasn't sure she'd heard him. "What?"

Slowly he raised his head to look her in the eye. "Did you kill your mother?"

The words shot ice through her stomach. Laura couldn't move. Couldn't talk. She concentrated on her breathing. In ... out. In ... out. If she was breathing she must be alive.

"I can't believe you're asking me that." Her words came out raspy.

Her father looked away.

They had nothing more to say to each other. After five minutes of silence, of looking around the glass walls like they were strangers, Laura got up to go back to her room.

CHAPTER 10

Laura first heard about her father's girlfriend in a letter from Kylie. She'd been in the hall four and a half months. Her trial was five weeks away. She was counting the days. Once the trial was over, she could finally go home. It would be a home without her mother, and that would be bad enough. But at least she wouldn't be *here*, treated like some cold-blooded criminal. Even the other girls in the hall whispered about her. *"She killed her own mother."*

Laura wanted to slap them, punch in their faces. But she'd seen the extra punishment people got for fighting—no time out of their rooms, for instance. Besides, if she hit anyone, it would only prove their point. She was violent. A girl who was capable of bashing in her mother's skull with a hammer would be capable of anything.

Hey, Laura, the letter started. *Hope you are doing okay in there.*

Kylie told her about classes at school, which had just started. Who was now dating, who had broken up. How there was a new girl, really pretty, and all the guys were falling all over her. Kylie thought she was stuck up, herself. Then came the paragraph that made Laura's heart stop.

So who's your dad's girlfriend? Me and Evy went over to your house one Saturday to see him. Just to say hi and say we were thinking about him. She was there. He acted embarrassed that we saw her. Maybe because it hasn't been that long since your mom's death. At least that's

*what I was thinking. Evy said the same thing on the way home. Like—
really? Isn't that kind of random? Anyway, he stepped out on the porch
and talked to us. She stayed inside . . .*

Laura read the paragraph three times. A girlfriend? Visiting at
her house? Less than five months after her mother died?

She felt sick.

Last thing she wanted was to go home and see her dad with some
other woman. How unfair was that to her mom? How could he *do*
this? No wonder he'd been acting so weird during their visits. The last
two weeks he hadn't come at all.

A week after Laura received the letter he finally showed up. Laura
had thought about little else for the last seven days. She took no time
getting to the point. "I hear you have a girlfriend."

He pulled his head back, then tilted it. As if to say *I knew your
friends would tell on me.*

"Who is she? And *why* are you with her?"

Her dad raised a hand. "I just … It's hard to explain it to you,
Laura. I've just been so lonely."

Like *she* hadn't?

"You *can't* be with someone else, Dad! That's just so … rude."

He shook his head.

"Mom would never do this, if it was the other way around."

Her dad flinched. "I didn't mean for it to happen. It just did."

"Who is she?"

He laced and unlaced his fingers. "Her name's Tina."

"Tina what?"

"Fulder."

"Fulder? What kind of name is that?"

No answer.

Laura folded her arms. "What does she do?" Probably some ditz
in that mortgage company he worked in.

"She's a policewoman."

"She's a *cop?*"

He nodded.

Laura's limbs stiffened. She shot to her feet and paced the room. Kicked her chair. Out the corner of her eye she saw Tats, the big guy behind the desk with decorated biceps, eyeing her through the glass walls. Fine. He could look all he wanted.

"*How* could you do this?" She leaned over her father, who sat there like some caught little boy. "A *cop?*" She'd grown to hate those people. A cop had accused her of killing her mom, slapped cuffs on her. Another cop had put on the leg chains. Drove her here to this dump. Nobody in the hall liked the police, *nobody*. Least of all *her*.

"She's a good woman, Laura."

"She's a *slut!*" Laura kicked her chair again. "Hanging around you when you just lost your wife."

"She … makes me feel better."

"Well, good for you."

Her father's expression changed. He looked up at her, eyes narrowing. "Don't you talk to me like that."

"How do you expect me to talk! I have to hear from my best friend that you've got a girlfriend? What's gonna happen when I get home? I *don't* want to see you with her. I *won't* let her into the house!"

"It's my house, too, Laura. In fact, I pay the bills."

"My mother's inheritance paid for that house, in case you forgot. And now you're bringing some other woman into it."

Her father's cheeks reddened. He stood up. "I won't stay here and listen to you talk like this."

"Fine, go! Why'd you come at all?"

He faced her, breathing hard. "Because I still don't want to believe the truth. Because I still want you to convince me you're not guilty."

The *truth?* The word pierced Laura to the core. She grabbed onto the back of her chair, squeezed it hard. Then, suddenly, she got it. All the pieces came flying into place. A girlfriend—who was a cop. Who had to believe, like all her other colleagues, that Laura was guilty. This woman, this Tina Fulder, was not only moving in on her father just after he lost his wife. She was telling him *his daughter* was to blame.

"*She* did this to you, didn't she?" Laura's voice was low.

Her dad ran a hand down his face. "There's all the evidence ..."

"You didn't believe the 'evidence' before."

"I don't want to believe it now."

"Then *don't*."

He hung his head.

Something in Laura died that minute. With her standing there, feeling the gumminess of her flip-flops, the stares of Tats, like he might have to come break up a fight. The dirtiness of the visiting room floor, its dusty smell and glass walls. Her dad looking totally removed from her. He might as well have been standing on the other side of the building.

She'd lost her mother. Her freedom. Her respect. Her *life*. Even God seemed to have turned His back. All she'd had left was her father. Now she'd lost *him*.

To a cop.

If her own father didn't believe in her, how could her mother ever receive justice?

Laura's insides went to jelly. Then froze solid. Like she'd learned to do before, she concentrated on breathing. In ... out. In ... out. When she opened her mouth, the words could only croak.

"*Don't* come back here. I'll see you at my trial. Where everyone else, at least, will believe me."

Laura flung back the door and stalked away from the one person she needed the most.

April 2013

CHAPTER 11

As soon as I clicked off the call with Cheryl King, I drove to her house, praying all the way. I could straighten out the false rumor she had heard about my spotting Billy the previous night. But how to calm the heart of a mother who was terrified for her son? Especially when I was terrified too. I *knew* how easily Billy's interrogation could go wrong.

As I pulled up to the curb in front of the Kings' house, I saw Cheryl peeking out the window. I'd told her I would be right over. She met me on the porch.

"I'm so sorry." I gave her a hug. She stiffened in my arms.

"Come on inside." She barely bothered to hold the door open for me.

We sat in two sofas in her living room, facing each other. Both of us perched on the edges of our seats. "Look." I held up a hand. "I did *not* see Billy last night. I never said I saw him. In fact, when Chief Melcher asked me about it, I insisted I hadn't seen him."

Cheryl blinked. "Then who told Bruce that Billy was anywhere near that area?"

"I have no idea."

Cheryl searched the carpet, as if the answer lay there. Anguish stretched her face.

I closed my eyes. How much to tell her? I couldn't let a mother hurt like this. But dare I ignore Chief Melcher's threat to arrest me if I "interfered" in his investigation?

"What is it? I see it all over your face, Delanie Miller. *What* do you know?"

I gazed at her, pulling my upper lip between my teeth. I could feel my world teeter. Again.

"*What?*" Cheryl leaned forward, hands balled in her lap.

"I ... did see someone last night. A man in the shadows of the Graysons' yard." Surely this information was wending its way through town already. If I didn't tell Cheryl, she'd hear it soon on her own. "But I know it wasn't Billy."

"How do you know?" Her expression changed. "I mean, I *know* it wasn't. But how do *you* know?"

"He was too short."

"Did you see his face?"

"No."

Cheryl leaned back against the couch. "At least it's something."

Apparently not enough for Chief Melcher.

She ran a hand across her forehead. "Maybe the chief will just question Billy and let him go."

"I'm sure he will."

"Because I know Billy wasn't anywhere near Brewer last night. Why would he be? That's six blocks from here."

It would be easy enough to mistake someone's identity in the dark. "He gets off work from McDonalds at nine, right?"

"Yes. Sometimes he has to stay a little over and do some cleaning up. But then he always drives right home."

"Did you tell Chief Melcher that?"

"Of course, but he didn't seem to care. Said he needed to hear it from Billy."

"Do you know what time Billy got home last night?" The timing was so very important. How well I knew what a difference ten minutes could make.

"Shortly after nine. Doesn't take long to drive here from the restaurant. I told the chief that too."

"And you know Billy stayed here and didn't leave again?"

Cheryl's face hardened. "Why would he leave? Where's he gonna go at night in this little town?"

"I understand. It's just that the chief's bound to ask your son if he stayed home. If you can back up his alibi, it would really help."

"He stayed home." Cheryl's voice was firm. "I *know* he did."

We looked at each other. Something about her—a flinching around her eyes?—gave me the impression she was lying. Maybe it was her emphasis on the word *know.* A chill trickled through me. If I'd sensed that, surely so had Chief Melcher.

I cast about for what to say next. "Did the chief press you on that, Cheryl? Did he demand to know where you were in the house and how you could be sure?"

"Yes. I told him everything. But still he took Billy away."

I nodded. As much as I wanted to know the "everything," I couldn't press this any further.

"Billy was *so* petrified." Cheryl winced. "He was practically cry-ing on his way out the door. And he looked so *guilty.* He can be that way around authority. Just going to the police station is enough to tie him in knots. But I've watched plenty true crime shows. I've seen how many times police misread somebody's fear. They automatically think the person's got something to hide."

I couldn't respond to that. Because it was all too true.

"What do we do now?" Cheryl got up and paced, the energy of her fright clearly too much to contain.

"All we can do is wait. Hard as it is. But I have to warn you, Billy could be at the station for a number of hours."

Cheryl halted. Her expression contorted. "I can't lose him. Isn't it enough that I lost Lester last year?"

More than enough.

"Billy's all I have now." She looked at me. "You know I had him late in life. I couldn't get pregnant, even though Lester and I had tried for years. Finally when I was forty ... Many times I wondered if that's why Billy is the way he is. Slow. Barely able to grasp concepts like math when he was in school. Maybe it was my fault. Maybe I was just too old."

"Cheryl, don't say that. You wanted him, you've loved him. He knows it, and that's what counts."

She flopped back onto the couch and picked up a pillow. Tossed it down. I couldn't bear the sight of her despair. Memories of my father flashed in my head—those first few days after my arrest when he still believed in me. He'd suffered so terribly. As I had. Then look what had happened to him ....

I could not sit back and watch this happen to Cheryl.

"Look." I leaned forward. "I promise you I'll do all I can to keep Chief Melcher from homing in on Billy. I already talked to him just this morning, insisting your son's not responsible for this. And I'll keep talking. I'm the closest thing to an eyewitness. My recollection has to count for something."

Cheryl focused on me and slowly nodded. "Thank you." The words were little more than a croak.

I stood. "I need to go now. I was on my way to see the Crenshaws."

Cheryl winced. "Tell them I'm sorry. Tell them Billy didn't do it."

"Yes."

What else could I do?

On the way out I put my arm around Cheryl again. This time she hugged me back.

Maybe she hadn't lied to me at all. Maybe I'd misread her, just like the police were so good at doing.

Maybe, somehow, I would slide through this. Help Billy and still keep the life I'd built. The life that demanded my constant deceit— and separated me from the God I so needed.

If I could just find the real murderer.

CHAPTER 12

As I was driving to the Crenshaws, still shaken from my visit with Cheryl King, my cell phone rang. Pete. I pulled over to a curb and answered. "Hi."

"You won't believe this, but they already hauled Billy King down to the station."

"I know." I told Pete I'd stopped by to see Cheryl.

Pete grunted. "And you told her you know Billy's innocent, didn'tcha."

"Yeah."

"Even after ol' Melcher-Belcher threw out his threats."

"I can't stand by and—"

"I know, I'm with ya. But things just got harder. You know who told the chief they saw Billy last night?"

My back straightened. "Do you?"

"Yup. Becky Myers."

The name shot through me. "Becky! She was at the shower. Left not long before I did."

"Yup. She lives on Brewer 'bout a block and a half up from where Clara was killed."

"How you'd hear this?"

"Oh, I got my ways. Made a few phone calls to friends who live on Brewer. And when I heard it was Becky, I called her directly. Said I was just tryin' to watch out for you. Which is true."

I stared out the windshield, stunned. Becky was a good friend of Dora Crenshaw, Clara's mother. And about the same age. Becky was a kind woman who'd never say anything bad about anybody. She wouldn't have told the police anything less than the truth.

"And she's sure it was Billy?"

"Absolutely positive. Becky told me she pulled into her driveway and nearly hit him as he was hurryin' down the street. He looked right at her, in her headlights, then kept on goin'. This was about fifteen minutes before you found Clara."

This couldn't be. Around 9:20 Billy was heading straight for the place where Clara was killed? I pictured the look on Cheryl King's face as she'd insisted her son hadn't left the house. Had she been in her bedroom, watching TV? Maybe she couldn't really be sure ...

"Don't look too good for Billy, does it," Pete said.

"No." Scenes from my own interrogation years ago flashed through my head. How much harder to prove your innocence when you were *at* the place of the crime. At this point I could only hope Billy told Chief Melcher everything. Why he was on Brewer that night. Where he'd come from and where he was going.

"Thing is, Del-Belle, fifteen minutes ahead of you puts Billy at the right place at the right time."

My stomach felt sick. "I know."

"Still don't believe he did it. I'm just sayin' it's real bad timin'. And Chief Melcher's gunnin' for a suspect."

As were Clara's parents, no doubt. All too well I remembered the consuming fire of needing to know who'd killed my mother. "I need to convince the Crenshaws it wasn't Billy. If they really think that, they'll put all the more pressure on Melcher."

"Might be a hard thing to do, in the midst of tryin' to comfort 'em. You could come across as tryin' to defend their enemy."

Pete was right. The only thing a grieving family had left was to pursue justice for the one they'd lost.

"Besides which, you'll dig yourself in deeper with Melcher."

If Pete only knew how much that terrified me. "Well, let me see how it goes. I do need to visit them."

"Okay, see you back at the house."

"You're not there now?"

"Heavens no, girl. I've hit the streets. I got to find out who woulda wanted Clara dead."

I managed a smile. "Be careful."

"You too."

After ending the call, I sat a moment longer, trying to collect my thoughts. And praying for guidance.

As if God had any reason to grant anything I requested.

Heavy-hearted, I pulled back into the street and headed for the Crenshaws. They lived on the outskirts of town in a two-story brick house. Dora had been a seamstress all her life, using a large back room in the house as her working area. Lately she'd been busy making Clara's wedding dress and all the bridesmaids' dresses. One of them was for me.

Pain stuck a knife in me and turned it.

It hit me then—half of Clara's wedding gifts were still at the church. They'd need to be cleaned out. And taken ... where?

Numerous cars lined the curb in front of Dora's and Dave's house. I recognized Clara's fiancé's blue Honda. Jerald had mostly likely been with the Crenshaws all day. In front of his car sat a beige Ford SUV. His parents'.

I walked up the porch steps and knocked softly on the door. Jerald's mother answered.

"Hi, Delanie." Marie's face was drawn. "Please come in, I know they'll want to see you."

I stepped inside the hardwood foyer. The smell of baked chicken and rolls filled the air. Too late I realized I should have brought something. What was I thinking?

"I'm so sorry to be empty-handed. I just haven't ..."

"Don't worry about it. They've got more than they can handle already." Marie headed toward the combination kitchen and family room at the back of the house. She gestured for me to follow.

I stepped into the room, feeling the heaviness in the air. Dave sat on a couch near Jerald. Jerald's father, Hank, sat opposite them in a gray armchair. Dora was in the kitchen, leaning against the counter, talking quietly with Jerald's older sister, Paula. Dora's sister, Gretchen, was also there, as well as their mother, Evy May. All of these women had been at the shower the previous evening. From joy to despair in less than twenty-four hours.

This had to be a dream. Maybe even now I would wake up ...

The men rose to greet me. I hugged them and all the women, murmuring how sorry I was, how enraged and stunned. As I looked into their faces, the weight in my heart grew heavier. Jerald's eyes were hollow, like those of an old man. The make-up on Evy May's lined face was tracked with tears. Nothing I could say or do would take away the grief in this house.

They graciously offered me food. Drink. All I could handle was water.

Dora's green eyes were red-rimmed, her typical graceful way of moving now rigid. She held herself like a statue threatening to crack. "We have plenty to eat, as you can see, and more in the oven for lunch." She waved a hand at the casseroles and salads lining the counter. "I've just been trying to put it all away. People have been so kind ..." Her face crumpled. She turned away. Gretchen wrapped her in a hug.

Fresh anger simmered within me. The *waste* of it. Of a precious life, so ready to be lived. Clara would never be married. Never have children. Never grow into the mature, incredible woman that she would have become. And for *what*? Who would *do* this?

Dora pulled away from her sister and wiped her eyes. She turned a circle in her kitchen, as if not knowing what direction to take next. "I have to get all this food put away."

Evy May laid a hand on her daughter's shoulder. "We'll do it, Dora."

"No." Dora's voice sharpened. "I have to keep busy. I have to do … something." She yanked open the refrigerator door and started shoving its contents around. Then, just like that, she slammed it shut and turned to me. "What did you see last night? I have to know."

"I want to hear, too." Dave Crenshaw sounded so weary, as if he'd walked a thousand miles. His expression bore the intaglio of anguish. Gazing at him, I remembered my own father, mourning his wife. "Just a little while ago we heard Chief Melcher took Billy King down to the station," Dave said. "We've been hearing about Billy all morning. He was there, right *there* when Clara was …" He swallowed hard. "Did you see him, Delanie?

Something inside me snapped. I pressed a hand against my mouth. No, no, I could not cry now. These people deserved answers, not to watch me break down. But I couldn't stop the tears, and once they started, they flowed for so many people. For Clara and her family. For Billy. For myself accused of murder those years ago, and my father. For my mom.

"I'm so sorry." The words sputtered from me.

"It's okay." Gretchen handed me a tissue.

They all watched as I pulled myself together, which took too long. I could feel their aching need to *know* who took their Clara. To see justice done.

"If you interfere anymore in this investigation, I will haul you off to jail."

But Clara's family had asked what I'd seen. How could I not tell them the truth?

I balled the tissue in a fist. "I saw a man. But it wasn't Billy."

The questions came fast. "How do you know?" "Who was it, then?" "What was he doing?"

My mouth opened, and out came the answers. All of them. Including how Mr. Grayson and I had measured the bush.

Dora held on to the kitchen counter, drinking in my every word. "But I heard that Becky insists she saw Billy."

"I'm sure she did. But it doesn't mean he was involved in this."

Dave shook his head. "I don't know. That boy ... He's had a crush on Clara for a long time."

"And I never *did* anything about it." Jerald thrust a hand in his hair.

Evy May patted his shoulder. "How could you know, he always seemed so harmless."

"But I should have seen it. I should have known ..."

My throat tightened. Had they not heard a thing I said?

"Well, we'll just see what Billy King was doing on that street." Dora's voice hardened. "Right now I'm not believing in coincidence."

The phone rang. Dave answered it. All eyes followed him, waiting to hear his end of the conversation. Would it be more news? Or simply another friend, expressing sorrow.

More news, it was. And of the worst kind. Chief Melcher was on the line, wanting the Crenshaw family to be the first to know. Billy King had been arrested for Clara's murder.

October 1995

CHAPTER 13

After a lifetime Laura's first day of trial arrived.

She'd been told it might last a week. Maybe more. She was being tried before a judge, not a jury, since she was a juvenile. This was good news and bad news, Devlon said. The good news was, they only had to convince one person of her innocence—the judge. The bad news? All the prosecution had to convince was that same person.

Judge George Myers was his name. He looked skinny, even with a big robe on. Had a long, angular face and thin lips. Laura didn't like him from the start. He was part of the System—which hadn't worked too well for her so far.

Laura got to dress in her own clothes. How cool it had been to put them on—until she noticed how tight her pants were. Sitting in juvey all day, eating starchy foods had made her fat and sluggish. When she got back home, she'd start an exercise routine. Eat fruits and vegetables and fish.

On the drive to the courthouse she pressed her face to the window, drinking in sights of the world. All those people in cars, going wherever they wanted. Did they have any idea how wonderful that was?

When she'd gone into juvey it was spring. Now it was fall. Still plenty warm in the Bay Area. The sun was shining, so glorious. She loved the feel of it on her face.

She'd been praying a lot lately, begging God to let her be acquitted. For months she hadn't prayed. But now there was something to hope for. God could still make this right.

In the courtroom she sat down at a polished dark wood table with her attorney. She'd been warned her trial would be open to the public. Apparently a lot of juvenile trials in California weren't, but her charge was a felony. So somebody in the System had decided people could come to gawk.

Laura's dad would be in the courtroom soon. Devlon had explained that her dad would be the first to testify—so afterwards, as her parent, he could sit and watch the trial. Laura hadn't seen him since that visit four weeks ago. Now she'd have to watch him on the stand, testifying for the *prosecution*. Oh, yeah, she'd heard it all from her attorney. How the prosecutor would ask her dad about the fights she'd had with her mother. No doubt by now her dad didn't think Laura might be guilty—he knew it. Just think how Miss Cop Girlfriend had managed to cement that idea in his mind.

Somehow when Laura went home, they'd have to work this out. Once she was acquitted, her dad would have to see that she didn't do this. Could never have done such a thing. The police had quit looking for any other suspect the moment they set their eyes on Laura. And she hadn't thought of one person who might be guilty, even though she'd had many long days to think about little else.

Devlon, on the other hand, had come up with a few startling possibilities. It was clear to both of them the real culprit had wanted two things: her mom dead and Laura found guilty for it. Because Laura had obviously been framed. It had taken weeks for that to sink through her head. That the evidence hadn't just happened to point to her. It had been planted, perfectly planned to do that.

The realization had cost Laura many a night's sleep. Who would do such a thing? *Why?*

Her dad had been at work but could have hired someone to do the job, Devlon had offered. Laura rejected that idea. He wouldn't have killed his wife, and he certainly wouldn't have framed his daughter for it. That was beyond all comprehension.

Laura knew only two things as she sat at the defense table, getting a feel for the room. First, Devlon would prove she hadn't killed her mom. Second, once she was freed, Laura would not stop looking for the real murderer until he was found, even if it took years. She would see justice done for this crime. Her mother deserved no less.

She looked over her shoulder and spotted her Aunt Nicky. The woman nodded at her. Laura gave her a small smile. Was she like Laura's dad now, believing Laura was guilty? Other neighbors and friends of her mom were also there. And a couple people Laura didn't know, scribbling on notepads.

"Who are they?" Laura asked Devlon.

"Reporters."

Reporters? She stared at them, wide-eyed. Why would they be here? Was her name being put in the newspapers? None of her friends had mentioned that. Did they just not want to tell her?

Laura hunched her shoulders. She didn't want to be watched like a hawk. Written about. Especially in the first few days of the trial, when the prosecution called all their witnesses and tried to make her look as bad as possible.

"Look." Devlon patted her arm. "They'll be here when you get to testify, too. Don't you want your own story out there?"

It was little comfort. She focused on the table, feeling the burn of eyes on her.

Court began. Laura's breathing hitched. She'd dreamed about this for weeks. How she'd have to sit through the bad stuff. But then she'd get to tell her side. And even during the prosecution's part, Devlon told her, he'd be questioning their witnesses. Trying to make their "ironclad evidence" look not quite so ironclad. He'd told her to be positive. He thought they had a really good chance of getting an acquittal. Especially with her testimony, which they'd practiced over and over. Devlon had said she'd be good on the stand.

Why wouldn't she be "good?" She would just tell the truth.

The prosecutor, Larry Cantor, was different than the man she'd seen at her arraignment. This one was short and round—the exact opposite of the judge. He had white hair and a red face. Big jowls that shook when he talked.

Laura hated him.

Cantor called Laura's dad to the stand. She tensed. Devlon patted her arm again.

Just before her dad swore to tell the truth, he shot her a glance. No smile. He'd lost weight. Looked way more fit. Younger. With a tan and new hair cut.

How *dare* he look all happy?

Almost like his life had never been so good. While she'd rotted away in a tiny cell. His life probably *was* great. Especially after what Devlon told Laura. Her father had inherited *all* of her mother's money. The part that had supposed to go to her? All given to him. Since she'd supposedly killed her mother, the law said she couldn't benefit from the inheritance. Something about a "clean hands doctrine." Oh yeah, hers were so dirty. So now, even with an acquittal, she'd have to fight her own father to get her money back—not that she would. Besides, what if there wasn't any left? What if he'd spent it all on his girlfriend?

Laura's breathing went hard and shallow. But she was not going to let her father see how much he'd hurt her. She closed her eyes and forced the emotions down.

The prosecutor jumped right in with his questioning. As promised, he asked her father about all the arguments between his wife and daughter. How Laura had acted. What she'd said. The more her dad talked, the worse she sounded. Laura hung her head. She hadn't really been that bad to her mom, had she? Didn't all teenage girls fight with their mothers?

Then Cantor asked about the last fight they'd had—starting two days before Laura's mom was killed. Her dad testified that it was worse than the others. Laura had seemed madder than before. More "volatile." And then there were the ill-fated words she'd sobbed into her father's chest out on the lawn after her mom was killed. "I didn't mean it."

Cantor repeated the words for effect. "What did she mean by that?"

"Objection, calls for speculation." Devlon's voice sounded impatient, as if Cantor knew he couldn't get away with such a question.

The judge didn't need to think about it. "Sustained."

Laura kept her eyes on her father. If he'd been allowed to answer, what would he have said? He wouldn't look at her again—not so much as a glance. Her lungs began to burn. Did she hate him? Or love him? Or both? She wanted to scream at him for his betrayal. But she couldn't lose him forever. Hadn't she lost enough? Somehow she had to win her father back. She'd show him. And she'd forgive him for turning on her. He was still grieving, that was all. Not thinking clearly.

But a tiny voice inside Laura said, *"Does he look like he's grieving? After finding a girlfriend so fast?"*

When Cantor was finally through with her father, Devlon rose to question him. A flicker of ... something ... passed across her father's face.

"Tell me." Devlon stood with hands clasped behind his back. "In all the arguments your daughter had with her mother, did she ever get violent?"

"No." Her father shook his head.

"Ever hit her mother?"

"No."

"Threaten her in any way?"

"No."

"How about at school? Was Laura ever in trouble?"

"No."

"Did she ever show any violent tendencies toward her friends?"

"Not that I know of."

"So ... this was a girl with absolutely no history of violence, as far as you know."

"That's right."

"Hmm." Devlon paced a few steps. "And that last argument you spoke of between Laura and her mother. You said they made up the day before your wife was killed?"

"Yes. Laura apologized."

"Did she show any signs of anger toward her mother after that?"

"No. It appeared the argument was over."

"When you saw Laura the next morning—the day of your wife's death—did she display any signs of anger then?"

"No."

"Did you think everything was all right between them?"

"Yes."

What was her father thinking as he answered these questions? Was he glad the answers helped her case?

Devlon switched to a new line of questioning. "Are you dating someone now, Mr. Denton?"

Whoa. Laura didn't know her attorney would do that.

Cantor objected. The issue was "beyond the scope" of his direct. Devlon shot back that Cantor had "opened the door" through some of his questions. The judge called both men up to the bench, where they argued in heated but low tones. Finally Judge Myers allowed the testimony. Cantor did not look happy. Neither did Laura's father.

Devlon again asked the question.

"Yes." Her dad shifted in his seat.

Devlon asked for the woman's name and what she did for a living. Laura's dad had to answer.

Her lawyer raised his eyebrows. "I see. On the San Mateo police force. How long has she served in that capacity?"

"Five years."

"And when did you meet Miss Fulder?"

Laura's dad looked down. "About two months after my wife was killed."

"Two months."

"Yes."

"You didn't know her before that?"

"No."

"Where is Miss Fulder living at this time?"

"At my house."

Laura froze. Tina was living *in her house?* Sure, Laura's friends had seen her there, but Laura had just assumed she came over a lot. She *lived there?* What could her father be thinking? What was supposed to happen when Laura got home? Like she was just going to accept this *cop* in her life?

Laura stared at her hands, seeing their cracked and dry skin. One of the many reminders of how hard her life had become. No fancy creams in juvey. Nothing soothing at all. When she got home she wanted everything to be as comforting as possible. It would be hard enough with her mother gone. No other woman was going to take her mom's place. Tina Fulder was moving *out.*

Devlon kept her dad on the stand for another hour or so. After awhile Laura tuned out. She just couldn't listen to her father's voice anymore. It hurt too much. By the time he was done testifying, every muscle in Laura's body felt like stone. This was only the first day. How was she going to get through an entire week of this?

Her father took a seat in the courtroom. Laura could feel his eyes on her back. She couldn't help but picture him going home to Tina. What they would talk about. How he would describe his day.

She hated Tina Fulder.

Before Laura could take a breath, Cantor summoned the woman who'd answered her 9-1-1 call to testify. Soon he was playing a tape of the call in court. Laura heard her own voice, screaming, crying. Begging for help. She squeezed her eyes shut and lowered her head. The sounds were like a knife in her heart. They brought back all the memories, fresh and raw. She could see herself in her mom's bed-room, feel the bang of her heart, smell the blood …

The tape ended. Laura's face was wet with tears, and she trembled in her seat. Judge Myers asked if she needed a recess. She shook her head. If she stopped the trial every time she felt bad, they'd never get done.

"Are you sure?"

She took deep breaths—and nodded.

"Okay." The judge motioned to Cantor. "Proceed."

Next up began the series of cops and paramedics who'd come to the house. What they'd seen, what they'd done. More reminders of the chaos. The nightmare. Laura pressed her mind deep inside itself. Maybe if she just didn't listen …

When lunch break came, she didn't want to eat.

By mid afternoon Laura felt sick. She couldn't take any more of this. But the day was about to get worse. Cantor called Detective Standish. Her lawyer had warned her that the detective may testify for a long time—a day or more. Laura hadn't seen him since she'd been arrested. The very sight of him made her stomach turn over.

The detective sat on the stand like he owned it, looking all factual and perfect. Answered questions like he had all the answers. Didn't take long for Cantor to ask him about the words she'd said to her dad all those months ago. *"I didn't mean it."* Yes, the detective verified he'd heard those words too.

Well, good for him. Clearly the man could read Laura's mind. Sure enough, those words had to mean she was a cold-blooded mur-derer, and then was sorry about killing her mother when it was too late.

The prosecutor moved on to questions about what Detective Standish had found at the scene of the crime. A pair of Laura's shoes with blood on them. The green shoes were brought out for everyone to peer at. The bloodied hammer with Laura's fingerprints. Every-body in court got to see that too. And on and on. The prosecutor made it sound like *everything* about Laura's life pointed to the fact that she killed her mom. By the time the day was done, Laura had to admit, if she'd been sitting in the courtroom listening, she'd have believed that, too.

She left the courtroom on weak legs. On the drive back to juvey, she didn't even look out the window. She could only stare at her lap and cry. And first thing tomorrow morning she'd get to listen to more of Detective Standish.

She would never survive the rest of the trial.

CHAPTER 14

Laura's trial dragged on. Detective Standish's testimony covered every minute they'd spent together in her two interrogations. Turned out that little camera in the top corner of the room had taped it all. She got to watch herself on a monitor, knowing everyone else in the courtroom was gawking as well. She saw her scared face, her tears, the denials. Couldn't everyone see she was telling the truth? Did they really think she was that good at lying?

She stole long glances at the judge, wondering what he was thinking.

The prosecutor was finally through questioning Detective Standish in the afternoon of the second day. By then Laura's insides had frozen over. She didn't know if she couldn't feel or just didn't care anymore. Every minute that ticked away had made her look worse. How could her attorney ever turn things around?

Devlon rose to cross examine, bristling with energy.

He took Detective Standish back to the afternoon of the murder. He'd found blood spatter on the shoes hidden in Laura's closet, correct? Had he noted any blood spatter on Laura herself? Her long-sleeved T-shirt? Her pants?

"She had quite a lot of blood smeared on her hands and shirt," the detective replied.

"I'm not talking about smears. Those she could have gotten from finding her mother on the floor and turning her over, correct?"

"Yes."

"Blood spatter is different. In your testimony you noted that it occurs at the time of attack. You found it very significant that spatter was on the shoes. Correct?"

"Yes."

"Did you find blood spatter anywhere else on Miss Denton's person?"

"No."

"Really? Not anywhere?"

"No."

Devlon paused, as if surprised. "Didn't you find that significant?"

"No."

"Why not?"

"You can't always figure where blood spatter will go."

"I see. So are you saying in this case the spatter went downward only? To the shoes?"

"I … no, I can't say that."

"You testified you saw spatter on the walls by the bed, did you not? Both the wall that the headboard was up against, and the side wall that ran parallel to Mrs. Denton's body?"

"Yes."

"So it did go upward as well as down."

"Apparently so."

"I see. If it went upward, and Miss Denton had been present at the time of the attack, wouldn't it have gotten on her clothes as well?"

"Depends on where she was standing."

"There was only one place *to* stand, wasn't there? In the three feet of space between where Mrs. Denton fell and that side wall?"

"Yes, but exactly where in that space? The defendant could have been near Mrs. Denton's head or more at her waist level."

Devlon consulted his notes, then launched into a series of

questions that came harder and faster. Hadn't the detective testified that the blood spatter on the side wall was found from the corner to eighteen inches out, then stopped, then started up again at thirty-eight inches from the corner? So there was a blank space of twenty inches? Why would that be? Wasn't it safe to surmise that's where the perpetrator had been standing? What else could have possibly blocked that spatter? And if that was the case, the spatter would have gotten on the person's clothes, wouldn't it? Is that not what the law of physics would require? Had the detective ever known blood to bend around nothing, going in two directions of its own accord? Yet there was no spatter on Laura's clothes, only her shoes, was there? Did the detective have any explanation for that?

Laura had to work to keep a smirk off her face. How long she'd waited to see Detective Standish squirm. Now maybe he knew how it felt to be pounded with questions. The only difference was—he was *guilty* of the things he was being accused of—ignoring the truth, homing in on her alone. *She* hadn't been.

But her attorney wasn't done. Next he wanted to know about the bathrooms and kitchen sink in the house. Had the police checked the drains for blood?

The detective admitted they hadn't.

"Wouldn't that be a standard part of a murder investigation?"

Later, when the detective slipped and mentioned the blood on Laura's hands, Devlon pounced on it. Did he mean to say the police had focused on her immediately as a suspect? So much so that they hadn't conducted the investigation of the crime scene as thoroughly as they should have?

The detective tried to explain his actions, but with every statement Devlon managed to corner him more.

"So what you're telling me is, *if* the perpetrator of this heinous crime washed the blood off his hands before leaving the premises, you *wouldn't know it*. Because you never checked for it."

"We did not check."

"If you had checked and found blood in a drain, wouldn't that have alerted you to the presence of someone else in the house other than Miss Denton? Since she clearly had not washed her hands when you arrived on the scene?"

The detective went around and around the question. On the fifth try, Devlon finally got him to admit that would have been something they'd have "looked at."

When five o'clock came and court had to stop for the day, Laura was surprised to find herself disappointed. She could have watched Devlon's show all night. That evening she went over and over Standish's cross examination in her mind. Was the judge seeing the truth? All the things that should have been done in the investigation—that weren't?

The next morning Devlon talked to Laura before court began. He looked rested and ready to fight, wearing a dark blue suit and red tie. Cantor looked dull in comparison, wearing his standard gray. "I need to warn you I'll be bringing out some information you haven't heard yet," Devlon said.

Laura didn't like the word *warn*. "Like what?"

"About a man at your mom's work. Apparently he had a crush on her."

Laura's eyes widened. "Somebody you think could have killed her?"

"I don't know. Thing is, the cops never looked at him."

The judge entered, calling court to order. Laura's heart tumbled around. Some man who liked her mom? Had he tried to make moves on her, and she said no? That could make someone mad enough to kill—if he was a sick person. Maybe, just maybe, this was the answer to her burning question.

As Standish sat down to testify, Laura tried to gather her whirling thoughts. The news about this man at her mother's work was exciting. But why hadn't she heard about him before, including from her own attorney? Wasn't this *her* trial? It was like the adults pulled all the strings, and she was just some puppet. The puppet who'd pay for their mistakes.

Devlon started in on Standish. "You testified about interviewing some of Mrs. Denton's coworkers at the hospital. Ever hear the name Roger Weiner? One of the male nurses at the hospital?

"Yes."

"Did you interview him?"

"No."

"I see. You testified you did interview Myra Bastion, Mrs. Denton's best friend at work?"

"Yes."

"And she told you about Mr. Weiner's obsession with Mrs. Denton?"

Another objection from Cantor. Laura wished he'd just shut up. In time the judge let Devlon continue. He repeated the question.

"She mentioned it."

"Why didn't you follow up on that?"

The detective tried to skate around an answer. Devlon finally got him to admit by then the evidence was "so against" Laura, they stopped interviewing people at her mom's work. Another example of their tunnel vision.

Devlon had to stop there with Standish. He'd told Laura he would bring out more of the information on Mr. Weiner during the defense questioning. There was only so much he was allowed to do during cross exam. The detective left the stand and courtroom without one glance at Laura. Well, good for him. The man who knew everything. He might not hold his head so high when she was acquitted.

The worst thing about Devlon finishing with Standish was that the prosecution took over again. Cantor started calling some of Laura's friends—*her own friends*—to the stand. One was Natalie Dross. Laura used to gossip with Natalie every day. They'd go to movies or the mall together, talk on the phone. Laura would have trusted her with anything. Now Natalie wouldn't even look at her.

Cantor asked Natalie to recount what Laura had said about her mother the last time they'd fought. Devlon objected that it was hearsay, and he and the prosecutor argued back and forth until the judge called them both up to the bench again, where they argued some more. In the end the judge let the evidence in.

The prosecutor looked so pleased with himself. "So what did Laura say to you about her mother?"

Natalie looked straight at Cantor. Laura had the feeling they'd practiced this. "She said, 'If you think my mom's so great, you can have her.'"

Laura couldn't even remember saying those words. But even if she had—so what? She wouldn't have meant it. How could that possibly mean she'd killed her mom?

As if Natalie wasn't bad enough, Cantor called in a second friend—Derra Tobert. And Derra testified Laura said the exact same thing to her. Laura couldn't believe it. She sat at the defense table, shoulders hunched, trying to keep it together. These girls got to live in the outside world. Got to go to school, and talk on the phone, and go to the mall. Who were they to say anything against her? Didn't they know they were helping the prosecution? Or did they think she was guilty, too? Just like her dad.

For the first time Laura began to fear getting out of juvey. What would her life be like? Her dad with some other woman. Both of them believing she was guilty. Friends who also thought she was guilty. Everywhere she went people would look at her and talk about her. How could she go back to school? Find her mom's real killer on her own? How could she ever resume a normal life?

Fact is, her life *wouldn't* be normal. Ever again.

CHAPTER 15

On the fourth day of Laura's trial the prosecution rested. Finally her own attorney could question people—who'd tell *her* side of the story. And she'd get to testify herself.

This is it, God. Please help!

Laura took her seat behind the defense table, more confident than she'd felt since the trial began. The reporters were still there. Now they'd hear the truth. And they'd *better* write it in their stupid articles.

Devlon gathered his notes and rose. He was looking good today in a dark pinstriped suit. His tie was a swirl of mauve and blue. Definitely cool.

Her attorney began by calling one of her mom's coworkers to the stand—Paula Dewey. Laura had never heard of her. Paula was a large, no-nonsense-looking woman. Older, with gray hair and green-framed glasses. She sat in the stand comfortably, like she had nothing to hide.

Turned out Paula supervised the nurses, including Roger Weiner, the male nurse who was "obsessed" with her mom, as she put it. Laura sat up straighter. Ever since she first heard the name Roger Weiner it had run through her head. Someone who could be guilty. Who'd actually killed her mother. Those kinds of things—jealous would-be lovers—happened in the movies, didn't they? And sometimes in real life.

Cantor wasted no time in interrupting. He objected to the word *obsessed*. The witness was stating an opinion. The judge sustained. Laura hated it every time Judge Myers agreed with Cantor. Made her wonder if the judge favored the prosecution. Devlon had reminded her the judge had agreed with him on some important issues. Laura didn't care. He could agree with Devlon one hundred times, she'd retorted, but the one time he sided with Cantor would be the one she'd remember.

Devlon tried another approach with Paula Dewey. "Did Roger Weiner work on the same shift and floor as Sally Denton?"

"Yes, at first."

"But then you moved him to a different floor?"

"Yes."

"Did he ask you to put him back on the same floor as Mrs. Denton?"

"Yes. Numerous times."

"Did you comply with that request?"

"No."

"Why not?"

"I'd moved him in the first place because I'd heard complaints from Sally of his behavior toward her."

Little by little Devlon extracted what that behavior was about. Asking Laura's mom to meet him after work. Making comments about her looks. Getting too close to her as he reached for something. Laura felt her blood go hot. How dare some sicko treat her mother that way.

According to Paula, other employees had noticed Weiner's behavior too. It had gone on for about a month before she moved him to another floor. He was a good nurse, but he'd been warned—no interaction with Sally Denton at work. So he technically "obeyed" by talking to her in the parking lot before and after their shifts. He'd try to park close to her, make sure he was walking to his car at the same time she was.

"Did Mrs. Denton make a final complaint about Mr. Weiner the day she was killed?" Devlon asked.

"Yes. The previous day he had accosted her in the parking lot at the end of their shift—'accosted' was the word she used—and forced her up against her car with his body. He told her she was 'going to be his' soon."

"What did you do with Mrs. Denton's complaint?"

"I began the procedure for firing Roger based on sexual harassment. Sally's previous complaints had already been filed and were on record. It would not take long until Roger was gone."

Laura's fingers curled. Why hadn't Detective Standish ever mentioned this man? *Why* wasn't her dad upset about Roger Weiner's actions?

Apparently Weiner heard what Paula had done. He argued with her about it, claimed Laura's mom was lying. He was so mad he quit on the spot and left the hospital. That was around one o'clock. Laura's mom got off at two.

By the time Laura got home from school around three-thirty, her mom was dead.

As Paula Dewey left the stand, Laura could barely breathe. If she saw Roger Weiner right now she'd leap at the man. Tear at his throat. He'd done this murder, hadn't he. Stomped out of work, mad enough to kill, and waited somewhere on their street until Laura's mom got home.

"But Detective Standish told you they didn't even interview this guy!" Laura hissed to Devlon during a break. "Why'd they let him go?"

"You heard what Standish said. The evidence already pointed to you. They got you in their crosshairs and never looked anywhere else."

"It's reasonable doubt, right? I mean, enough to show the judge I didn't do this?"

Devlon raised a hand. "And I'm not done yet. I'll raise plenty more.

But the thing is, sometimes it's not enough to say the defendant didn't do it. You have to point the finger at someone else who could have."

Laura rubbed her arms. "Do you think he did it?"

"I think he's a strong possibility. And right now that's all we need."

But what would happen when Laura got home? Wouldn't the cops turn to Roger Weiner as their next suspect? Would he get mad again and come after *her* this time?

"Listen, Laura." Devlon put his hands on her shoulders. "Good news is, he's not likely to come after you. Because bad news is, they won't even talk to him."

"*Why?*"

"Because they'll go on saying you did it. You just got away with it, that's all. As far as they're concerned, there *are* no other suspects."

No. This was too much. "So he'll just *get away* with it?" No, this could never be. Her mom deserved to rest in peace. Her mom deserved justice.

Her attorney looked away. Slowly nodded. "I'm afraid so."

At lunch, once again Laura couldn't eat. She could only think about what the prosecutor and Standish would say to the public after she was acquitted. She could imagine the newspaper articles. "*The judge got it wrong. Justice was not done for Sally Denton.*" Everybody would still say she was guilty. Everybody.

She wouldn't be able to stay in San Mateo. She'd have to go … who knew where? Some other state. Start over again. Maybe her dad would be so glad to see her go, he'd give her some money, tell her to be on her way. And why shouldn't he? He'd inherited plenty from her mom.

That afternoon Devlon called more of her mom's coworkers to the stand. Each one told how Roger Weiner had acted toward Sally Denton. And two of them said, when they first heard her mother had been killed, they immediately thought Weiner had done it.

Of course Cantor moved to strike their statements. The judge agreed.

Back in juvey that night, lying on her hard cot and staring at the ceiling, Laura thought about her new life after she was acquitted. Where she'd go. What she'd do. The thought of leaving her home town to live all by herself was petrifying.

How do you start a new life alone, after you've lost everything?

April 2013

CHAPTER 16

An hour after hearing the news of Billy King's arrest, I drove away from the Crenshaws with thickened blood in my veins. Clara's parents and family at first had been stunned and saddened by the news. Then, quickly, their feelings turned to anger. *How* could he have done it? *Why*? Nothing I could say would have persuaded them Chief Melcher was wrong. They'd lost Clara, now they wanted, *needed* justice for her. The faster that happened, the faster they could find some sort of closure, however frail. They were so wrapped in their pain I couldn't bring myself to argue with them.

"I'm so sorry," was all I could say. Lame words spilling from me, again and again. "So very sorry."

Now my brain felt numb. Where should I go now? What could I possibly do?

The overwhelming helplessness of my own arrest and trial came flailing back, threatening to choke me. This is what Billy was feeling now. Like me, he'd probably be stuck in prison until his trial. The thought of gentle Billy in jail for even one night was too much to bear.

Something had to be done *now*.

I pulled over to the curb and picked up my cell to call Andy. His thoughts would be clearer than mine. But before I could tap his name, the phone rang.

Pete.

I answered the call.

"Del-Belle, you okay?" Pete's gruff voice sounded scratchy with emotion. "I guess you heard."

A sob rolled up my throat. I wanted to hit something. Scream to the mountaintops. "Cops are terrible people, Pete! I hate them *all*."

Seconds ticked by. I gulped down air, trying to get hold of myself.

"They're not all like Melcher, Del-Belle. Had a few police in my own family. They were honorable men."

"I'm sorry. I just …"

"I know. This ain't goin' well. But sounds like you're thinkin' about more than just Billy. You have a run-in with some other cop in the past?"

Sickness spread through my stomach. Why had I said anything? My two worlds were about to collide, trains on the same track. And I couldn't find the brakes.

"It's just Melcher." I swiped at a tear. "I *told* him. He won't listen."

"Yeah, well. Trouble is, he's got louder voices to listen to than yours. Like Becky Myers, who wouldn't lie about seein' Billy on the street. And Cheryl King, who *did* lie about Billy bein' home all night."

"How do you know that for sure? Just 'cause I told you?"

"I was at her house when she heard about Billy's arrest. She'd been tellin' me the same thing she told you—he never left home. Until that call came. Then she just fell apart."

I could imagine. "Did she admit to you she lied?"

"Didn't have to. I could see it all over her face."

I'd seen the same thing. Just hadn't wanted to admit it to myself. The queasiness in my gut grew stronger. "Billy lied too, didn't he. Told Melcher he was at home."

Cheryl's words echoed in my ears. *"Billy looked so guilty. He can be that way around authority."* Billy's own fear would push him into denying he was anywhere near Clara last night. And the more he lied, the guiltier he'd look to Melcher. To any cop.

"Apparently that's just what Billy did. After I heard the news I beat feet down to the station. Tried to get Hank Shire to talk to me."

Hank had been the first responder at the crime scene. Seemed like a nice man. Nothing like Melcher. Still, he was a policeman.

"Turns out Hank was in the interrogation room with Melcher and Billy. All Hank would tell me was, 'Nothing he said was the truth.'"

I laid my head back against the seat rest, memories of the interrogation about my mother's murder flashing through my head. I'd never lied to Detective Standish, not in the slightest. Yet he'd twisted the truth into his own sinister story. *"Let me tell you how it happened, Laura."* How much more ammunition Melcher would have now, hearing Billy's false statements. Added to that, my own account that I'd seen a man in a dark hooded sweatshirt. Billy had been on Brewer Street. Wearing a dark hoody.

And Clara's car had been at the curb, engine running, driver's door open. She must have gotten out of her car quickly. Most likely for someone she knew.

Who, if not Billy?

"Pete." My throat was tight. "What do we do now?"

"We hunt around and find out who else would have wanted Clara dead."

"I was just with her family for a couple hours. No one there has any idea, other than Billy. *I* have no idea."

Pete grunted. "They're probably glad the suspect's been found so fast."

"Exactly. They're clinging to it. How do you take that away from them?"

For once Pete had no answer.

I checked my watch. It was almost 3:00. Andy would be picking me up for dinner at 6:30. What great company I'd be.

"Pete, I forgot to tell you I won't be making dinner tonight. I'm going out with Andy."

"No worries there. We'll rustle somethin' up."

I ended the call and tossed down my phone. No point in calling Andy now. I'd be seeing him in a few hours.

With a sigh I pulled back onto the street—and found myself heading toward Brewer, where Clara had been killed. I parked across the street from The Spot, eyeing the fluttering crime scene tape. The mound of flowers people had left was growing. I saw a small stuffed teddy bear. Some cards and candles.

Something within me turned inside out. I slid from the car and crossed the street. Walked toward Clara's shrine, a lump in my throat. My thoughts jumbled as I surveyed the scene. I pictured Clara sprawled on the sidewalk in the dark. The hooded figure in the Graysons' yard. Those memories morphed to those of my mother. Her blood, her battered body. Yelling at Detective Standish in the interrogation room. Being hauled off to jail. Back then a murderer had walked the streets of my hometown and killed my mother. What murderer walked *these* streets, here in the quiet town of Redbud? Had he visited this spot where I now stood? Watched grieving friends and family bring Clara flowers?

Vaguely I registered the sound of a vehicle pulling to the curb across the street. Two car doors opened and closed. Footsteps approached. I glanced in their direction and saw two men, one with a microphone and another with a TV camera. Behind them sat a WTVQ van—the ABC station in Lexington. The man with the camera swung it up and turned it on.

I jerked my head away.

"Ma'am, I'm Barlow Watkins." The reporter stepped onto the sidewalk. "I'd like to ask you a few questions."

"No thanks." The cameraman had come around and was filming me from the side. I turned my back to him.

"It'll just take a minute." Watkins stepped in front of me once more. His voice was gentle, full of concern. "You're Delanie Miller, aren't you? The one who discovered Clara Crenshaw's body? I've been hoping to speak with you. We stopped by your house, but no one was home."

Reporters. I should have known they'd come. I focused past Watkins to the flowers left for Clara. Suddenly it hit me what a story this would be for the local media. A beautiful young woman on the way home from her *wedding shower*. In small, typically safe Redbud.

How fast would the media convict Billy King?

"Miss Miller?" Watkins raised his eyebrows. "Is it okay if I ask you a few questions? I'm going to do a segment for tonight's news from here. I hoped to include you."

"I don't want to be on camera." I worked to keep fear out of my voice. This was the last thing I needed. What if someone had moved here from the California Bay Area and recognized me?

"You don't have to be. I'd just like to understand from you what you saw last night."

What I saw. My gaze cut to the reporter. "Have you talked to the police?"

"Just came from the station. I know they've arrested a man named Billy King. Apparently he had a crush on Miss Crenshaw. You know anything about that?"

I stared at Watkins. It had already begun—the public molding of facts to fit Melcher's scenario. The twisting of quiet, slow-minded Billy King into a hidden killer, a jealous bomb waiting to explode.

In my mind I pictured Bruce Melcher's rage-filled expression as he stood in my kitchen, his finger stuck in my face. *"I'll haul you off to jail!"*

Arrested. My background checked …

I could not talk to this reporter.

"Do you, Miss Miller?"

"Yes." The word popped from my mouth.

Watkins waited but I said no more. "What do you know?"

I pictured Billy in jail. Remembered how numb I'd felt in juvey all those years ago.

"I know that Billy would have done anything for Clara. Chief Melcher arrested the wrong man."

The cameraman eased in front of me, still filming.

"How do you know he's the wrong man?"

No way for me to keep quiet now. I *couldn't*. In a matter-of-fact tone I told Barlow Watkins what I'd seen the night Clara was killed. The figure that stood by the bush just down the street—a figure too short to be Billy. Barlow wanted to see the bush. I walked him down to the Graysons' yard and pointed it out, the cameraman following. Told the reporter how Mr. Grayson and I had measured the bush.

"Have you told all this to your police chief?" Watkins and I remained in front of the Graysons' house.

"Yes. Absolutely."

"What was his response?"

I looked back up the street toward the yellow crime scene tape and Clara's flowers. Dare I speak the answer ready to spring off my tongue? How incendiary it would be. How the media would eat up the controversy.

But maybe that's just what we needed here. If Chief Melcher was going to play his game in public, so could I.

"Miss Miller?"

My heart fluttered. I lifted my chin and stared directly at the camera. "Chief Melcher came to my house and told me flat out if I interfered anymore in his investigation he would 'haul me off to jail.'"

CHAPTER 17

When I pulled into my driveway, exhausted and railing at myself for what I'd done, Colleen's and Nicole's cars were out front. Pete's was gone.

A chime from my cell phone signaled a message. It was from Andy. *Can't wait to see you tonight. Love you.*

I managed a tired smile and texted back. *Love you too.*

You doing okay, Del?

Hanging in there. :)

I stared at the smiley face I'd added as a way to soften my answer. It looked ridiculous.

With a sigh, I grabbed my purse and got out of the car.

Inside the house I found Nicole on the couch, watching TV with a blank expression. I gave her a hug. "Where's Colleen?"

"In her room."

I surveyed her. "You okay?"

She shrugged. "Been a hard day."

Tell me about it.

I headed for the kitchen, hunger gnawing at my stomach. I hadn't eaten all day. From the fridge I pulled a small container of yogurt. I slumped at the kitchen table and spooned it down, barely tasting. Over and over in my mind I relived the words I'd said to the

Lexington reporter. *Why* had I done that? Even if the news was only local, I couldn't afford to be seen on TV.

Why had I done it? For Billy.

Colleen appeared from the hallway. She'd traded the knee high hose and pumps she always wore to work for her Dr. Seuss socks. Her short brown hair looked only a little better than when she'd gotten out of bed. Colleen's perpetually frazzled appearance was her trademark.

She was full of news from her work at Granger's Gift Store. People had come in and out all day talking about Clara's murder—and then Billy's arrest. "A lot of people pegged Billy even before he was taken in." Colleen sat on the big couch next to Nicole and tucked her colorful feet beneath her. "They're all saying how so many of those crazy people in the past who shot up schools or movie theaters or whatever were quiet and not right in the head."

I took a seat across from Colleen and Nicole on the smaller sofa. Would people like that change their minds after hearing my story on the news?

What would Andy say about what I'd done?

What would Chief Melcher do?

Nicole turned off the TV. She focused on her lap, lacing and unlacing her hands. "I couldn't concentrate in any of my classes today. All I could think of was Clara. I just still can't believe it." A tear rolled down her face.

Colleen patted her on the leg. "None of us can, honey. This is just ... too much."

"We'll get through this together, Nicole." I gave her a wan smile. She nodded.

A headache had set in. I pressed a hand to my forehead. "You both need to know Billy didn't kill Clara. I'm absolutely sure of that."

"It's hard to believe he would." Colleen waved a hand in the air. "But from what I've heard Chief Melcher thinks he's got his guy. Still, I say no way Billy did this. He loved Clara. He told me so. I knew they'd never get together, but still … I felt so sorry for Billy. His heart ached over her."

My brain flashed to Billy standing next to me at the crime scene. "Either of you know a Susan in town? Blonde woman. Someone who'd tell Billy that Clara wanted to be more than a friend to him?"

Nicole screwed up her face. "What?"

"Billy tell you that?" Colleen asked.

I nodded.

She seemed to ponder that. "So what else have you heard today?"

I pushed away the pictures of Billy and began detailing my going to the Graysons' and measuring the bush. My time at the Crenshaws, and Chief Melcher's not so friendly visit. I didn't tell them about my talk with Billy's mother, Cheryl, and how she'd lied about Billy being home. Colleen would likely repeat it to all the Granger customers the following day, and that wouldn't help Billy.

"I can't believe Melcher came into your own house and told you that!" Colleen sounded incensed.

I nodded. "Pete was here. He heard it."

Nicole made a face. "Sounds like the chief of police doesn't want to know the truth."

I pictured Detective Standish eighteen years ago, facing me across a wooden table. "It's not that he doesn't want to. It's that he thinks he *does* know the truth, so anything not fitting into his scenario has to be wrong."

"Poor Billy." Colleen closed her eyes.

I checked my watch. Time to change clothes for dinner with Andy. I wanted to be ready early enough to see the news before he arrived.

"Let's watch the local ABC news," I told Colleen and Nicole. "I'm supposed to be on it."

"Really?" Nicole's eyes widened. "What did you say?"

I gave her a grim smile. "Enough to get me in more trouble."

The front door opened—and Pete appeared. "Hello, ladies." He shuffled over to his favorite chair and sank into it. "Whew. What a day."

"Want a Coke, Pete?" It was his favorite drink. I rose.

He waved me back down. "Don't you worry, I'll get it."

I ignored him and headed to the kitchen to pour the soft drink. Brought it back to him.

"Thanks, fine lady." He smiled up at me through his scruffy beard.

"What did you find out?" I sat down again on the small couch.

Pete took a long drink. "Ah, good." He set the glass on the nearby table. "Talked to Phil Tranke." Phil owned Redbud's only drugstore. Clara had worked there a few years ago. "Phil thinks it's nuts they arrested Billy. He's got all kinds of ideas about Clara's murder. Like— what if we're lookin' at this all wrong? What if whoever killed her was a total stranger? Maybe some druggie on the street that she stopped to help, and things got outta hand. Remember six months ago Phil had a burglary at his store, and one of the things missin' was a lot of cold medicine—the stuff you need to make methamphetamine. There's been more and more problems with meth around here lately. Thing is, the murder seems so random. Not like it could have been planned. A woman's driving home at night. She stops—for what, we don't know. And she's killed."

Colleen worked her mouth. "The person could have known Clara would be driving home on that street around that time. Everyone in town knew about her shower."

Pete stroked his beard. "Maybe. Phil also says Billy wasn't the only guy sweet on Clara. He saw a number of other men hit on her when she worked at the store."

Clara had never mentioned any of that to me. "Like who?"

"Aaron Kater, for one."

Of course. Aaron. "I saw him at the crime scene just this morning. He seemed heartbroken. He did mention dating Clara in the past."

"Phil was there too, right?" Pete shifted in his chair. "That's what made him think of Aaron. Something about the things he said—before you arrived."

I lowered my chin. "Things can be taken the wrong way. And besides, it's all just conjecture, Pete."

"Yup. But conjecture's all we got right now. Unless you want to go with the Billy idea."

"What if Billy did do it?" Nicole said.

Three heads turned in her direction.

She pulled her mouth to one side. "Well, everything does point to him. He was there at the right time. Wearing the dark hoody you saw, Delanie. Plus he lied about all of that."

I couldn't believe what I was hearing. "But why would he hurt Clara?"

"He probably didn't mean to. Maybe he waved her down, and she got out of her car, thinking something was wrong. When she got close he tried to kiss her or something. She pushed him away, and he just … lost it. Started choking her. And he couldn't stop until it was all done. Then he panicked and ran."

I stared at Nicole. "How can you think this about Billy?"

"He *lied*, Delanie. Why would he do that?"

"But you *know* him."

She averted her gaze to the couch. Ran a finger over the cushion. "Maybe I just thought I did."

"What does that mean?"

Her throat convulsed. My insides went cold. Clearly Nicole thought she knew something.

"A comment he said to me last week. I didn't think much of it then, but …" A tear rolled out of Nicole's eye.

Colleen touched Nicole's knee. "What did he say?"

Nicole sniffed and wiped her cheek. "We were at church. He asked me if I was going to Clara's shower, and I said yes. He got this angry look on his face." Nicole raised her head and looked me in the eye. "He said, 'I have to stop her.'"

Pete drew his head back. "Stop her from doin' what?"

"I don't know. I asked him, but he turned away. Now I think … maybe I should have known. Maybe he was talking about Clara marrying Jerald."

"She was gonna be more than my friend." Billy's words ran through my head. Had he really expected Clara to break up with Jerald and be with him? And when she didn't …

No. Not possible.

"But Billy wasn't the man I saw by the bush." How many times did I have to remind people of that? "He's *too tall.*"

Nicole laid a hand against her jaw. "Look at this objectively. The man's height is what you remember, Del. But memories aren't always reliable. I learned about that in my psychology class."

Colleen tilted her head. "I've heard that too—that people think they remember who they saw committing a crime, but they're wrong. Eyewitness accounts are the least reliable evidence in court, did you know that? Saw it on the news once. But jurors tend to treat them like they're the most reliable."

Now there were *two* of them? I looked helplessly to Pete. He stroked his beard, focusing across the room. His gaze seemed to pierce through the wall. I could tell he was gearing up for a story. Frustration banged around inside me. I didn't want a railroad story right now. I wanted him to tell Colleen and Nicole they were *wrong*.

Pete leaned forward, arms on his legs and hands laced. "Back in 1995 or so I was engineer on the leg from Seattle to Wenatchee, Washington. I was with my conductor, Manny. It was the dead of winter and real cold. Trip took five and a half, six hours if there were no problems. You had to go through the Cascade Tunnel, which was all uphill goin' east. One point two percent grade. Goin' east we were always in the number six notch." Pete looked to me. "Notches had to do with how fast you were goin'. They ran from number one through eight."

My eyes flicked to the clock on the wall. I needed to change clothes for dinner so I could watch the 6:00 news. But I barely felt the energy to get off the couch.

"Anyway, there's only one main track runnin' each direction, of course. If a second train's comin' the other way one of 'em's got to move to a siding. Amtrak was comin', so before hittin' the tunnel we got over to wait. Then Amtrak radioed our dispatcher and said he saw a man at Bay Seven in the tunnel. Bays held equipment and stuff—a little indentation off the track. So the dispatcher tells us to stop and pick up the guy. He was way out in the middle of nowhere and likely to freeze to death if we didn't fetch him."

Nicole frowned. "How'd he get there?"

"Well now." Pete spread his hands. "That's a mystery, ain't it. What's the guy doin' there where he shouldn't be? Franklin and I started knockin' around theories. Neither of us came anywhere close to the truth."

Like—why was Billy King on Brewer Street last night?

"So we stop and pick the man up. A hobo, drunk as a skunk. He climbs up in the cab, mighty glad for the warmth." Pete pinched his nose. "Guy smells like he hasn't had a bath in months. I says, 'Man, what are you *doin'* out here?' Connor—that's his name—says he'd hopped a ride on another train with a few other hobos. Ended up gettin' into a fight with one of 'em, and the other guy threw him off. He went into the tunnel for shelter." Pete chuckled. "If he was even thinkin' that clearly. Guy was dead drunk."

"People really did that in the '90s?" Colleen planted a fist against her waist. "Hopped free rides on trains like that?"

Pete shrugged. "Sure. Don't mean it was legal. But how else were the tramps supposed to get around?" He stuck a finger in his beard and scratched his chin. "After awhile Connor starts groanin' 'bout his foot. And the guy won't shut up. 'Oh, it hurts, it hurts.' So Manny turns on the cab light and says, 'Let's have a look.' Connor's wearin' boots, and sure enough, looks like the right one has blood on it. Manny tells him to take off the boot. Which he does. Now the sock's *real* bloody. Connor, he still has no idea what's goin' on. Manny says, 'Better take off your sock.'"

Pete leaned back against the couch and scratched his chin again.

Colleen raised her eyebrows. "And ...?"

Pete sniffed. "Two toes fell out."

"Oooh!" Nicole screwed up her face.

"Connor just stares at 'em. Then he says, 'Are those *my* toes?' I point to his foot with three toes left and say, 'Looks like it, Bud.' Manny takes a closer look at the boot the guy took off. You can see a mark over the top of it. Apparently when Connor got thrown off the train, his foot was run over."

Nicole hugged herself. "How could he not know that happened?"

"Too drunk, is all. Amazin' what you miss when you drink too much."

"So what happened to him?" Colleen asked.

"Manny used our first aid kit to wrap up the foot. We radioed the dispatcher that we'd need an ambulance at the Redondo Crossing in Wenatchee." Pete gestured toward Colleen. "We're tryin' to help Connor, see? So what does he do? Get's all scared that the railroad cops are gonna arrest him for train-hoppin' when we stop. He keeps harpin' at us to let him off early. Man's so afraid of gettin' into trouble, he ain't even worried about his toes or freezin' to death." Pete spread his lips. "I convinced him he wouldn't be arrested. We stopped at the crossin' and the ambulance was there. They carted him off. Left his two toes behind though. Manny swept 'em out of the cab before we headed off again."

Nicole managed a nervous laugh.

If Pete had told this story two days ago, we'd all have laughed ourselves silly. How many times had he regaled us with stories about his railroad escapades? About how his conductor served as the "side-wall heater chef" in the days of the older locomotives, using the electric heaters on the side of the cab to cook deer, moose, bear, and wild meat chili. Or the time a train carrying corn derailed one hot summer, and the corn fell into a nearby stream. In the heat it fermented in the water. Bears followed their noses, ate the corn, and got drunk. Pete saw five to six bears staggering around or lying on their backs with their paws in the air. Colleen, Nicole, and I giggled about that one for days. Before Clara's death, even thinking about that story would set me off.

Now I wondered if I would ever find anything funny again.

Pete took a drink of his Coke. "So you get why I told you that story?"

Colleen pushed up her lower lip. "Comic relief?"

"More than that." Pete held up a finger. "One, sometimes the truth is way more crazy than you'd ever guess. Two"—another finger went up—"sometimes people who ain't thinkin' straight—like Billy—are so worried 'bout gettin' in trouble, they do stupid things to avoid it. Like Connor wantin' to get off the train early in the freezin' cold—with two less toes. Like Billy lyin' to the police about bein' on Brewer Street last night when he coulda just told 'em the truth."

"Then why was he there?" Nicole's tone held a silent plea, as if she wanted to be convinced.

"I don't know." Pete cocked his head. "Could be a crazy reason. Could be somethin' he's ashamed to admit, like wantin' to see Clara drive by on her way from the shower."

Problem was, now we might never know. The more scared Billy became, the more he'd dig in his heels. Insist on the lie.

Wait. Something Pete had said earlier to me that day ...

"What if he didn't lie?" I focused on Pete. "You asked me that before. What if Billy *wasn't* anywhere near Brewer Street last night? And Cheryl really is telling the truth about him being home. She's never admitted to anything different."

"Becky saw Billy." Pete sighed. "Told me so herself."

"Maybe she's wrong. Like Colleen said, eyewitnesses aren't always reliable. If *I'm* not reliable about the height of the man I saw, why is *she* any more reliable?"

"She saw his face," Pete said. "Right in her headlights."

"I know. Still, you're assuming she's right."

"Maybe you're both right." Nicole lifted a shoulder. "Becky saw Billy there, and you saw a different man." Her voice trailed off. "Wearing the same hoody."

I gave her a look. "Could be two similar sweatshirts. Maybe one was dark blue and one was black. There are millions of hoodies out there."

I put a hand to my forehead. My mind was running in circles. And I *had* to get ready for dinner with Andy. I pushed to my feet. "All I know is, we have to stop thinking we know everything. With every detail, we're making a lot of assumptions. We have to step back from those assumptions. Try to look at things in a different way. Or …"

My head lowered. At that moment I wanted to be anywhere but in Redbud. I wished I'd never come to the town.

"Or what?" Colleen's voice was gentle.

I focused on the floor between my feet. "Or an innocent person could go to jail for a very long time."

I turned toward the hallway and made for my bedroom, feeling three pairs of eyes on my back.

October 1995

CHAPTER 18

Laura's trial went into a second week. By that time her emotions were totally fried. But she had to pull herself together. On this day, she would take the stand.

She wore a new pair of pants her dad had bought for her. (Imagine that—he'd buy her clothes but testify against her.) And a long-sleeved green blouse that matched her eyes.

As Laura took her seat at the witness stand, she allowed her gaze to cruise the courtroom, catching the eyes of her Aunt Nicky and her dad. Laura quickly looked away. How different everything was from up there. Everyone looking at her—not just at her back, but her face. Everyone hanging on every word. The reporters were practically salivating.

She hadn't slept the previous night. After all her preparation with Devlon, what if she came unglued? Really messed up? Plus, he'd told her it wouldn't be easy. First she'd have to relive the whole awful story about finding her mother. Relate every detail. And that was just when her own attorney was questioning her. When he was done Cantor would have his chance. And don't you know that horrible man would just as soon skin her alive.

It wasn't until her testimony about finding her mom that Laura started to cry. She hated that. Tried to hold back the tears, but then her throat got all choked up. She went through three tissues from the nearby box. Clutching them in her hand, wiping her eyes. Good thing she wasn't wearing mascara. It would all be gone.

And then came the questions about the words she'd spoken to her dad on the lawn. "'I didn't mean it.' You remember saying those words, Laura?" Devlon's tone was gentle.

"Yes."

"Why did you say that?"

Laura looked at her lap. The tissue in her hands was twisted and wet. Her throat ached, head too. Her whole body felt tired and bruised. "Because I'd been fighting with my mom up to the night before. I'd already said I was sorry, but ... To see her there on the floor, so ..." More tears came. Laura swallowed hard. "At least the last time I'd talked to her, everything was fine between us. But I couldn't help but remember our argument. I just felt so bad for everything. For every time I'd said hard words to her. And I was afraid my dad would be thinking of our last argument. I guess I just wanted him to know I was sorry about it. And to forgive me for ever treating her that way."

Laura leaned forward and squeezed her eyes shut as fresh tears fell. Devlon waited her out.

"Laura. *Did* you kill your mother?"

A sob escaped her. *"No!"*

Devlon took her through all the so-called "evidence." He asked about her fingerprints on the hammer. Laura explained how she'd hung a picture in her room and used that hammer. Of course it would have her fingerprints.

By lunch break, Devlon was done with her. Laura got off the stand, legs trembling. She couldn't look at a single person in the courtroom, including her dad. Especially her dad. She tried to tell herself she no longer cared what he thought—she'd told the truth. But she couldn't help hoping ...

All Laura could do during that break was drink water. Her attorney encouraged her to eat. She needed fuel, he said. But her stomach couldn't take it.

That afternoon when Cantor faced her, ready to pounce, Laura sat like stone. *Breathe … breathe …*

He went over all the "evidence," as if the judge hadn't already heard it from Detective Standish. And he made a huge deal about the "missing" ten minutes. Cantor pounded her about her "claim" of standing on the porch, looking at pictures in a catalog. How could she have been there that long and not seen the door hanging open? In truth, hadn't she gone straight inside, argued with her mother, and killed her?

"No!" Laura leaned toward him, her voice shaking. "And you have to quit saying that!"

"So it's your testimony you were looking at pictures for *ten minutes.*"

How many times did she have to go over this? Devlon had warned her to keep her cool on the stand, but she was about ready to throttle the prosecutor. "It's not just my 'testimony,' it's the truth. People look down and miss things around them all the time. You haven't heard of someone running into a person or a wall because they're reading something? I *wasn't looking at the door!*"

Devlon gave her a laser look—*calm down.* Laura shifted in her chair.

But Cantor wasn't through. He turned to the green shoes—*her* shoes—with her mother's blood on the soles and in spatter on the top. During her own attorney's questioning, she'd said she had no idea why they had blood on them or why they were found underneath a pile of dirty clothes in her closet. But if she didn't get blood on them and hide them, then who did? Why would someone walk in off the street, kill her mother, and make it look like she did it? Did she have enemies? Was she fighting with someone at school? Could she name one person who hated her enough to do this?

Laura took a deep breath. "Maybe that man at my mom's work. Roger Weiner."

"Did he know you?"

"No."

"Had you ever even heard of him before?"

"No."

"Then why would he want to do this to you?"

"I don't know."

He nodded, as if he'd just made a major point.

"What's your shoe size, Laura?"

"Eight."

"Eight. Do you know any man whose feet would fit into your shoes?"

"I … no."

"Well, whoever committed this murder had those shoes on. Right?"

"Maybe they didn't."

"Any other way they'd get blood spatter from your mother on the tops of them?"

He'd trapped her. Laura's own attorney had referenced blood spatter and how it worked when he questioned Detective Standish. "I don't know. Maybe they were just … sitting on the floor nearby."

Cantor badgered her so much about the stupid shoes, Devlon had to object. The judge told Cantor to move on.

Laura tried to steady herself.

The prosecutor veered into another old topic—Laura's words to her dad. "*I didn't mean it.*"

"You had just found your mother dead. Why would you be thinking about an argument you'd had with her?"

"I already *told* you why. I felt bad for arguing with her."

"You were thinking of an argument that you said had been resolved?"

"It had been."

"And yet that was foremost on your mind. At the moment of finding your mother dead."

"It wasn't 'at the moment' I found her dead. Right when I found her, I went to her. Hoping she was okay. I called 9-1-1."

The prosecutor eyed her.

Laura wanted him to drop dead. "You tell me—what are you *supposed* to say when you see something like that? Something so awful you couldn't even imagine it? There's no 'right thing' to say. Your mind isn't even working. Everything slows and turns and goes upside down. Your whole word just … explodes."

Cantor changed to yet another subject—details of her arguments with her mother. He did everything he could to make Laura sound like a terrible daughter who'd just as soon see her mother dead. And then he went on to her mother's will. Another hard subject, now that Laura knew her dad had been granted all the money that was supposed to come to her. She could've used that money, now that she knew she had to leave home. But she couldn't show her bitterness on the stand. Cantor would love for her to do that. He'd claim her bitterness supported his theory—that she'd killed her mom for money and now was ticked that she wouldn't get any.

Laura's veins steamed as she answered Cantor's questions. She kept both hands in her lap, out of sight. They fisted and dug craters into her legs, but her expression remained calm. And her answers never waivered. She couldn't have killed her mother for money, because she didn't know about the will. Had never even thought to ask. Laura didn't want for anything, and she'd been promised a car that summer. Inheriting a big pile of money any sooner wouldn't have changed anything.

As Cantor consulted his notes for how to attack her next, Laura kept her eyes lowered. Speaking of a car—she didn't have one. And had no money to buy one. How was she supposed to leave town and live on her own when she didn't even have a car?

Laura was on the stand all day. When Cantor was finally done dragging her through the mud and hanging her from a tree limb, Devlon came back to ask some follow-up questions. He was much more gentle with her, and she tried to relax. But by then she could hardly think straight. All she wanted was to go back to her hard cot at juvey and sleep.

But of course that night sleep wouldn't come—again.

For the rest of her trial Laura sat at the defense table like a zombie. Something inside her had gone into a coma. She could hardly listen to the testimony, hardly feel anything. All she could do was count the minutes until the judge let her go home.

To a dad who didn't want her. And some female cop who dared live in *her* house.

Not to mention the reality that she would probably never see justice done for her mom.

On day nine of the trial both sides were done with their questioning. All that remained were the closing arguments.

Cantor got up first.

The prosecution's argument would be hard to sit through, Devlon had warned Laura. The prosecutor would be able to talk as long as he wanted, making all his arguments for her guilt, and they'd just have to sit there and listen.

"Can't you object?" she asked.

"I can, but it's not likely. It's sort of frowned upon during a closing argument, unless the other side makes some egregious claim. And I don't want him taking revenge by interrupting *me*."

Fine then. Laura would just tune Cantor out. These days she did what she had to in order to survive.

But when it came time, she *couldn't* tune him out.

Not when he went through every piece of "evidence" they had, step by step, showing how each one pointed to her and her alone. The hammer. The shoes. The footprints. And then there was the supporting evidence. The "missing" ten minutes. Laura's recent argument with her mother. Her words to her father as they hugged on the lawn.

"You know." Cantor raised his forefinger. "Sometimes in the worst of moments is when a person's true self comes out. There's no time for judging the words you're about to say. No energy to hold them back. What slips out is from the heart. A brutal honesty that, were it not for the trauma at hand, would have remained hidden.

That moment is when Laura Denton sees her father for the first time after killing her mother. And what is it that slips out of her mouth at that vulnerable moment? *'I didn't mean it.'"*

Cantor paused, letting the words hang in the air. "'I didn't mean it.' That's as close to a confession from Laura Denton as we will ever get."

Then there was the fact that the police had not a single other suspect in this case. If Laura didn't kill Sally Denton, *who did?* "Oh, the defense worked hard to give up someone else. Someone with an obvious crush on Mrs. Denton. But a crush does not a murderer make. And the evidence against Laura Denton mounted so swiftly, the police made the obvious choice—to arrest her for the crime."

Cantor shook his head. "I've seen a lot of things in my career. But this one, this case will stick with me. You have a teenager who's given everything she needs. She lives in a good home with good, loving parents. The teen herself seems well adjusted. Gets good grades in school. No prior trouble with the law. And yet underneath ... something simmers. Something sinister and evil. Perhaps it started with Sally Denton's inheritance from her mother. Laura looked at all that money her mother now possessed and thought *'I want that for myself.'* Maybe she pushed away the thoughts for a while. But they grew and boiled inside her. Until one day, after a final, heated argument with her mother, Laura Denton had enough. And in that moment she grabs a hammer that's sitting in her room and goes after her mother with it. With the first blow she hits her mom hard enough to knock her down. But Laura Denton doesn't stop there."

Don't listen, don't listen, don't listen. Laura focused on her lap, breathing hard, fingers twisted together. Cantor was describing a monster, not her. How *unfair* this was, that he could go on and on. That he could tell such *lies.*

"No, she doesn't stop there." Cantor's voice rose. "She stands over her mother and hits like this." He pantomimed leaning over and swinging a hammer down and up three times. "She keeps hitting and keeps hitting until her mother's skull is bashed in, and blood is on the walls and on her, and her victim's face is almost unrecognizable." Cantor stopped for a dramatic pause. When he continued, his voice held a grim quiet. "When it's all over she realizes what she has done. That she will be punished. So quick-quick, she stuffs the bloody hammer under a pile of clothes. Takes off her bloody shoes and hides them as well. She sees the blood on her hands and clothes. Cunningly, knowing she doesn't have time to wash those clothes, she smears more blood on her hands and T-shirt. So she can claim she tried to help her mother when she 'found' her."

Even with her eyes lowered, Laura could see Cantor turn toward her. Laura's gaze raised to him, her head unmoving. The prosecutor was glaring at her. Slowly his pointing finger came up. "That girl there, your honor, is a killer. A cold-blooded, heartless killer of her own mother. The woman who brought her into this world. Who nurtured her. And to this day I've seen not one whit of remorse. Only lies and pleas of 'I didn't do it.'" His finger shook at her. "This girl deserves to be punished for the crime she committed. It would be an outright travesty—to the victim and to her husband—to allow this murderer to go free. I ask that you do what justice demands—and find her guilty."

Cantor held his pose, then dropped his arm. "Thank you."

He returned to his seat.

You're so welcome. Laura shot him a dark look.

"All right, thank you. Mr. Brooks?" The judge showed no expression. Did he agree with Cantor? Could he see through the lies?

Devlon arose, shaking his head. "Your honor, that was a lot of theatrics from the prosecution. And a lot of supposition. You'd think we were trying this case in front of a jury. Let me just remind you of the facts."

Step by step Laura's defense attorney broke down the case. He covered her complete lack of a criminal record, her good grades in school. The life that she had, complete with promise of a car that coming summer. Why were her fingerprints on the hammer?

Because she'd used that hammer to hang a picture in her room. Interesting that her fingerprints weren't bloody ones. Wouldn't they be, if she was the one who used that tool to bludgeon Sally Denton to death? Much more likely that someone else, wearing gloves, used that tool. And once the murder was over, that Someone also pulled a pair of Laura's shoes from her closet and made sure those shoes were covered in blood spatter. Perhaps the perpetrator flicked the bloody hammer at them. Then he hid the shoes and the hammer in the most convenient spot for the police to later find—under Laura's clothes in her own closet. And how could the court know this is what happened? If Laura had been wearing the shoes during the murder, why wasn't spatter also on the bottoms of her jeans? Why was there no spatter on her T-shirt? Or anywhere else on her clothes? It was certainly on the wall, starting from the baseboard all the way up to the height of Laura's head. And the pattern clearly stopped where the perpetrator had stood, then started up again on the other side.

"So where's that blood, your honor?" Devlon raised his hands. "Nowhere on Laura Denton. *Nowhere.* Except for a pair of shoes she hadn't even worn that day, hidden in her closet."

This was clearly a very cunning, purposeful killer, Devlon continued. Someone who not only wanted Sally Denton dead, but also wanted her daughter to pay for it. Leaving her father, Gary Denton, alone and suffering, his family annihilated. Who would want to do something that sinister? Perhaps the man at Sally Denton's work who was so obsessed with her that he was fired due to his harassment. That man's involvement in this crime remained a huge unknown due to one fact—the police's complete ignoring of him because they'd decided they had their suspect. To this day the police and prosecution had paid this dire possibility little heed.

Devlon's voice rose. "It is unconscionable that an innocent sixteen-year-old could go to jail for years because of the incompetence of law enforcement."

He turned to the testimony of those who'd worked with Laura's mom, all of which pointed to a perpetrator other than Laura. And he went over Laura's own testimony.

As Laura listened, the dread in her chest began to ease. She'd heard all the defense arguments, sure, but never put together in such a perfect package. Forget what Cantor had claimed. When the judge looked at everything the defense was presenting, there was no way he could find her guilty. All the answers were there in front of him. Laid out. Stacked in order.

"Your honor, this entire case is such a travesty," Devlon said in closing. "This young girl has already lost her mother. And now she's lost six months of freedom. She needs to get on with her life. She needs to be reunited with her father and rebuild what family they have left."

Laura's heart plummeted again. They had no "family" left. Getting out of jail would just exchange one terrible problem for another.

By the time Devlon was done, Laura felt totally drained. She managed a small smile as he took his seat next to her. "Thank you," she whispered.

He patted her arm.

"All right, sounds like that'll do it." The judge shifted in his chair. "We'll meet back here tomorrow afternoon at two o'clock. I will have my verdict at that time."

He banged his gavel and rose to leave. And just like that the trial that would decide Laura's fate was over.

CHAPTER 19

The night her trial ended, Laura lay on her cot, staring at the ceiling as she had on so many nights. Would this be her last night here? She knew it would, even as misgivings whispered in her mind. She was petrified of being freed only to face carving out a new life by herself. But staying in jail would be so much worse. Plus, if she was found guilty she wouldn't stay in juvey. She'd be shipped to California Youth Authority. A place ten times worse than here, she'd heard. Juvey was hard enough, with lots of inmates in for crimes like stealing from a store or possessing drugs. But CYA was all hard time. Full of murderers and gang members. People who'd just as soon knife you as look at you. Laura would never be safe in a place like that. She had no idea how to defend herself from that kind of people.

She'd rather die than go to CYA.

Please, God, please. You know I'm innocent. Let me go home!

The next morning Laura could do little but pace the length of her bed. Three steps down, turn around, three steps up. The hours until two o'clock would never pass. So many things ran through her mind. Over and over, she saw her mother's bloody face, the broken body. Heard Cantor calling her a "cold-blooded murderer." Saw her own father on the stand.

What was her dad thinking this morning? Did he even care?

Lunchtime came. Laura didn't eat. As the hour approached for her to leave for court, her blood flowed cold, then hardened. When they let her out of her little room, she didn't look back. She'd never have to lay eyes on the horrible four walls again. She walked out of juvey for the last time, feeling sun on her face.

Within a few hours she'd be home. In her own room. Tonight she'd sleep in her own bed. How incredible.

How terrifying.

In the car she couldn't feel anything. Not even her own body. Her feet and ankles seemed miles away from the rest of her. She walked into the courtroom on someone else's legs. Sat down at the table using someone else's muscles. Devlon said a few words to her, but she couldn't process them. Could only hear her own shallow breathing. The sputter of her heart.

Laura's dad was there. And her aunt. Laura could feel them looking at her back.

It took forever to get everyone settled, including the judge. He called the court to order. Sat and shuffled a few papers. Laura slipped her hands beneath the table. Locked them in a tight grip.

The judge began to speak.

Devlon laid a hand on Laura's shoulder.

The world slowed … slowed, until it nearly stopped turning. The whole scene felt surreal, like she hung near the ceiling, looking down at herself. Laura squeezed her eyes shut, clinging to the judge's words, every muscle within her pulling, *waiting* for the "Not Guilty."

"… I find the defendant, Laura Ann Denton, guilty of second degree murder …"

What?

Laura's muscles locked. For a split second her mind went white.

Guilty?

No, couldn't be. She'd heard wrong—

The judge's voice singed her ears. "I will set sentencing for two weeks from today …"

Devlon gripped her shoulder until it hurt. Laura's muscles

unlocked, then turned to water. She started to tremble. First her legs, then torso, then whole body. She turned to her attorney, head shaking. Wanted to scream *Why? How?* But her throat wouldn't make a sound.

Noises behind her. Someone weeping. The prosecutor stood, looking so proud of himself. Judge Myers left. Cantor started packing up his files.

Laura couldn't get up.

A bailiff came to put cuffs on her. They'd take her back to juvey. *Back.*

"I can't go!" She jerked away. "I didn't *do* it!"

"Calm down." Devlon's voice.

Calm down! For what? So they could drag her back to that little cell? The hard bed and stained walls? So they could throw her in *CYA?*

Wails spurted from her mouth. "I didn't *dooo it!*" Laura fell to her knees.

Hands reached for her. Many hands. People calling her name, lifting her up. Her ankles wobbled, and the world dimmed. She caught a fleeting glance of her father watching her, forehead crinkled and tears on his face. "Dad!" She flung out an arm toward him, but someone caught it, pinned it. She felt the cuffs, and the world dimmed more, and her head tipped back, the room spinning ...

S p i n n i n g ...

rocks in her stomach and chest, breath blocked in her throat and people yelling and her knees giving way and the courtroom going black, blacker, until she saw noth—

April 2013

CHAPTER 20

D el!" Colleen called from our gathering room. "They're running the news story next!"

"Okay!" Quickly I put the finishing touches on my makeup and inspected myself in a full length mirror. I'd put on a blue cashmere sweater and black skinny pants and heels for dinner with Andy. Had only half managed to chase the stress and lack of sleep from my face. It would have to do.

I hurried from my bathroom. Pete, Colleen, and Nicole were still sitting where I'd left them fifteen minutes ago. I resumed my own seat, feeling my heart flutter. Once this news story hit the airwaves, what would happen to me? What would Chief Melcher do?

Commercials ended. The news returned.

"Here it is!" Nicole leaned forward.

An anchor woman led into the story of a "heinous murder in Redbud of a young woman driving home from her wedding shower." From there the scene switched to the reporter I'd spoken with, Barlow Watkins, standing in front of the yellow crime scene tape on Brewer. He told of Clara's strangulation and the arrest of Billy King, a man who "reportedly had a crush on Miss Crenshaw." According to Redbud Police Chief Bruce Melcher, King was spotted near the scene of the crime by two people around the time of the murder.

Two? Anger rose within me. Melcher had to mean Becky and *me*.

"But one of the eyewitnesses strongly disagrees with Chief Melcher. Delanie Miller, who discovered Miss Crenshaw's body, insists the person she saw in the shadows wasn't tall enough to be Billy King. According to Miss Miller, Chief Melcher isn't interested in what she has to say."

Nicole's eyes widened. "Uh-oh."

The picture switched to my face. I looked haggard yet defiant, the blaze of injustice in my eyes. The sight sent a shockwave through me. How many times I'd seen myself like that in mirrors during the days of my own trial. During all the years following.

I watched, muscles tense, as the reporter asked me more about Chief Melcher. And my response: "Chief Melcher came to my house and told me flat out if I interfered anymore in his investigation he would 'haul me off to jail.'"

Colleen and Nicole gasped. Pete turned to me, his mouth drawn inward. *Oh, boy*, he mouthed.

The story wrapped up in another half a minute. I barely heard. My ears rang with my own words.

The picture switched back to the news anchor and another story. How life moves on.

Colleen grabbed the remote and muted the sound.

For a moment none of us said a word.

Nicole pulled her bottom lip between her teeth. "Is he gonna put you in jail?"

I shrugged—*who knows?*

"Nah." Pete sat back and folded his arms. "As much as you got him riled up, Del-Belle, in a way you've protected yourself. How can he make any move against you now, with the media lookin' on, and all the town knowin' how he treated you?"

"Yeah, Pete's right." Colleen sounded almost as defiant as I had. "Now old Melcher's stuck by his own words."

I ran a sweaty palm over my pants. "I don't know. If people in town really believe Billy did this, they *will* look at me as interfering with justice. And they'll support Melcher."

Nicole made a face. "Melcher's not very popular in this town anyway. People like you way more. I'll bet they'll side with you."

I gave her a crooked smile. Kind words. But Clara was dead, and somebody needed to pay. That changed the balance.

The doorbell rang. *Andy.*

I rose, apprehension swirling in my veins. What would he say about what I'd done?

"Hi, Beautiful." Andy wore a dark blue sport coat and silk multicolored tie. He stepped inside and hugged me for an extra long moment. When he drew back, he studied me with a warm smile. "You look terrific."

My heart lurched. To the very core of me, I loved this man. If only he could have been beside me during this terrible day. Andy could make anything better. "Thank you."

He glanced at the faces of my roommates, the muted news on TV. "Something about Clara?"

"Yeah." Nicole gave me a meaningful look. "Delanie was on, too."

Andy raised his eyebrows. "You were interviewed?"

Thanks, Nicole. "I'll tell you about it in the car."

We said our goodbyes and headed outside. I was silent as we pulled away from the curb. The more I thought about what I'd done, the more frightened I felt. Something would come of this. Something bad.

CHAPTER 21

S o what happened with your interview?" Andy asked as we hit the edge of town. He shot me a sideways smile, but it faded quickly. Maybe he didn't approve of my talking to the reporter.

My hands pressed together. I had yet to tell Andy how Melcher had threatened me with jail that morning, and the chief's final remark about my "rich boyfriend not being able to help."

It struck me then for the thousandth time—how much I kept from Andy. I'd grown so used to guarding the secrets of my past, I didn't know how to share my present.

"First I need to back up and let you know what happened this morning." Staring through the windshield, I told him about Melcher's visit. What he'd said. How Pete had heard it all.

Andy's jaw set. "He really said that to you?" A rhetorical question. "Why didn't you tell me this earlier?"

I shivered. The evening wasn't cold, but my body could not shake its chill. "I had so many people to see, and …"

"But I called you hours ago. Didn't you think I'd want to know?"

I turned my head and focused out my window. "I knew we'd see each other tonight, when we could really talk."

Silence.

"Okay." Andy lifted a hand from the steering wheel. His tone did not match the word. "So what happened on the news?"

I told him.

A little smile crept over Andy's face. Hadn't expected that. "Well, sounds like you gave it right back to him."

"You're not mad at me?"

"Why should I be mad at *you*? I'm furious at Melcher for what he said. He deserves this. Now everyone knows what a jerk he is."

"Oh." I took a long breath. "A minute ago you seemed ..."

Andy shook his head. "I just don't like it when you don't tell me things."

I shifted in my seat.

"Pete says Chief Melcher won't be able to 'haul me off to jail' now. Because people will be watching him after the newscast."

"Pete's right." Andy fell silent again. After a moment he cleared his throat. "Something I need to say, though, Del. Even though I've been at work all day, I've been hearing things through phone calls. The evidence—other than what you saw—all points to Billy. I know you think he didn't do this. At first I thought the same. But you can't let your emotion cloud the facts."

I stiffened. "It's not just emotion. I know what I saw."

"You saw a shadow of a figure. Didn't even see his face, right? Becky Myers saw Billy up close. Yet he denies he was there and has no alibi. It just doesn't look good."

First Nicole, now Andy. If *they* wouldn't listen to me, who would? I folded my arms and stared out the windshield. "He *didn't* do it."

"Okay." Andy held up a hand. "But what if he did? And meanwhile you go around defending him? People will remember that."

The faces of Phyllis and Doug Bradshaw flashed in my mind. What were they thinking? They didn't approve of their son dating me in the first place. "Is this about your parents?"

Andy threw me a glance. "Why are you bringing them up?"

"Because they don't like me." And when his mother saw the news, she'd probably have apoplexy. The Bradshaws and anyone linked to them simply did not make spectacles of themselves on television.

"They like you just fine."

"No, they don't." Impatience laced my voice.

"Del. We are not talking about my parents."

I closed my eyes. The day had been bad enough. Did I need to make it worse by picking a fight with my boyfriend—something I'd never done?

"I'm talking about you and your reputation in Redbud. I'm just suggesting that as much as you like Billy, you might pull back now from saying anything more. Because if you're proven wrong, I think you'll live to regret it."

Tears of frustration bit my eyes. I tried to blink them back and failed.

"Hey." Andy reached over to squeeze my arm. "I don't want to make you cry. I just ... want to protect you, that's all."

Since the beginning of our relationship, Andy had viewed himself as my protector. As if I was somehow lost and needing direction. He was three years older and supposedly therefore wiser. Little did he realize I'd lived through twice what he had in my lifetime.

"I know." I dug a tissue out of my purse.

"Look. Just let me say one thing, all right? Then we'll change the subject."

Like there *was* any another subject right now. "Okay."

He tapped a finger against the steering wheel, as if considering how to begin. "Sometimes people surprise us. Sometimes they're not at all what they pretend to be."

My gaze darted to his face and hung there.

"I know you've seen it on the news or heard stories. Everyone swears they know a certain person, and that person would never do x, y, z, but then it turns out they did. And the friends and family members say 'how can this be? It just doesn't fit with what I know.' Or sometimes people who may be disturbed don't show it outwardly. They're quiet and easy to overlook. Until *bam*, they blow up."

Shades of the town's gossip Colleen had heard. I turned my head away. My heartbeat felt like a hard grind.

"Do you hear what I'm trying to say, Delanie? I just don't want you hurt more than you already are in case something like that happens."

I rubbed my hands together, focusing on my fingernails. Why didn't I paint my nails? It would be so much more refined and fashionable. So would living in my house by myself, instead of gathering a faux family. And I should have a job. Be like a normal person. I'd bucked all those things to be *me* in this new life I'd created.

Except I wasn't being the real me at all. Never could be.

"Delanie?"

Words stuck in my throat. "I hear you. Thanks."

Andy sighed. "Okay then." He slid his arm across my shoulder and massaged my neck. "I'm done. And now—this evening is about us. No one else."

My chest felt tight.

I could think of little to say the rest of the drive, or as we sat down to dinner at a secluded corner table in the best restaurant in Lexington. Andy told me about his real estate deals—which had worked, which were giving him trouble. I responded at all the right times, but it was obvious I was still upset. Andy kept up the conversation, pouring out energy for both of us. I loved him for that.

After our meal was finished, he pushed aside his coffee and reached across the table for my hand. "Delanie." His eyes were so warm. "I love you."

My throat constricted. How had I ever found this man? "I love you too."

He took his hand away to reach into the pocket of his coat. Brought out a blue velvet box and pulled back its top. A large stunning diamond in platinum gold sparkled in the lamplight.

All air left my lungs.

Andy watched my face, nervousness pulling at his mouth. Never before had I seen him show such an expression. "I want to be with you forever, Delanie Miller. You're everything I need. Will you marry me?"

I couldn't speak. A montage of memories flooded me. My father and mother kissing in front of a Christmas tree. My father's grief at her death. The long days in juvey, when all I wanted was the family I'd lost. The horrible years and further shocks following my guilty verdict. The day I bought my house in Redbud. The day Pete moved in. My first date with Andy. The nights I'd fallen asleep dreaming of this moment. Clara's smile after her wedding shower—"You're next, Delanie!"

Andy still held out the ring. "I—I know it's a bad time. Sorry for that. I just … after what happened to Clara, I want you near me always. Starting now."

I looked at him, fresh tears in my eyes. His mother would hate this.

"Sometimes people aren't what they pretend to be."

Love for Andy flushed through me. The last thing I would ever do was hurt this man. And if he found out how I'd lied to him about who I was, my childhood, my parents—*everything*—he *would* be hurt. I could never, ever let that happen. Ironic, how he thought he would be protecting me from now on. Just the opposite. Whatever it took, however hard it was, I would protect *him* from discovering my deceit. For Andy. For me. For our life together.

I gave him a shaky smile. Took the box from his hand and slipped the gorgeous ring onto my left fourth finger. "Yes. You know the answer is yes!"

October 1995 — January 2004

CHAPTER 22

Two weeks after her guilty verdict, Laura Denton was sentenced to serve time in the California Youth Authority until she turned twenty-five. She would be moved by the end of the year.

Eight and a half years in CYA.

By the time the judge handed down her sentence, Laura already knew what was coming. Devlon had warned her. No crying out, no fainting like she'd done at the verdict. Laura heard the words fall like stones from the judge's mouth but barely felt a thing. In the last two weeks she'd gone numb. The days blurred by, nothing mattering, nothing to fight for. Letters had stopped coming from her friends. Did they believe everything they read in the papers? Had their parents made them quit writing? No matter, either way. Laura was alone.

Her mother's real killer would never be brought to justice.

A week after the sentencing, Laura's father showed up in a surprise visit. When they told her he was there, the anger in her wanted to declare she wouldn't see him. The love in her, however beaten and bruised, moved her feet out of her room and down the hall.

They faced each other in the glassed enclosure, both standing. Her dad looked like he'd aged ten years.

"Hi." His hands hung awkwardly at his sides, as if he didn't know what to do with them.

"Hi."

"I came to see you before …"

"Before they ship me off to CYA? Somebody in there'll kill me, you know. That's what happens in that place."

Her father's face turned grayer.

Laura's nerves sizzled. She wanted to punch him. She wanted to throw her arms around him and never let go. "You still think I did this? You really believe that?"

He shook his head. "I … don't know."

"Which means you do." Her voice was razor sharp.

He gazed at her, pain zigzagging his face. "Did you?"

She closed her eyes, so weary. "Like you didn't hear my answer enough in court?"

Her father gave a slow nod. Looked away.

Weakness rushed Laura's legs. She sat down in one of the plastic chairs. Minutes ticked by, both of them staring at nothing.

Laura took a breath. "You gonna come visit me in CYA?"

He flinched. "You want me to?"

Yes. No. Who knew? What she wanted was her *life back*. Her mom alive. And her dad. School. Friends.

"You still have that same cop girlfriend?"

Her father lowered himself into a chair. Focused on his hands. "Yeah."

"You gonna marry her?"

He shrugged.

"I'll bet she tells you how guilty I am, huh. Fills your ears full with it."

"We … don't talk about it."

"Oh. Your daughter and your *dead wife* aren't worth talking about?"

He looked up at her, eyes glazed. "Laura. *Don't.*"

Her heart turned over. If only she could hug him. Cry into his chest. But he sat across from her, a world away.

Laura closed her eyes. How hard she was becoming. How cynical.

And she wasn't even in CYA yet. She heard how that place changed people. She couldn't let herself get worse. Age twenty-five was a lifetime away, but it would come. And she'd have the rest of her life. Somehow ... some way she had to keep some part of who she was. Who she'd been.

She picked at a pulled thread on her ugly cotton pants. "So you gonna marry her or not?"

Her dad sighed. "I don't want to talk about Tina. I want to talk about you."

Tina. Laura hated that name. "What's there to talk about? You think I'm guilty. That I'm going where I deserve. And no matter what you say, I know your girlfriend convinced you of that. After all she is a *cop.*"

"You're still my daughter."

"What good does that do?"

His jaw flexed. "I'll always love you."

She looked down and shook her head.

More silence.

"Are you happy with her? *Tina?*"

"Why do you keep asking about her?"

Laura bristled. "Maybe because she's your life now. Mom's gone, I'm in here rotting away. And you just go on with your new, happy existence."

He swallowed. "It's not all happy, Laura."

Well, cry me a river. "It should be miserable! You shouldn't be sleeping at all, thinking about me in here for some horrible thing I didn't do. You should be working day and night to get me out of here! Instead it's like you're ... somebody else. You don't even know me anymore." The *injustice* built in Laura, higher and higher until she could stand it no more. She pushed to her feet. "You know what—I don't want to see you in here again. I *can't.* It hurts too much, and there's nothing left to say."

Laura turned away and headed for the door. Sobs clogged her throat.

She whirled back. Tears prismed her vision. "Tell you what." She jabbed a finger toward her father. "Come see me in CYA—when you *know* I'm innocent."

She flung open the door and stumbled to the desk where Tats waited.

As she was escorted down the long hall to her room, Laura sobbed aloud. She wanted to scream. Wanted to run back and tell her father she hadn't meant it. Instead she hung her head, watching the scuffed floor slide beneath her plodding feet. In her room she flopped down on her cot, her back to her roommate, and stared at the wall. Her heart tremored, ready to burst from her chest.

Laura knew her father would never come see her in CYA.

CHAPTER 23

On November fifteenth Laura was transported to Ventura County in Southern California, the only CYA that accepted girls. As Laura began the intake process at the facility part of her was still scared past comprehension. Another part didn't care. If somebody here—a *real* killer—wanted to knife her, so what? Death didn't matter much when you had nothing to live for.

She was put in a tiny room with brick walls. A small, hard cot—like she'd had in juvey. A little desk. A white toilet and sink. At least she was by herself, no roommate. The day room was a large area where she and other inmates could go when let out of their cells. There was a family visiting room—not that she'd have any visitors. And a pay phone in the day room to call family. Not that she'd be using it.

"Don't look like a victim," inmates at juvey had warned her. They were the ones with brothers and sisters and cousins in CYA, who filled her ears with tales of the horrible place. But how to not "look like a victim" when you're not tough and had never been in trouble with the police in your entire life—until they decided you'd killed your mother?

Laura tried to keep to herself, which lasted about an hour the first time she was let out of her cell into the day room. A huge girl with frizzy blonde hair sidled up to Laura, her eyes slitted. "I heard you killed your mama." She spoke with a Southern accent. How she'd ended up in California, Laura had no clue and didn't want to ask.

"They said I did. But I didn't."

The girl rolled her eyes. "Yeah, right. Nobody in here's guilty."

Laura protested. Made no difference. The girl looked at her like she was scum. "I can understand killin' somebody else, but your own *mama*?"

Word soon spread. No one liked Laura. After a month it started to get to her. Stuck in here was bad enough. Couldn't she have one friend? After the second month she quit telling people she was innocent. No one listened. And she may not have had friends, but no one bothered her either. Apparently she was considered quiet but dangerous. If she'd killed her own mother, who knew what she was capable of?

They went to school in the days, for what it was worth. If anybody got out of control, if a fight erupted, they were all sent back to their rooms. On non-school days she was in that tiny cell by herself for twenty-three hours a day. Laura thought she would climb the walls.

How could she do this for *eight and a half years?*

Laura missed her mom more than ever. And her dad. Was he married by now? Did he ever think about her?

She felt herself slipping away to some remote, alien place. Sometimes she couldn't feel anything. In group counseling sessions she never said a word, no matter how hard the counselor tried to draw her out. They all saw her as a murderer. What was there for her to say?

"Hold on to you—the real you," she told herself over and over. Some day eons from now she'd be out. She'd be twenty-five with no family (that cared anyway), no job, and no money. She'd have to make it on her own, build her own family. She'd find a man who loved her. She would be a mother some day. But she couldn't do that if she was all hardness and cold. She needed to keep the ability to love in her heart. Somehow.

God was no help. He didn't do prison.

The first year dragged by …

…

…

…

And the second …

…

…

Laura earned her high school degree.

Now what to do with herself within those four walls? There were some vocational classes, but she wasn't interested in any of them.

Girls came and went. Few were in for as long as she. By the time she got out she'd be older than any of them. *Twenty-five.* Sounded ancient. Women were married by twenty-five. Had kids and careers. She'd have nothing.

She turned nineteen in March 1998. On her birthday she sat on her cot, trying to remember the sound of her mother's voice. The memory was gone.

Her twentieth birthday was spent in the infirmary, weak-limbed and high-fevered with flu. She dreamed (hallucinated?) that her mother was in the room, calling to her. Promising Laura that one day the real murderer would be caught and brought to justice. Laura awoke chilled and sweaty. Wishing she could return to the dream. In real life, as far as the System was concerned, her mother's "murderer" *had* been caught. The case would never be reopened.

When Laura was finally well, she returned to her little room with her head full of thoughts about Roger Weiner. She'd not allowed herself to dwell on him before—too frustrating. Now she couldn't help herself, thanks to the dream. Where was Weiner now? When she got out, could she find him? Somehow make him confess?

Laura began to fantasize about seeing the evil man on trial. Watching police lead him away in cuffs to prison. Hearing her own name exonerated.

The new millennium dawned. New for everyone else. Around the world people were partying. Living it up. Laura was asleep before midnight.

Her twenty-first birthday was spent in her room, in lockdown. A fight had broken out, and three girls had been beaten. When something like that happened, everyone paid.

Happy birthday, Laura.

A tiny piece of her had wished for at least a letter or card from her father. But—nothing.

November 2000 skulked around, and her fifth year was done. Laura could barely remember what it was like to live on the outside. Wake up when she wanted to. Get into a car and ride down the street. Go to a movie. The mall. Wear her own clothes.

By her twenty-second birthday Laura felt like she'd lived a lifetime in CYA. Few girls there were older than she. Laura watched them argue in the day room, cuss each other out. Carry their anger on their sleeves. For what?

Maybe they knew something she didn't. Maybe it was better to live an angry life than to not feel at all.

Three more years to go.

Dreams of catching Roger Weiner, sending him to jail, had faded. What was the use? The police hadn't believed her when it mattered most. Now they never would.

After Laura's twenty-third birthday something shifted inside her. She had only two years left. And fear of getting out began to set in. CYA was hellish. But it was a hell she knew. What would happen when she was free? She didn't know how to fend for herself. Couldn't remember how to make her own decisions.

A new fantasy overtook Laura—reconciling with her father. Maybe he'd contact her before she was released, offer to let her stay with him until she got on her feet. He'd throw his arms around her and tell her how sorry he was. That he now knew she was innocent. Anything he could do for her, anything at all … And if his new wife (surely he'd married her by now) didn't want Laura around, he'd put his beloved daughter up in an apartment somewhere. By then all her high school friends would be long scattered, busy with their families and careers. The media would have forgotten the murder case. There wouldn't be so much as a peep when she returned to the Bay Area.

But there remained one huge problem. She would have a felony—for *murder*—on her record for the rest of her life. How could she possibly get a job? Who would ever hire her?

Over the next few months Laura began to dream again of bringing her mother's killer to justice. Roger Weiner *did* matter. In proving he was the real culprit, she would also free herself.

No more fantasizing—she had to convince her father of her innocence. She couldn't do this alone. And maybe she could even convince his cop wife. (Somehow Laura would have to stomach being around the woman.) With Tina on her side, investigating with the mind of an officer, they'd get somewhere.

On her twenty-fourth birthday, with just one year left, Laura wrote her dad a letter.

CHAPTER 24

One month after Laura wrote her father, she received a reply.

She sat on her familiar hard cot, holding the envelope. It had been slit open, the letter resting inside. CYA staff read all incoming and outgoing mail. Laura turned the envelope over and over, afraid to take out the piece of paper. So much in her life had gone wrong. She'd long ago given up on God. Now she was asking Him to help her just this once. In desperation, Laura had gone so far as to make a pact with God. If He would just bring her father back to her, she'd believe in Him again.

She took a deep breath and slid out the piece of paper that could change her life.

Dearest Laura,

I can't tell you how happy I was to see your letter. I've read it over and over, and still carry it in my pocket.

There is so much to tell you. So much to talk about. I just can't begin to cover it on paper. Years ago you told me not to come see you unless I believed in your innocence. Now I'm coming to see you. I've been in contact with CYA and learned about the visitation process. In two weeks I've got a few vacation days coming, and I'm using it to drive down there. I'll see you then—and we'll talk about everything.

All my love,

Dad

Laura read the last word and froze. She stared at the letter, trying to process. Trying to *feel*. Years had passed without good news, years in which she'd stuffed her emotions deep inside. Now, reading this incredible letter, she wanted to experience happiness. She wanted to jump and shout, but all she could do was sit there.

Maybe she'd read the letter wrong.

She went over it again.

Hard breaths came first. A sense of her chest bursting. Tears came next, flooding her eyes and smearing her face. Then it came, an old feeling she could barely remember. Happiness. Insane *joy* zig-zagged down her nerves, sparked out from her fingers. Laura pushed off the cot on wobbly knees and tipped her head toward the ceiling. At first the words wouldn't come. They caught in her throat, thick and jumbled. Then, in an instant they broke free.

"Thank You, God, Thank You, God, thank You, thank You, thank You …"

She snatched up the letter and spread her arms. Turned in circles. Then clutched the blessed piece of paper to her chest.

"Thank You, thank You, thank You …"

In the next two weeks she talked to God often. She still didn't know why He'd allowed her mom to be killed. Why He'd allowed her to go to jail. But now, finally, He was going to fix it. Her life was going to go on. She even asked for a Bible and began to read, starting with the New Testament. The words soothed her. Filled in the hard-edged cracks. She began to sense a change in herself. A softening, a reawakening of feeling. Not a night-and-day difference by any means, but … something.

The first weekend, when visitation took place, crept by. For the first time Laura did not sit in her room. She took a seat in the corner of the day room, watching her fellow inmates and their families talk and laugh. Hug one another. One more week, and that would be her.

The next Sunday she stood in the day room awaiting her father, palms sweaty and heart fluttering. When the doors opened for families to come in, he was the first to enter.

They caught one another's eye across the room. He looked older, with grayer hair. Laura couldn't move.

Her father closed the distance in long strides. He pulled her into his arms and held on tight. Laura buried her face in his chest, taking in his once-familiar smell, the years of absence melting away. She sobbed, and he held her tighter. For a long moment they stood, ignoring the chatter all around them, the scrape of chairs. When they finally pulled away, she saw his eyes were filled with tears too.

"It's so good to see you." His voice was raw.

She swallowed hard. "Good to see *you.*"

They found two seats as far from everyone else as possible. Sat facing each other, holding hands. Laura had a million things to ask but couldn't speak another word. She saw new lines cut into her dad's face. Crinkles around the eyes. Deeper ones around his mouth. He would be … what? Forty-nine now?

Her father squeezed her fingers. "You look so different. Shorter hair. Much more mature."

Laura could only nod.

"You're still so pretty. Like your mom."

Another sob threatened to crack from her throat. Laura forced it down. "Are you … still working at the same place?"

"Yeah. I'm a VP now."

"Oh. That's great."

He lifted a shoulder.

They sat awkwardly, searching for words across the years.

Her dad rubbed her hands. "I'm sorry I doubted you. I'm so, so, sorry …" His voice caught and he shut his eyes, unable to continue. Laura watched remorse and pain seize his face.

After a shuddering breath, he pushed on. "I didn't believe it at first. But the more I heard from the prosecutor … He insisted you did it. That you'd lied to him from the beginning. I felt my world crashing in. I'd lost my wife in the most horrible way. Now I was losing my daughter. Meanwhile Tina was there, soothing me. Giving me support. My life was a nightmare. All I could do was throw my attention on her. Just to save myself. But at least I was living a free life. There you were, in jail. Being accused. You had nothing, no one else to focus on. Except your trial and an acquittal. And I just … left you there."

He broke down again. Laura's pulse surged. She gripped his hands and cried with him. "It's okay, Dad. It's okay."

It was some time before he could pull himself together. Laura got up and fetched them both some tissues. Thrust one into his hand, still hardly believing he was sitting in front of her. It all seemed so surreal. "Did Tina tell you I was guilty?"

"She *knew* you were. She tried to get me to see it through objective eyes, she said. Not through my loving father's eyes. She said the sooner I dealt with it, the sooner I could heal."

Of course she would say that. "And after awhile you believed her."

Laura's father worked his jaw back and forth.

"Is she still a cop?"

"Worse. She's made detective."

Worse? "You still with her?"

He looked at the floor. "It's not going well."

"Oh. I'm sorry." No she wasn't. "What's happening?" Other than the fact he was realizing the horrible woman had managed to separate him from his daughter …

Her father shook his head. "We got married a few months after you came here. I thought she was everything I needed. But after a couple years she started to change." He shrugged. "Maybe it wasn't change. Maybe I was just seeing the real Tina. She became demanding and caustic. Always wanting to spend more and more money. Impress her friends, the neighbors. Twice we've separated. Both times she convinced me to take her back. I've tried all these years. But I just can't … And now in less than a year you're getting out. You'll need a place to live. I want you to come home, Laura."

The words filtered through Laura's head, stunning and warm.

"Do you want to come home?"

"Yes." She could barely talk.

He smiled. "Tina will never accept it. That's why she has to go."

Laura stared at him. "You going to divorce her?"

Her father nodded. "We'll be a whole lot better off without her, you and I."

She leaned across his legs and hugged him.

"Does she know you're here visiting me?"

"She knows."

"Guess she's not happy about that."

"No."

Laura rubbed a finger over her pants. "Does she know you think I'm innocent?"

"Yes. I was so overwhelmed when I realized … I couldn't keep it from her. She hasn't let up about it since. Just harps and harps, like she's obsessed. Honestly, sometimes I wonder if she's coming unhinged. I finally just told her I'm not talking about it anymore."

So many questions. "Why do you believe I didn't do it now?"

Her father stared across the room. When he looked back at her, he seemed to gather himself. "Your bedroom—I hadn't touched it in all these years. Everything's still there. Your clothes, pictures on the wall. Everything."

Her room was still like it had been? Laura couldn't imagine it. To see that room again, just like she'd left it. Sleep in the same bed, under the same covers. Even in her wildest fantasies of going home, she hadn't pictured that.

"The door has been closed. I never went in there. I couldn't. And then one day after Tina and I'd had a huge fight, I just … did. I stood near the doorway, gazing around the room. Remembering. And then—out of nowhere—a memory hit me. A memory I'd never had until that moment." Her father stopped, rubbed both palms against his jeans. "I saw you, the day your mom was killed. You were leaving the house in the morning, carrying your backpack. You'd apologized to me for arguing with your mom. And there you were, walking out the door into the bright day. I remembered the sky, how blue it was. And how it matched your shoes."

He stopped.

Laura's mouth creaked open. Her shoes. The *blue* ones.

Her father watched the significance of his statement play across her face. He nodded. "Yeah. The ones you insisted you'd been wearing all day."

Laura swallowed hard. "How ... you saw that scene, just like that? After all those years?"

His eyes teared up.

"Why? Why then?"

Her father shook his head. "Don't know. I guess stepping into your room ..."

Laura looked away, not sure whether to laugh or cry. Great that he'd had the memory. But why'd it have to take so long? Why couldn't he have remembered when she was arrested? When she was on trial? At least sometime in the last eight lonely years?

"I'm so sorry." Her father blinked hard. "I can't explain why it took so long to remember. I only know the day your mom was killed I was in such shock. And then everything happened so fast ..."

Laura raised her chin. Let it fall.

"When I remembered that scene I got so lightheaded I sat down on your bed. For the next few days I kept going over and over it. Trying to shake the memory loose. But no. It wasn't just wishful thinking. It was real."

Laura could only breathe. In and out, in and out. *Why* had it taken a memory to make her father believe in her?

"And that's when I began to see it. To understand everything you were trying to tell me. As crazy as it sounds, as much as it feels like some TV show, you *were* framed."

He looked into her eyes—and must have seen the ambivalence swirling there. "I'm sorry. I know I keep saying that, but ... I can never say it enough."

No. He couldn't.

Laura licked her lips. Now was not the time to sort through all her feelings. Visiting hours would be done before they knew it, and there was still so much to talk about.

"It's okay, Dad."

"I started going over all the 'evidence' in my head. And started realizing how easy it would have been for someone to pull your green shoes from your closet, make sure they got blood on them. Every piece of that trial I started seeing in a new light. Through the defense's eyes, not the prosecution's."

Indignation still threatened to spill out of Laura. She held it back. "You think it was Roger Weiner?"

"Absolutely. Think about it. If he was out for revenge, what better way to do it? He'd kill your mom because she rejected him. Frame her daughter for the murder. And leave her husband with nothing. The whole family would be ruined." Laura's dad shook his head. "I can almost imagine him telling her all that when he came into the house. When he surprised her in our bedroom."

Laura's eyes widened. Could that be true? Could her mother have died *knowing* the coming ruin of her husband and daughter? She'd have fought with everything she had. She'd have fought for *them.*

Her dad ran a hand across his forehead. "We have to prove your innocence. Somehow. I'll fight for you to my dying day."

Warmth gushed through Laura. Yes, she'd waited years to hear this. Far too long. But at least she *was* hearing it. At least she had a plan now, after she got out. She didn't have to be afraid anymore. Didn't have to worry about facing life on her own.

"Do you know where Roger Weiner is? We have to bring him to justice for Mom."

"I know. And no, I don't know where he is. But I'm going to start looking for him. We've got eleven and a half months. By the time you get out I hope to have gathered all the evidence I can. And in the meantime I'm divorcing Tina. She doesn't know it yet, but I've already seen an attorney."

"Sounds like she won't go easily."

Her father gave her a wry smile. "No. And she'll try to take me for everything she can. But we haven't been married all that long. And most of my savings came from your mother. I'm not going to let Tina take your mother's money from *you*."

Laura blinked. She hadn't thought for years about inheriting her mother's money. Not since the trial, when Cantor claimed that was her reason for committing the crime.

Her dad looked at the large round clock on the day room wall. "How much time do we have?"

So little. "Fifteen minutes."

"Okay." He shifted in his chair. "Listen. I'll keep coming to see you as often as possible. I'll try for once a month. I'll write you too. And call. But if I find new information about your case, I'm not going to give details in my letters or on the phone. I know they listen to calls and read everything. I just don't trust the System anymore."

No kidding.

"When I visit I'll give you all the latest news."

"Okay."

"We'll do this, Laura."

She nodded.

"I know we've lost a lot of time. But now we have years to make it up. I'm going to do everything I can to help you. You can still have a wonderful life. Put this behind you, once you're proven to be innocent. We'll put it behind *us*."

Laura smiled. She believed everything he said would happen. She had to.

"Yes, Dad. We will."

CHAPTER 25

After Laura's father visited, the days eked by, their hours longer and stingier than ever. Sometimes she thought they moved even more slowly now that she had hope. In his second visit her dad brought her a calendar. Laura began marking the days off until her twenty-fifth birthday.

One.

By one.

By one.

Her father remained true to his word and came every month. He started divorce proceedings against Tina. In June she moved out of the house. She'd hired a lawyer and had vowed to "break him." He was seeing her true colors like never before. "That woman," he told Laura, "is a witch."

Information on her case was moving slowly. Her father couldn't even locate Roger Weiner. Then finally in September he had breaking news. He and Laura had hardly sat down in the day room before he blurted it out. "I've found him!"

She sucked in a breath. "Where?"

Her father smacked a palm against his leg. "He's in jail. *Jail*, Laura. Been there for years. He was convicted of assaulting a woman. Thank God she survived, but he almost killed her."

Laura's limbs went cold. "Where'd he do it? When?"

"He'd moved to Arizona. Apparently he was working in another hospital. It was a lot like the thing with your mom. He set his sights on some coworker, but she wouldn't have anything to do with him. One night at the end of her shift he caught her in some storage room. He'd beaten her unconscious before someone heard noises and went to investigate."

Laura's mouth opened, then shut. So similar. She felt terrible for the woman and her family. But surely this would help their case. Weiner was a man now proven capable of deadly assault.

"This is *huge*," she whispered.

"Yeah."

Laura thought of the calendar in her room. She'd stopped Xing out the squares and was now counting down until her release on March 15. One hundred eighty-one days to go. "What do you do now?"

"I'm trying to get the transcript of your trial. I want to go over every word."

"Are you going to meet with Cantor, tell him what you know?"

"Not yet. It'll take a lot to get his attention, and if I don't go in with more than this from the beginning, I'll probably never get another chance."

"What about your memory—that I was wearing the blue shoes that day?"

Her father shook his head. "So what? That's not evidence to Cantor. He could say I'm making it up."

True. "Speaking of 'evidence,' he's still got all the stuff, right? My green shoes? The hammer?"

"He'd better. Because at some point we'll need them again."

Laura rocked back in her chair, elated. This could really happen. They could really prove her innocence one day. Which would force the police to look for the real killer.

For the rest of that visit they could talk of little else. Except that

Laura's father did tell her the divorce was coming along and should be final by the time she got out.

"No more Tina in our lives." He grinned.

She grinned back. "No more Tina."

How she hated that name.

October came … and November. Laura's father had little more to tell her. "I've decided to call Cantor and set up a meeting—if he'll see me. I told you I got the court transcripts. But no one will let me see the boxed-up evidence. Apparently Cantor's the only one they'll let open that box. Somehow I'm going to have to convince him."

Laura stared at her lap, processing the news. "What's new to see, though? The same spots on the shoes. Blood on the hammer. Cantor will explain them just like he did before."

Her dad closed his eyes. "There has to be something. *Something*. And I'm going to find it."

In December, with the day room decorated for Christmas, Laura's dad looked worn as he entered. One glance at him and dread etched her veins. She sat him down and laid a hand on his leg. "What's happened?"

He shook his head. "It's just Tina. What I ever saw in that woman …"

"She giving you a harder time than usual?"

"The divorce is almost done."

"Oh. That's good, isn't it?"

"*Almost* is the important word. Tina's still fighting over the settlement. Now she's found out I've been asking about your case. Guess somebody in the D.A.'s office told her. She called me, smirking about it—because it'll help *her*. She said she'll use it against me in court. Say I'm so crazy that I believe in my guilty daughter's innocence. That you've turned me against her. That you're just after the money. Again. And you should never get it, which eventually you will, if I get to keep it. So more should go to her."

Rage knocked up Laura's spine. How *dare* that woman say a thing against her. And to treat her father like that! "So what, Dad? She can talk all she wants. Doesn't mean her threats will work. And even if you do have to give her more money, in the end you'll be rid of her."

"It's not that, Laura. If it was just the money ..." He shook his head. "It's what she can do against *your* case. I know she's talking to Cantor. She'll do everything possible to keep us from moving forward."

Laura's mouth dropped open. "She'd *do* that?"

"You have no idea how set she is on getting every penny out of me. And because I've fought her, she's turned vindictive. She'll use her 'inside knowledge' of our family to convince Cantor I've gone over the edge. That I can't deal with the reality of your guilt."

No. "Can she really stop us?"

Her father ran a hand across his jaw. "Detectives and prosecutors are tight. They work together all the time. No telling the lies she's saying about me. And Cantor has every reason to listen to her. Listening to *me* means putting his conviction at risk. What prosecutor's gonna do that?"

Laura couldn't talk. After everything that had happened, this couldn't be real.

When visiting hours were over, she returned to her room with lead in her stomach. *"I'll fight for you to my dying day."* Now her father may not be able to keep that promise.

After that visit Laura's days seemed to grind to a near halt. She prayed and prayed for God's help. But hatred toward Tina Fulder boiled in her heart. Would God listen to her if she hated someone? Even if that person deserved it?

Eternity passed.

Finally the year 2004 dawned. By the time Laura would see her father in his mid-January visit, she'd have less than sixty days to go.

She called him collect the week before his visit. Never imagining what was to come.

"Dad, hi."

"*Laura.*"

Her breath caught. "What's wrong?"

"I …"

She could hear him pulling in air. Trying to talk.

"The divorce is through. Thank God."

"Oh. *Good.*" Laura waited for more but nothing came. "Dad, what *is* it?"

"So much has happened. I don't even know where to start."

Laura could only grip the phone.

"First, Roger Weiner's out of jail."

"What? Already?"

"He didn't serve all his time. He came up before parole board, and they let him go."

Laura could hardly process that. A guilty man, back out on the streets, while *she* was still in prison?

"Then *we've* got to put him back in jail, Dad. For Mom's murder! Go to Cantor about him."

"I've tried." Laura's dad sounded so defeated. "He wouldn't see me. The case is done, the 'guilty' suspect has been convicted. Cantor finally talked to me—and told me to stop calling."

Laura stared at the drab wall. So this was it? She could never prove her innocence. For the rest of her life she'd be branded as a murderer. And never see justice on behalf of her mother. How could she live with that?

"But, Laura …"

For the *rest of her life.* "Yeah."

"Now I've found … something new."

"About my case?"

A beat passed. "Yes."

Laura's pulse snagged. "Tell me."

"I can't … I'll need to come see you."

"I want to know now!"

"I can't. Not on the phone."

Laura smacked the wall with her palm. Why was her entire life about waiting? "You're still coming next week, right?"

"Yes. I'll tell you then. Everything. I'll have to tell you *everything*."

The way he said that last sentence. With such pain in his voice. "Will it help us? Just tell me that much."

More silence.

"Dad?"

"Yes." His voice choked.

He *had* found evidence against Weiner!

"Okay. Good, Dad. *Good*."

What was that sound? Was he crying?

"I love you, Laura."

"I love you too."

"I love you so much. And I loved your mom. It's my fault. I should have protected her."

"You couldn't have known what he'd do, Dad."

They needed to hang up. Collect calls were so expensive. "I'll see you next week, Laura."

"Okay. Can't wait."

She placed the phone in its receiver and slumped against the wall. Finally. *Finally!*

The week leading to her father's visit would never pass. Laura paced her room. Prayed. Tried to sleep the time away. Sleep wouldn't come.

Five days later Laura was called into the floor supervisor's office. Told to sit down. What had she done? Girls were never called into that room unless there was a major problem.

Please, whatever it is—don't take my father's visit from me!

Florence Wright was tall and stern-looking, with short hair and a square jaw. But at the moment she looked almost compassionate.

Laura sat, her heart tilting. *What?*

"I'm so, so sorry to tell you this, Laura." Ms. Wright sat beside her, placing a hand on her shoulder. "I have sad news."

Laura stopped breathing.

"This morning your father was in a car accident. They did everything they could to save him. But by the time rescuers could get to him, he was dead."

April 2013

CHAPTER 26

The morning after my engagement I lay in bed staring at my out-stretched left hand. Emotions warred within me. Hope. Joy. Relief. Fear. Dread.

If I had known what was to come on that day, I would have pulled the covers over my head and never moved.

As it was, I ogled my ring, hardly believing it was there. The pain and shock of Clara's death still gripped me. And yet … here was this promise of new life. A family. What I'd dreamed of for so many years.

After I said "yes" the previous night, Andy and I had talked for hours about so many things. I could still barely process it all. He'd brought up the subject of where we would live. Where I might find a job—if I wanted. Andy made it clear that I didn't have to work. If I was content to stay home and take care of the house, that was fine with him.

"Do you want to move into my place in Redbud?" he asked. "Or would you rather go to Lexington, where we could find a much grander house?"

I squeezed his hand. "I don't need a grand house. I'd much rather stay in Redbud, where I know people." There I could be close to my own house, which I wouldn't sell. As far as I was concerned, Pete, Nicole and Colleen could stay right where they were.

Andy and I had also talked about our engagement. With the town of Redbud still mourning Clara, this wasn't the time to announce it to the world. "I'd love to run through the streets shouting you'll be my wife, but ..." Andy winced.

I thought of the dreams I'd had about this moment. How I'd be calling everyone I knew. Now the very idea seemed callous.

"You won't need to shout in the streets. All we need is for Colleen to see my ring. She'll tell everybody who comes into Grangers, plus those passing by on the sidewalk."

Andy gave me a rueful smile. "Oh, boy."

"I'll just tell her we want to keep it a quiet engagement for now because of Clara. Colleen will make sure to include that bit of information when she's spreading it across town."

Andy laughed.

When I'd arrived home Colleen and Nicole were still up. As expected they made a huge fuss over my ring, oohing and aahing. I assured them they needn't worry about moving from the house once I was married. And I cued them in that Andy and I wanted to "keep the engagement quiet" for now.

One thing Andy and I hadn't discussed at dinner was money. Andy had plenty of his own; he didn't need mine. Months ago I told him I'd inherited substantial funds from my parents. But he didn't know the real story of that, of course. Nor did he have any idea how much.

I should tell him the amount soon. Keeping such information from a boyfriend was one thing. Now that we were engaged, Andy deserved to know. Besides, I spent time every few weeks on my computer, adding up bills and moving enough money to a local bank from my offshore accounts to cover them. He'd be bound to wonder what I was doing.

I turned the diamond on my finger, watching it glisten in the morning light. A sense of entrapment nagged deep in my gut. Now I had all the more reason to keep the Secret of how I came here. Even as I should be totally honest with the man who'd pledged me his life.

My cell phone rang, jarring my nerves. I picked it up from my bedside table and checked the ID.

Cheryl King.

I took a breath—and hit *answer.* "Hi, Cheryl."

"I saw you on TV last night." No *hello.* But when your innocent son sat in jail, who wanted to waste words?

He *was* innocent, right?

"Thanks for standing up for Billy. I can't believe Chief Melcher threatened you like that."

Something in her voice ... exoneration? As in—the end justified the means? I still believed she'd lied to me and Melcher about Billy's being home the night Clara was killed.

"The Chief's just not willing to listen to anybody." Cheryl's voice caught. "I can't *stand* to think of Billy in jail."

I couldn't either. "We'll keep working on it, Cheryl. We'll think of something."

Useless words. Billy King would likely spend years in prison. The thought squeezed my heart.

"Have you been allowed to see him, Cheryl?"

"I've tried. But not yet."

"Does he have an attorney?"

"They appointed him a public defender. I don't have the money to pay for a lawyer."

A public defender. Billy would get the minimum of help. "Let me know when you see him. I'll want to visit him too."

That last sentence barely made it out of my throat. The mere thought of entering a jail flooded me with horrific memories. I pictured Billy behind bars, helpless and scared. How could I witness that?

After Cheryl's call I tried to take a shower and dress quickly, but the phone kept ringing. *"I saw you on the news last night."* Friends. Neighbors. Women who'd been at Clara's shower. If I'd become engaged two days ago, they'd all be calling to congratulate me. Now I made no mention of how my life had radically changed. Many of the callers said they'd never believe Billy King had done this. With each conversation I felt a little more hope. Maybe if the townspeople got up in arms over Melcher arresting the wrong man, he'd succumb to the pressure and start looking at other possibilities for suspects.

Then Clara's mother phoned. I saw the name *Dora Crenshaw* on my cell—and stilled. I braced myself before answering.

"Hi, Dora."

"I saw you on the news last night."

I sat down on the bed.

"Do you really think Billy is innocent?" Grief and weariness and something akin to indignation tinged her tone.

"He's not who I saw that night, Dora. Someone else was there on Brewster. Hiding."

"Maybe that was Billy."

"The man I saw wasn't that tall."

"How do you *know*?" Her voice rose. "You didn't *see* his face, and meanwhile my daughter is *dead*!"

My throat closed. I hung my head, the phone pressed to my ear, and could not think of a single word to say.

"Well, I think he did it, you hear me? He killed my daughter. Someone who would never hurt him or anybody. And I don't think you should be telling people he didn't!"

"Dora, I'm so sorry. I—"

"She was your *friend*, Delanie!"

"I know. And I loved her."

"Then stop talking against her."

My fingers tightened on the phone. "I didn't mean to talk against Clara."

A sob broke from Dora. "Really? What exactly would you call standing up for the person who choked her to death!"

A click sounded in my ear.

I sat like stone, staring at nothing. Then threw the cell on my bed and lowered my face in my hands.

January — April 2004

After her father's death the passing days no longer had meaning for Laura. She stopped the countdown to her release date. She didn't even want to get out of CYA anymore. At least she had a bed to sleep in, food to eat. What was she going to do on the outside? She hadn't even driven a car for almost nine years.

As for pursuing her case, whatever her father had discovered about Roger Weiner, he'd taken it to his grave. And she had no energy—or money—to track it down herself.

Grief for her father alternated with roiling anger. Florence Wright had told Laura her father was in a one-car accident. He'd been driving up Highway 1 on the coast, lost control of his car, and plunged over a cliff. Swerve marks leading up to the scene told the tale. So did his body. The autopsy showed a high level of alcohol.

How could he do that to her? Get drunk and then go out driving? He'd always loved Highway 1, Laura knew that. The ocean, the winding road. She'd driven it with him more than once when his Porsche was new and shiny. But to be so careless. Just when she needed him most.

If only he'd never walked back into her life.

With less than two months left, Laura began having private counseling sessions twice a week—both to help her deal with her father's death and plan for getting out of CYA. Her counselor was a black woman named Yolanda. Spoke her mind but full of empathy. Said she had three daughters of her own. She mothered Laura, let her cry on her shoulder. Listened to everything she had to say—including her claims of innocence. Not that they mattered much anymore.

"Listen," Yolanda told her in February. "I've been making some calls. You've got an inheritance coming to you, did you know that? And from what I hear, it's pretty substantial."

Laura lifted a shoulder.

"Well, that should matter to you. You're gonna have to have money, aren't you? And that house your dad owned, it's coming to you also."

Laura shivered. She couldn't imagine walking into that house, with all its memories of two dead parents.

Yolanda sighed. "Fine then. I'll give you time to think about this. But like it or not, you're being released next month, and you're gonna have to make a living. And I'm not about to let you go without preparing you all I can."

Laura tried to think about it—amidst her grief. But it was no use. The pain over losing her father so soon after finding him was more than she could bear. And that loss brought up the sadness for her mother all over again.

Laura wanted to be mad at God, wanted someone to blame. Instead, lonelier than ever, she found herself turning to Him for comfort. She read the Bible more. Prayed more. Even if sometimes all she could say was, "God, help me, help me, help me."

Then, almost as an afterthought, the day she'd waited nearly nine years for arrived. On March 15, Laura's twenty-fifth birthday, she was declared free—and released from prison.

Out she walked.

Yolanda had arranged with Laura's Aunt Nicky to come pick her up. Laura had spoken to her dad's sister on the phone. "We know you're innocent, Laura," Aunt Nicky told her. "Your father told us about what he remembered. Your Uncle Ted and I want you to come stay with us until things are settled."

What he remembered. What about the final information on Weiner he'd discovered just before he died? The mere thought made Laura's heart skip. But she didn't want to talk about details over the phone.

Walking free into the afternoon air on that auspicious day, her aunt by her side, was almost more than Laura could process. She had to be dreaming. In truth she was back on her cot, locked in her room. The forever years behind her could not have ended. Laura slid into her aunt's car and fiddled with the seatbelt, the experience out-of-body. She heard herself speak, forced a smile, but she felt removed and alien. How could she ever live in this outside world?

When she could find her tongue, Laura posed her burning question.

"Aunt Nicky, did Dad tell you what he found out the last week he was alive? Some way to prove Roger Weiner killed my mom?"

Please, please.

Her aunt raised her eyebrows. "He did? I'm sorry, I don't know anything about that."

With those words Laura's dream of being exonerated and seeing justice done for her mother died.

CHAPTER 28

For the first two weeks out of CYA, Laura barely dragged through the days. Her aunt and uncle asked nothing of her. They just wanted her to "heal" and "get on her feet."

Time blurred by, meaningless. Laura couldn't feel much of anything. And she had no future. Why even get out of bed?

As for Roger Weiner, he was out there somewhere on the streets. Maybe still in Arizona? Maybe he'd attacked another woman by now. Or even killed again. She should do something to stop him. But Laura was powerless. All the same, she couldn't stop thinking about him. In her dreams she testified against him on the stand. Saw him handcuffed and led off to jail.

"Laura," her aunt said gently one day, "at some point you'll have to start living your own life and stop obsessing about this man."

"But he killed my mom!"

Her aunt's head shook. "But you can't prove it. You never will be able to prove it. A terrible injustice has been done. But at some point you need to move on, hard as it is. If you don't, you will allow your past to rule you forever. This has already taken nine years of your life. Don't let it take any more."

Laura hung her head, tears falling. "*How* can I move on? It's so *unfair*. My mom deserves for him to be punished."

"Yes. It is unfair. Many terrible things in this world should never happen. But they do. And some wrongs aren't righted on this earth. Sometimes the innocent are punished, and the guilty go free." Her aunt's eyes glistened. "In the end, God will judge. But we can't always see a happy ending to the story in our lifetime. What we *can* do is make the best of the life we have left. Let God help you do that."

A rational voice within Laura said her aunt was right. She couldn't be the victim forever. And she couldn't spend the rest of her life seeking a justice for her mother that would never come. Even if her mother's killer was found—then what? Her mom would still be dead. Laura would still have lost nine years of her life. What she accomplished in the future would be up to her. And wasn't God faithful enough to see her through?

But this wasn't the future, it was *now*. And right now Laura had no strength or desire to do anything. She couldn't even pray.

The days muddled on.

Then her aunt and uncle made an announcement. They had to start talking about Laura's inheritance. Apparently her father had changed his will just after the divorce. Taken Tina out completely and left everything to Laura. Her father's lawyer, Russ McConally, was acting as executor.

Did she *have* to deal with this? Laura still had no energy. But her aunt and uncle pushed her to meet with McConally. "You have to take care of this, Laura," Aunt Nicky said. "Your father did this for you, and he wants you to have his estate."

Heavy-hearted, Laura went to the appointment they set up for her. Aunt Nicky drove. Laura watched the buildings stream by on El Camino. In nine years little had changed. How could that be, when she'd changed so much?

Laura was not prepared for the shock of that meeting.

Her father's estate, McConally told her, was worth over five million in cash and stocks alone. Plus the house, which was worth another two and a half million. It was owned free and clear, since her parents had paid cash for it.

Seven and a half million dollars. Laura couldn't even imagine that kind of money.

After hearing that, she couldn't process anything else McConally said.

"Understand," Aunt Nicky explained on their way home, "that seven and a half million is *after* the divorce settlement. Tina got over a million. She wanted much more—over half the estate, can you believe it? She'd only been married to your dad about eight years. And she hadn't helped earn any of that money. In fact she did all she could while they were married to spend it. Early in those years she'd even sold what jewelry your mom had and used the money to buy her own pieces."

"My *mother's jewelry*?" That was too much. Laura's mom had never been big on jewelry, but what she'd had, Laura had wanted as reminders of her. Those pieces were more than just gems, they were history. *Her* history. And they'd gone to *Tina*? "How did Dad allow that?"

Aunt Nicky shook her head. "You'd just been sent to CYA, Laura. Your dad thought you were guilty. In his mind you didn't deserve anything from your mom. Please know he lived to regret that."

He'd better have. What he did was unthinkable. Some other woman getting her mother's jewelry? Made Laura want to spit. "*Why* didn't he tell me?"

"Probably very hard for him to admit. I'm sure he was going to."

Like when? Once Laura got home and found the jewelry gone? She folded her arms and looked out her window. What else had her dad not told her?

They drove in silence.

"So was this jewelry-stealer mad to only get a million dollars in the divorce?" Laura asked after a moment. *Only.*

"Furious. One thing's for sure, seeing the way she's acted. She married your dad for his money."

The words chased Laura's anger away. Had her father been that used from the beginning? She thought of him driving his expensive sports car. How that could have turned a gold-digger's head.

"I don't think she ever loved your father." Aunt Nicky's voice edged. "But she sure loved his money and his house. Thank heaven the divorce was final before his accident. At least Tina Fulder's out of the picture for good."

At least. Laura hoped she never had to meet the woman face to face.

In the next few days the enormity of the inheritance began to sink in. Seven and a half million dollars. All Laura's. She could start a new life anywhere she wanted. Who cared if she couldn't find work— she wouldn't *have* to. If she was careful with the money, invested it properly, she'd be set for life. All she had to do was wait for the courts to handle the probate process. Unfortunately that could take a year or longer. More waiting.

In the meantime, what to do with herself?

Laura had lost so much. Her mother and father. Her freedom. Now a new world lay ahead of her. If she could just push through her grief. If she could just hang on a little longer until the money was hers.

Two days later, when her aunt and uncle were both at work, the doorbell rang. And Laura's new nightmare began.

April 2013

I t was some time before I could recover from Dora Crenshaw's call. Finally I ventured from my bedroom out to the kitchen as Colleen and Nicole were eating breakfast. My phone remained in the bedroom. Colleen took one look at my face and stilled. "What's wrong on this morning after you just got engaged?"

At that moment I wished Andy hadn't asked me to marry him. Our engagement should have come at a time when I could fully rejoice. Now any thought of my future happiness brought a new wave of guilt. Clara was dead. And I'd hurt her grieving parents.

I waved a hand at Colleen. "Phone calls. Not everyone likes what I said on the news last night."

"Like who?"

I could only shake my head.

From my bedroom my cell rang. I poured myself some coffee and slumped down at the table.

Colleen soon left for work, and Nicole went off to her college classes. Pete emerged for his breakfast routine.

In the bedroom, my phone had rung with five more calls.

Pete studied my face, then clumped over to the refrigerator and pulled out two eggs and a package of bacon. "You gettin' some pushback 'bout your interview last night?"

I focused on my coffee mug. "The worst. From Dora."

Pete grunted. "You had to know some of that would be comin."

"But from Clara's own parents! I can't hurt them, Pete. I can't *do* this."

"Tell the truth, you mean?"

My cell phone rang again. I lowered my chin.

"You got somethin' else to tell me?"

Colleen must have whispered the news to him. "I'm engaged." My words dulled the air.

Pete cracked an egg into his cast iron pan. "Don't sound too happy 'bout it."

"Life is complicated, Pete."

"You're tellin' me." The second egg went into the pan. Followed by three pieces of bacon. They started to sizzle.

Movement out the front window caught my eye. A car I didn't recognize pulled up to the curb. A man got out.

Pete studied the figure as he came up the walk. "Who's that?"

"No clue."

The doorbell rang. I pulled to my feet to answer.

It was a reporter. Wayne Hollander from the Cincinnati newspaper. *Cincinnati. In Ohio.* Would I answer a "few questions" about the case?

My muscles chilled. "I can't talk any more about that."

"If you could just tell me—"

"I'm sorry. No."

I shut the door. My heart banged around in my ribs.

Pete saw my stricken face and gestured with the spatula in his hand. "You don't have to talk to them anymore, Del."

Didn't I? Yesterday I'd vowed to help Billy all I could. How could I turn away this opportunity?

Because of Clara's family, that's why. I'd done what I could for Billy, now I needed to keep silent.

But in the core of me, I knew that was only half of it. I was afraid for *myself.* My face being seen by more people, by someone who might recognize me. Now I was actually engaged. All those years in CYA, longing for a family. I was on the verge of having it. And I couldn't lose that. I *couldn't*.

I was going to sacrifice Billy for *myself*.

On weak legs I stumbled to the couch and sank upon it. I lowered my head and heaved into sobs. Pete soon sat down beside me, putting an arm around my shoulders.

"I don't want to be on TV anymore, Pete." My voice cracked and ran all over the place.

"You don't have to be."

"But Billy ..."

"You said your piece. You've done what you can."

If Pete only knew what I feared. The truth churned inside me, fighting to come out. *Just be free of it, Delanie, tell him and be done with this.*

But once I told the truth I could never take it back. And my life as I knew it would be over. Then what would happen to Billy? With my integrity in the mud, no one would believe me on the witness stand. For once I had to see justice done. The false suspect cleared. The real killer brought to justice. Clara deserved that. So had my mother ...

I wiped my cheeks with the back of my hand. Sat bent over, staring at my knees.

"Don't you worry 'bout Dora Crenshaw, now." Pete curled his gnarled fingers around the back of my neck.

"It's not just her. Lots of other people in town must feel the same way."

Pete grunted. "Partly out of convenience, I suppose. People have been scared to death that a killer's runnin' the streets. Now to think he's in jail—that takes a big load off everyone's mind."

My cell phone went off again.

Throughout that morning it continued to ring. A few calls I answered. Most I didn't, but those people left messages. Some encouraged me. Others said Melcher was right, and who was I to mess up an investigation?

A second reporter came to my door, this one from another Lexington TV station, with cameraman in tow. Pete spotted the two outside and said he'd take care of it. I hid in my room like the coward I was and listened to him turn them away.

Next came a call from Colleen at Grangers. "I've seen four reporters in here today, and I'll bet you more are on the way."

Four?

"They all want to know about the case, Delanie. And they all want to talk to you."

I sat at the kitchen table, trying to eat a late breakfast. "Did you tell them you're my roommate?"

"Sure. I imagined you'd want to talk to them just like you did yesterday."

My stomach felt sick. I pushed the food away. "Colleen. Please don't do that again. Tell them nothing. I'm through talking to the media."

Apparently the reporters were keeping Colleen busy enough that she wasn't spreading the news about my engagement. Not one person had mentioned it.

In the next hour two more reporters showed up at the house. I began to panic. I wanted to escape—anywhere. But what if they spotted me and followed? And where could I go? As much as I wanted to run to Andy, I couldn't bother him during his work hours.

Next, Jack Grayson called. Reporters were outside his house, he said, taking pictures of his yard and The Bush. "They won't leave us alone. I talked to the first two, but after that it gets old, you know?"

"I'm so sorry, Jack. I didn't mean for this to happen."

"Not your fault. Just wanted you to know what's going on over here."

I clicked off the line and stared out the window, trembling. Clara's death was horror enough. Then Billy's arrest. Now this. Surely, the media were at the Crenshaw's house as well. Would Dora go on camera declaring I was wrong? Would Redbud neighbors and friends start arguing publicly, this quiet little town turning into a cat fight as the world gawked?

"I'm goin' downtown." Pete shuffled toward the garage. "Gonna see what's happenin' down there."

I wasn't sure I wanted to know. "Text me."

He stopped at the door. "You be okay? Just don't answer if someone comes knockin.'"

I nodded.

After Pete left I could do little but pace the house. I tried to pray, but God seemed to have moved even further out of reach now that I was engaged. The diamond ring on my finger burned. I'd pledged to give myself in honesty to a man who didn't even know my real name. Who had no idea I could go to jail if law enforcement discovered what I had done just before arriving in Redbud. *After* already serving time for supposedly killing my mother. Andy didn't deserve that kind of shock. He would be crushed.

A chime sounded from my phone. It was a text from Pete. *Three news vans on Brewer. More reporters at the police station.*

I stared at the words, knowing this wouldn't stop. The media had been at my own trial. What if Billy went to trial—and cameras were allowed in the courtroom? I'd have to testify on *TV*.

A shaking began in the pit of my belly. In my mind I heard Pete's words from his grimmer railroad stories. During his engineering career he'd hit seven people on the tracks, and the memories still haunted him. *"Takes a long time to stop a train when it's barrelin' along. If someone steps in front of it, there's no savin' 'em, no matter how hard you brake."*

I thrust a hand in my hair and begged God to save me. He wasn't listening.

I texted Pete back. *Are you talking to them?*

Nope. Observing.

Five minutes later he texted me again. It was just as I'd expected. *Drove past the Crenshaws and saw the WTVQ news van. Dora and Dave were on their porch, talking to Barlow Watkins.*

No doubt they were setting the record "straight."

Around 11:30 Andy called. I answered with trepidation. "I hear there's a lot going on in Redbud," he said.

I sat on the couch, wrung out. Pete still had not come home. "Reporters are everywhere. They're trying to get to me. I keep turning them away."

"I think that's the right decision, Del."

"Dora Crenshaw called me. She's furious about what I said on TV."

Andy sighed. "I was afraid that would happen. You doing all right?"

"Sure." I fiddled with my ring.

He hesitated, as if not believing me. "I told my parents about our engagement. Didn't want it to get to them through someone else."

"I'll bet your mother is thrilled."

"Delanie, come on."

"I'm sorry."

"You've got to quit this negativity against my parents. Puts me in a very bad position."

"I know. I'm sorry. It's just … a hard day. Even though you made me happy last night."

"Yeah. Know what you mean."

We fell silent.

"All right, I need to go, Del. Love you."

"Love you too."

I ended the call, dwelling on more negative thoughts of Andy's mother. Phyllis would be so perfectly groomed at my wedding. She would do her best to smile. For the rest of my life cold Phyllis Bradshaw would be all I had for a mother. My own wouldn't be there to see me marry the man of my dreams. Nor would I have a father to walk me down the aisle.

Pete. He would do it.

At noon, with butterflies in my belly, I turned on WTVQ news. Their lead segment featured Watkins, standing once again at the crime scene on Brewer. Then it flashed to his interview with Dora and Dave, both with tears in their eyes. "Two days ago we were looking forward to our daughter's wedding in June," Dora said. "Now we're barely holding on, getting through each hour. Each minute. We don't even know yet when we can have our daughter's body for a funeral." Her voice cracked. She turned away from the camera.

Dave wrapped an arm around his wife's shoulder. "We do want to say thank you to the Redbud police for arresting the perpetrator of this horrible crime so quickly."

Watkins pulled the microphone to his own mouth. "What about the statement of Delanie Miller? She claims the person she saw hiding in the shadows the night of the murder isn't Billy King."

Dave Crenshaw firmed his mouth. "She's wrong."

My body tingled. The people in this town would end up hating me.

How ironic. I'd gone to great lengths to hide my real identity in Redbud and guard the reputation I'd earned as Delanie Miller. Now townspeople were turning against me anyway.

But I shouldn't care, even now. I shouldn't be worried about reporters. If I had any integrity at all I'd be driving to the county jail, trying to visit Billy. I'd keep standing up for him.

What had I become? Where had my dreams of justice gone?

The news story ended. I flipped to another local channel and caught the story again. At least I wasn't part of the segment. But they showed my picture, naming me as a witness who insisted the man who'd been arrested was innocent.

I flicked off the TV and bent over, arms at my waist. My bones felt like they were coming apart. That video of me and my picture would live forever on the Internet, long after the media had moved on to other stories. What if someone who'd known Laura Denton stumbled upon it?

What if my aunt and uncle saw it? Pain and longing shot through me. It had been years since I'd so much as talked to them. I *missed* them.

My phone rang. *Bradshaw* appeared on the ID. Andy's mother. This was all I needed.

The cell rang three times before I brought myself to answer. "Hello?"

"Delanie, it's Phyllis." The tone sounded so … formal. "I wanted to tell you best wishes on your engagement."

"Thank you."

"You couldn't get a better man, if I do say so myself."

"I agree."

A beat passed. My tongue felt like lead.

"I couldn't help but hear about your news appearance last night." Phyllis's voice dropped in tone. "I started getting calls right after the segment."

Of course. From her country club friends, wondering at the behavior of her son's girlfriend. What would they say when they heard we were engaged?

"Now that you're joining our family, I would suggest that you refrain from discussing your opinions with the media. You never know how they'll twist your story. And it's always best to keep out of controversy."

Hadn't I known she'd do this? My fingers gripped the phone, a dozen responses crowding my head. For Andy's sake I pushed the clamoring ones away and laid hold of an obeisant, smoothing reply.

"You're right. I'm sorry I ever spoke to that reporter. I've told Andy I won't do it again."

"All right then. Good. And I was so sorry to hear about Clara."

Such controlled empathy in her tone.

"Thank you."

We ended the call, and I threw my phone across the couch.

For the rest of that afternoon one hour blurred into another. At some point Pete returned. Then later, Nicole and Colleen. I hadn't even thought about dinner. We ordered pizza. I managed to force down one piece. It was the most I'd eaten all day.

At evening news time, like a moth to flame I sat on the couch and numbly watched as Pete flipped through channels. All local TV stations covered the story. This time Melcher made his own appearances, always declaring they "had their man." Reporters pressed him for information on the evidence, but he would only say they were "gathering it, and there was plenty."

Plenty?

But Melcher didn't stop there. As for "Miss Miller's assertions" that he had threatened to "haul her off to jail," Melcher declared, they were "complete fabrication and totally unfounded."

The first time I heard the words, I gripped the arm of the couch, my limbs going cold.

"That liar!" Pete shook his forefinger at the TV. "I'm not lettin' him get away with this!"

By the third time we listened to Melcher lie, all four of us were more than incensed.

Someone from the Crenshaw family also appeared on each news show. First Clara's parents, then her sister, Paula, followed by her Aunt Gretchen. In one way or another they accused me of interfering in the investigation. "Delanie was my sister's good friend," Paula said. "We were all together at the shower just before this happened. I don't understand why she's saying these things."

Maybe because they were true. But who would believe that now?

The remaining pizza was growing cold on the coffee table as the last "Redbud Murder" news segment ended. None of us had eaten much, focused as we were on the screen. Nicole's eyes kept flicking to me, as if pleading reassurance. *What will happen to our home, now that you've gone and taken a stand against half the town?*

Pete muted the TV. For a moment we sat in silence, each of us stewing.

"Did you hear from Chief Melcher today?" Colleen asked.

"Not a word."

Nicole raised a shoulder. "He won't threaten you again. For all he knows someone would hear him next time."

Pete grunted. "Somebody already did."

My gaze fell to the floor. Melcher may not be overtly threatening me, but it was clear I'd now made a serious enemy. He would rejoice to see me brought down.

I closed my eyes and pictured him putting me in handcuffs …

My phone rang. I checked the screen. *Cheryl King*. Exhaustion swept over me, trailed by guilt. What had I done all day to help her son?

With a reluctant hand, I picked up the cell. "Hi, Cheryl."

"Delanie. Did you *see*?" She sounded terrified, desperate.

A rubber band pulled tight around my chest. "What?"

"My poor Billy's picture is plastered on national TV! Now everyone in the country thinks he's a murderer." Cheryl's voice broke in two.

No, no, no.

"And that interview you did yesterday with WTVQ? That was on there too, every word of it."

Dread flooded me. I buffed my forehead hard, trying to think. This couldn't be true, Billy's mom was just confused.

"Are you sure, Cheryl? Where did you see it?"

"On CNN!"

April 2004 — March 2008

CHAPTER 30

When the doorbell rang at her aunt and uncle's house, Laura ignored it. She'd been lying in bed, unable to gather the energy to do anything. Probably some salesman anyway.

The bell sounded again.

Laura sighed.

Someone started banging on the door. Hard.

Who in the world?

When it didn't stop, Laura pushed to her feet and trundled down the stairs.

She swung back the door—and found herself facing a woman in a black jacket and pants. Her straight black hair glossed to her shoulders, blunt cut to perfection. Flawless skin. Oval face and eyes dark enough to laser right through a person. Barely controlled rage contorted the woman's face.

"It's about time." The coral lips sneered. "You must be the famous Laura Denton."

Laura shrank back. There was only one person this could be.

"That's right, I'm Tina. The woman your father walked all over. Dragged through the mud, chewed up and spit out. And now—cut out of his will."

Laura tried to close the door.

Tina stuck her foot in the threshold. "Oh, no, you don't, Miss

Mommy-Killer. You're going to listen to what I have to say." She shoved her way into the foyer. Laura stumbled back.

With great satisfaction Tina closed the door. Laura looked at her with frightened eyes.

Tina raised a forefinger and pointed it at Laura. "You are *not* getting *one penny* of your father's money, got that? It's *mine*. I will fight you in court until the day I die. I will fight you until you've got no strength left. *If* you have any to begin with."

Anger burst in Laura's lungs. "That money's not yours! It came from my mother."

"Who you killed, remember? Cold-blooded murdered her to get that money, and now you're trying to get it again."

"I did not—"

"Oh, save your breath, Laura." Tina's eyes narrowed. "I know you did it, as much as you tried to convince your poor father otherwise. And the courts know. They'll *always* know. And guess what—you still can't inherit that money. It may be coming from your father now, but he got it from your mother. And by law you can't reap any rewards from your own crime."

Who did this woman think she was?

"Get out." Laura stalked around Tina and flung open the door.

Tina smiled—the most evil smile Laura had ever seen. "Oh, I'll leave, but that won't help you any." She stepped closer. "I'm a detective, remember? I can hound your life. I wouldn't do one tiny thing wrong if I were you. Because I'll be all over you."

Laura's teeth clenched. "Get *out*."

Tina moved into the doorway. "Leave town, Laura. Don't fight me on this. You'll be sorry. And in the end—you'll lose."

She threw Laura a final, taunting smile. "Have a good day."

Tina stepped out onto the porch. Laura slammed the door and locked it.

Ten days later Laura received formal paperwork from the courts. Tina was suing her for her father's estate.

CHAPTER 31

Laura tried to prepare herself emotionally to fight for her inheritance. With no money of her own in the meantime, she had to stay with her aunt and uncle. She wanted to pay for rent and food. Desperately she tried to find work, but no one would hire her. When filling out applications at first she left the lines asking about any felonies on her record blank. Only to be nearly hired—then summarily dismissed when the background checks came in. After that she told the truth, trying to explain she'd been wrongly convicted when asked for details. The looks on people's faces when they learned the nature of her "crime" were more than degrading. After slinking out of office after office, Laura gave up.

"When I win my case," she told her aunt and uncle, "I'll pay you back for all you've done for me."

"Don't worry about it." Uncle Ted patted her shoulder. "You've been through enough. We're glad to help."

They were good, good people. The only positive thing in her life as an outcast.

Laura found a lawyer, considered one of the best in cases regarding inheritance. Lou Traxton was in his sixties, gray-haired, thick-jowled and big-bellied. Intimidated by no one. In their first meeting, with Aunt Nicky by Laura's side, Traxton tried to answer her roiling questions about Tina Fulder's claim.

"How can she even *do* this?" Laura had begun the meeting with a notebook and pen in her lap for taking notes. She'd certainly learned how convoluted the law could be, and she didn't want to miss anything. But now she found no energy to record what her lawyer said. She could barely sit there without crying.

Laura shoved the notebook and pen into her aunt's hands.

Traxton leaned back in his swivel chair, fingers steepled. "A will contest is generally difficult to prevail on. The applicable law here is a part of the California probate code known as the 'slayer statute.' It states that a person who feloniously and intentionally kills the decedent is not entitled to any inheritance from that person. However, there's a loophole, and that's what we'll argue. The statute only bars a convicted murderer from inheriting *directly* from the victim. It doesn't address situations such as yours, in which the inheritance is indirect."

Aunt Nicky was scribbling furiously.

"So how can she claim this, with that loophole?" Laura spread her hands. "Especially when she wasn't even married to my dad when he died?"

"Well, she'll argue her side. She has standing to fight this new will because she was treated more favorably in a prior one. She has numerous causes to raise a challenge. In this case she's claiming your father was under 'undue influence' in changing his will."

"From who?" Laura already knew the answer.

"You. According to the claim, once your father started visiting you in jail, you persuaded him of your innocence—even though the evidence shows otherwise—and as a result, he changed his will and cheated her out of her money."

Laura leaned forward. "So *I'm* the bad guy here?"

"According to Tina Fulder Denton."

Laura winced. She couldn't stand to hear her own last name attached to that woman.

"Potentially she can also argue based on the 'clean hands'

doctrine, a different part of the Civil Code that prohibits a person from profiting by his or her own wrongdoing. The general public policy establishes the idea that one should not be unjustly enriched. Under this doctrine she could say it doesn't matter that your inheritance is indirect. You'd still be profiting from your crime."

"But I didn't *do* it!" Tears bit Laura's eyes.

Traxton sat forward, resting both elbows on his desk. His voice gentled. "Laura, according to the courts, you were convicted and are guilty. The only way your claims of innocence would ever matter would be if your verdict was overturned."

Which was never going to happen. Unless she could somehow discover the information about Weiner her father had taken to his death. And Laura didn't even know where to begin.

Her throat tightened. "So. She'll win, right? I'll lose. Again. What's the point of fighting?"

Traxton lifted a shoulder. "Don't be so sure about that. Fact is, your father wrote his will after you were convicted. After you'd served the majority of your sentence. That's a strong presumption in your favor. He purposely chose *you* to be his heir, despite your criminal record."

"But I 'influenced' him!" Laura's voice rose. "I cast some sort of magic spell and forced him to take out Tina's name and put mine in."

Traxton inclined his head. "See how stupid her argument sounds?"

Aunt Nicky patted Laura's leg. Laura looked away out the window. Tried to pull herself together.

"How long is all this going to take?" Her voice sounded toneless.

"Hard to say. Two years or more."

Laura's heart sank. *Two years.* After all her time in CYA. The crossing off of days, one by one. Did God expect her to wait forever for her life to begin?

And even if she won, what then?

Sitting in the plush chair in Lou Traxton's office, Laura looked

down the long corridor of her life and saw only one thing—the scarlet red brand of *Murderer*. No matter what she did, no matter how
much money she had, that would always be on her record. She would
spend the rest of her life trying to convince people she was innocent.
And who would believe her?

By the end of the meeting Laura could barely talk.

She spent the next two days in bed. When she did drag herself
up, it was only to stare mindlessly at TV. But what to watch? Channels were filled with either shows about crime or family comedies.
Neither of which she could stomach.

Weeks passed.

In time Laura pulled herself out of her lethargy. She had no
choice. And she started praying again, reaching out to the God she
so needed. Even if she couldn't feel Him sometimes, wasn't it enough
that she willed herself to believe He was there? But—what was she
supposed to do with herself? She had no money and no job. She
could go to school—if her aunt and uncle would cover the cost. "I'll
pay you back many times over when I win," she told them.

But what if she didn't?

"Laura." Aunt Nicky gave her a hug. "You know we'll help you.
And if you never can pay us back, that's okay."

In some ways, regardless of winning her case, she would never be
able to pay these people back for all the love they'd shown her.

Traxton put her parents' house on the market. Laura never could
bring herself to even walk through the door. She couldn't bear to see
what was once her home. Couldn't bear to see her room so perfectly
preserved from the life she once knew. The house sold for $2.6 mil-
lion. After realtors fees and closing costs, the remaining funds—over
$2.4 million—were held as part of the estate.

Laura ended up going to the community college in San Mateo,
starting with summer classes. It was a two-year college, one in which
she could fulfill all her general education requirements, then transfer
the credits to a four-year California university. Laura had no idea

what she wanted to major in, so getting the required classes out of the way suited her just fine. She loaded up her schedule, taking as many credits per semester as she could.

She had to take public transportation until she could finish a driver's education course (for her own piece of mind) and renew her long-expired license. That accomplished, Uncle Ted bought her an old car for a couple thousand dollars. "It's not much." He shrugged. "But it'll get you to class and back."

She could only hug him, tight-throated.

But paranoia struck as soon as Laura sat behind the wheel. What if Tina saw her, made some excuse to pull her over? Laura drove slowly, like some old person.

The year 2004 gave way to 2005. Laura had fallen into a mind-numbing routine of attending classes and studying. In her free time she cleaned the house and did the grocery shopping and errands for her aunt.

Laura made a few casual friends in college but in general remained aloof. If she became too close to anyone, she'd have to talk about her life. The last thing she wanted was for the other students—and teachers—to know about her record. Besides, she was older than most of the students, who were right out of high school.

In March she turned twenty-six. A full year out of CYA—and little to show for it. How would she ever lead a normal life? She longed to fall in love, get married. Have children. But what man would accept her?

The lawsuit dragged through the courts. And to make matters even worse, some reporter started following the case. Now and then an article about the "convicted killer" after her mother's inheritance would appear in the newspaper. Sometimes in class other students would look at Laura strangely, and she'd think, *They know, don't they.*

She stopped trying to be friends with anyone.

Occasionally there would be some meeting or hearing about the lawsuit. But Tina and her lawyer would always fight as hard as they could. "Why shouldn't I just let her have the money, God?" Laura wailed more than once to the heavens. But in reality, she still couldn't stand the thought of that woman getting her own mother's money. Such blatant unfairness would be the bitter icing on her already inedible cake.

In the spring of 2006 Laura, then twenty-seven, completed her classes at the community college and graduated with her AA. She had no plans of going on to a university, no plans for her life. The lawsuit against her still had not been settled. She remained penniless. She couldn't ask her aunt and uncle to continue fronting her education. And once again she fought depression. That last semester she'd barely been able to force herself to study.

Then one day soon after graduating, when she least expected it, Laura found herself face to face with Roger Weiner.

CHAPTER 32

Well, look who we have here."

The voice behind her was male. Not one she recognized. Laura turned from loading groceries into her car. The man stood tall, maybe 6'2". He had short brown hair and deep set eyes. A hard face. He wore a smug expression as he leaned casually against her car.

Laura took a step back.

He smiled, and it wasn't friendly. "You don't know who I am, do you?"

Laura looked around, searching for others in the parking lot.

"You *should* know. Your attorney spent enough time in the court-room trying to pin your mother's murder on me."

Laura's mouth creaked open, but no words would come.

"Yeah, that's right. Good ol' Roger. Let's tell everybody *he* did it."

Air shoved into Laura's lungs. "Wh-what do you want?"

He tilted his head. "To see what you looked like up close. Amaz-ing how a killer can look so normal."

Laura's nerves vibrated. She slammed the trunk of her car. "Get away from me."

"Hey, hey." Weiner straightened. "Don't get all bent out of shape. I'm nothing to be afraid of."

What? "Tell that to the woman you attacked in Arizona. Tell that to my *mother*." Laura choked on the last word.

"Come on now." Weiner crossed his arms. "What's the point in going on with that story? You've served your time, it's all done."

"*Why* did you kill her?" Tears bit Laura's eyes. She wanted to smash this man's face in. Tear out his heart.

"Last I heard, *you* did it."

Laura's fingers curled into fists. Weiner glanced at them and laughed. "What, you gonna hit me now? Attack me? Come on, take a shot. Get yourself arrested and thrown back in jail."

Laura went weak. Her body shook.

Weiner leaned in, his face close to hers. "Even if I did kill your mother, there's no use now trying to pin it on me. It's *over*, Laura. Move on."

Move on. How could she ever do that now, after looking into this man's eyes? Such evil there. This face, this voice were the last her mom had seen and heard.

This man was a *nurse*?

"Why are you here?" Clearly he was enjoying torturing her.

He shrugged. "I drove to the grocery store."

No way. This could not be coincidence. "You followed me."

"Don't flatter yourself. I came here and recognized you. That's all."

"Why are you back in the Bay Area?"

"What, I can't return to the land of my birth?" Weiner spread his arms. "I like it here."

Laura backed farther away. "Don't come near me again."

"Or you'll what? Call the police?"

For a moment Laura thought she might throw up. She clenched her mouth shut and stumbled toward the car door. Opened it and flung herself inside. Flicked down the locks. She fumbled for the car keys in her purse, hating herself for her own weakness. Here was the man she'd wanted to hunt down, the one responsible for ruining her life—and she was *running away*.

Weiner moved back from her car and watched, a smirk on his face.

Laura slammed the keys into the ignition and thrust on the engine. She surged her car forward and drove off, back ramrod straight.

Weiner lifted a hand in a mock goodbye.

The rest of that day Laura raged around her aunt and uncle's house. Nothing they could do proved of any comfort. Her uncle offered to call the police—but to report what? Weiner was right. Laura was the "guilty" one when it came to her mother's murder. No law enforcement would believe anything different. And Weiner hadn't so much as touched her.

The next day Laura barely left her bedroom. She hated Weiner. Hated Tina. Why didn't these people just leave her alone? Hadn't she been through enough? For two years after leaving CYA she'd fought for some semblance of a life. In two minutes it had been snatched from her. Laura found herself right back where she started—obsessing over Roger Weiner. Dreaming of how to bring him to justice.

When was her life ever going to be normal?

After a day of drowning in her misery, Laura pulled herself together. Maybe she was just too tired of being the victim. Maybe it was the prayer. Whatever the case, Laura felt a calming in her spirit. She had a future, even though she couldn't see it right now. She had to look forward. She would drive herself crazy looking back.

Whenever the court system finally got in gear and she won her case over Tina—*God please let that happen!*—Laura would rebuild her life. She'd move far away to some safe, small town where no one knew her background. Where she could start over.

The days slogged on … and still no word about her inheritance trial.

Laura's aunt and uncle continued to be so kind. But she knew they wanted their house back to themselves. Who could blame them for that?

Once more the wild dreams of bringing Weiner to justice faded. If there was any chance of them becoming a reality, Laura would fight for it. But she had nothing. No evidence to take to the prosecutor. And if she tried to contact Cantor now as her father had done, wouldn't Tina hear about it and further sandbag her case? The money was the only promise Laura had left. *That*, she could win. She didn't dare do anything now to sabotage her chances.

And so Laura waited. Again.

At last in late June Laura heard the news she'd been waiting for. The trial regarding her inheritance was set for the following month.

Once again she counted days.

CHAPTER 33

"Y ou ready?" Aunt Nicky squeezed Laura's arm. They stood outside the courtroom with her Uncle Ted. It was time for the three of them to go inside. Laura could hardly feel her body.

She managed a nod.

But how could she get through this? Laura could just imagine Tina's pointing finger, her righteous indignation at this "murderer" trying to inherit the money that was "rightfully hers."

"Don't worry," Laura's attorney whispered as she took the seat beside him. "If we don't prevail here, we'll appeal."

Sure. More time waiting, her life on hold. Only to attend another hearing and be dragged through the mud *again*.

Tina Fulder entered, looking almost dowdy. A plain gray dress, her hair pulled back. Little make-up. Like she was some poor, trampled-on librarian. Laura wanted to smack her. She could hardly stand being in the same room with the woman.

"*Don't* give her mean looks." Traxton kept his voice low.

Laura closed her eyes. *Breathe, just breathe …*

The probate judge, Nathan Lang, looked past retirement age. Heavily lined face, sparse hair. Small eyes that flicked over the courtroom as if recording every detail.

He hates me already.

The hearing was everything—and more—Laura had expected.

Tina on the stand, telling the court how her father *knew* she'd murdered her mother. How he'd mourned over that for years. Until he started visiting her in jail. Somehow Laura had managed to manipulate him—to the point of convincing him to seek a divorce and change his will. His behavior at home became "erratic" after that. Nothing Tina said or did would get through to him. They'd had a "happy home" until he began seeing Laura again. In his last days he was drinking too much—and that ended up costing his life.

The last accusation was a kick in the stomach. Laura was now responsible for the death of *both* her parents?

Then came her chance to testify. Laura felt like a robot taking the stand. In her mind, her main argument remained that she didn't kill her mother in the first place. How she wanted to tell them about Roger Weiner's guilt. That just a month ago he'd confronted Laura in a parking lot and practically admitted to killing her mother. But her attorney had warned her—say nothing about Weiner.

In the attorneys' final arguments it came down to one roiling issue: did the judge really want to see a young woman who'd murdered her mother now profit from that heinous crime?

The trial took four days. By the time it was done, Laura hardly cared what happened. She was shot down all over again. Worn and raw. No matter where she was—in the courtroom, in the restroom, in bed at night—she felt the untenable weight of her conviction. It was a blazing scarlet letter that would forever define her. Taint all she might accomplish in life.

The probate judge took a week to make his decision. When Laura and her supporters returned to hear the outcome, she felt beyond numb. She'd lost everything. God had somehow decided to deal her His worst hand. And now she would have to face more loss.

Laura was in for another shock. The judge ruled in her favor.

At first his words merely hit the armor around her heart and bounced off. Her aunt and uncle turned to her, joyous.

"You won, Laura." Traxton grinned. "You won."

Comprehension rocketed through her. She opened her mouth, but no words came.

Judge Lang leaned in Laura's direction and raised his forefinger. "Miss Denton, I have to say I found in your favor on the strict sense of the law. The plaintiff did not prove undue influence in this case. So I chose to uphold your father's will. But I can't say I'm happy about it. As a convicted murderer, you are indirectly inheriting from your own victim. I suggest you do *nothing* illegal from this day forward. Consider this your chance for a new beginning, one lived within the law."

The judge's words pummeled Laura. She was a *murderer*. Always would be.

Roger Weiner's face hovered in her mind.

Aunt Nicky put an arm around Laura as they left the courtroom. "Don't worry about what the judge said. What matters is—you won."

Laura could feel no victory.

Outside the courthouse, Tina stepped in front of Laura, eyes glittering. Aunt Nicky tried to turn Laura aside, but Tina pushed in front of them. "You'll never see a *dime* of that money. I promised you that before, and I promise you again. *Not. One Dime.*"

Laura could not sleep that night.

Tina filed an immediate appeal. Once again the inheritance was on hold. Laura and her attorneys went before the three-judge panel on the Court of Appeals. By then she was on medication for depression, fighting thoughts of suicide. What did life matter anymore? Even God had gone silent.

Her attorneys argued her side, and Tina-the-witch's lawyers argued hers. The panel of judges interrupted with questions. When the hearing was over, again Laura had to await the decision. Weeks later it finally came through written papers. The Court of Appeals had upheld Judge Lang. The inheritance would go to Laura.

The day they received the news, Laura's aunt and uncle wanted to take her out to dinner to celebrate. Laura couldn't do it. Surely as she sat in a restaurant, the neon sign of *Murderer* would still be seen by all. And once again Tina couldn't leave Laura alone. She called a few days later. "You'll pay for this." Her voice sounded like steel. "There's a God in heaven. There's a judgment day for murderers. And when that day comes, He will make you pay."

CHAPTER 34

On October 22, 2006, Laura received the balance of her inheritance after the attorney had been paid—over $6.7 million. The first thing she did with the money was to write a check to her aunt and uncle for half a million dollars. Aunt Nicky gasped when she saw the amount.

"This is way too much! We haven't spent anything near that on you."

Laura shook her head. "If anything, it's too little. You've been my only support. My only family. You deserve it."

She needed to start her life over—which meant leaving the area. Too many memories in San Mateo. And Tina was still there. But it would be so hard to leave Aunt Nicky and Uncle Ted. They had become her second parents.

Laura prayed a lot, asking for God's help, His strength. Slowly she fought through her depression and was able to take a little less daily medication. She bought a new car—a reliable Toyota Corolla. And a laptop computer. She spent hours online looking at towns all over the country. She needed to go *far* away. Far from Tina Fulder and the many haunting memories.

Laura worried about the majority of her money being tied up in stocks. She didn't want to be giving out her new address to a bunch of companies. Detective Tina could easily track Laura down if she had a mind to.

Before the end of the year Laura sold all the stocks and got into a cash position. She would take the tax hit and pay the IRS in 2007. She opened an offshore bank account, using her aunt and uncle's address, keeping half a million in the U.S., scattered in various accounts.

She'd decided on moving to the South, where people were known to be friendly.

In late February Laura loaded up her car, hugged her aunt and uncle a tearful goodbye, and set out across the country.

She landed in a suburb of Atlanta with about 20,000 residents. Not too big, not too small. Laura paid cash for a modest house (they were so cheap compared to California!). She filled the house with furniture. Found a church and tried to settle in. Met her neighbors, who were quick to welcome her to the neighborhood.

Laura didn't yet know what to do with her time. Transfer her college credits to a nearby university and finish school? But what to major in? Sometimes Laura could do nothing but sit around her house all day, still fighting the depression. She called her aunt and uncle often. But talking to them only increased her loneliness.

After four months in her new home, Laura received a letter sent from San Mateo. She held it in her hands, staring at the writing, knowing it had not come from Aunt Nicky. Heart beating sideways, Laura opened the envelope. The one piece of paper contained a few lines, no signature.

Think I wouldn't find you, Laura?
Remember what the judge said. Don't you dare do anything wrong. If you do, I just might have new reason to appeal for all that money you stole from me.

Laura dropped the paper. Her fingers burned.

For the next week she did not leave her house. When she finally ventured outside she spotted her next-door neighbor in his driveway and managed a wave. He threw her a hard look and turned away. A few days later she had a similar experience with her neighbor on the other side. Two days after that a note was left on her doorstep.

We know what you are. Leave this neighborhood now, before it's too late. Your kind doesn't belong here with our families.

Laura stumbled to the couch and collapsed upon it. Hugging herself and rocking, she cried and cried. Tina had done this. Even now that woman could ruin her life.

Laura had to move. She'd try to be more careful. Maybe next time Tina wouldn't find her. She searched for new towns and ended up in Tennessee. This time she chose to rent a home until she found the right one to buy. On the rental application form she left the questions about any criminal convictions blank. She moved in and once again tried to settle. Met neighbors, found a church. Eventually sold the house in Georgia.

After five months in her new place Laura received an eviction notice from her landlord. The terms of the lease were broken. Laura had a criminal record—a *conviction for murder*—that she'd failed to disclose. A detective in California had alerted the landlord to the truth.

Laura left the house with only her clothes and her car. No way to move the furniture without leaving a trail. Besides, where would she move it? Wherever she went, Tina would find her.

At the bank she withdrew ten thousand in cash.

She drove aimlessly through southern states, staying at hotels under fictitious names, paying for everything with cash. She called her aunt and uncle but never told them where she was. What if their phone was bugged? Laura couldn't trust a simple conversation anymore.

Christmas 2007 came and went. Laura was alone. Even God seemed to have abandoned her.

One evening in January 2008, in a hotel room in North Carolina,

Laura stared at a bottle of over-the-counter sleeping pills. She spilled them out on the bathroom counter. Counted them. She could do this. *Should* do this. It would be so easy to just go to sleep …

She swallowed the first two pills—and then it hit her. If she died without a will, with most of her inheritance still intact, Tina would likely end up with all of it. What a final, utter victory for her nemesis.

Laura flushed the rest of the pills down the toilet.

When she awoke the next morning after twelve hours' sleep, a new thought flamed in her mind. She *would* live. She *would* build a family someday. She *would not* let Tina or Roger Weiner win. What happened in the past would not define her future. She would embrace her aunt's wise words and truly, completely "move on."

There was only one way to do that. Laura Denton had to disappear. Somehow she had to forge a fresh identity, someone Tina couldn't find. Someone who did not carry the stigma of *Murderer*.

Laura lay on the hotel bed, thinking about Judge Lang's words: *"Do nothing illegal from this day forward."* His ruling in her favor seemed so tenuous, even though upheld by an appeals court. Tina could be right. If Laura was ever caught doing something illegal, maybe her inheritance could be taken away from her. Tina and some sleazy attorney would surely think of some loophole in the law. Some way to lay claim to the money.

Assuming a fake identity was certainly illegal. Especially when walking away from a felony.

For two more days Laura considered her choice. She wrote the pros and cons on separate sheets of paper. Read and reread them before tearing the lists into pieces.

How could she even think of doing this? She would be caught forever in a life of deceit. How could she ever pray then? How could she live as a Christian?

Still the pull of a new, fresh start would not go away. And in the end it came down to this: she could not have any kind of meaningful life as long as Tina Fulder could find her. And Laura so wanted to *live*.

But how to find a new identity? And how to take her money with her?

Laura scoured "how to disappear" websites on her computer. Read other sites about moving money offshore in a way it couldn't be traced. She took pages of notes, developed a plan. Somewhere along the way she pushed down all thoughts of living in deceit. This wasn't about lying. This was about self preservation.

Systematically Laura began to implement the steps of her plan.

She called her aunt and uncle, throat squeezed tight, and thanked them again for all they'd done for her. Laura knew she could not contact them again. That phone call hurt almost more than she could bear.

After that, Laura settled deep into herself, blocking out emotion, blocking out the past. Just. Looking. Forward.

On the Internet she found someone who would sell her a new identity, complete with a birth certificate and social security number. The man, identified only as "Bonn", assured her the social security number was from someone who was dead. Who'd been born the same year she had—and had a clean record.

Laura hoped she could believe him.

She chose the name Delanie Anne Miller and printed it on the birth certificate. Bonn filled out the rest and signed the document. Her social security number began with 372. "Which means you were born in Michigan," Bonn said. "Remember that."

She applied for a drivers license from North Carolina under her new name.

Now to take care of her money.

In a convoluted series of steps, Laura added Delanie Miller to her offshore account, using her aunt and uncle's address. Then she took off her real name. When she settled in her new life, she would change the address for Delanie. Then she would move all the money from that bank to another, severing all banking ties to her old name. As for her money still in the U.S. Laura broke it into smaller accounts, slowly withdrawing the funds under $5000 at a time. She ended up with a duffel bag full of bills. If anyone found it, they'd think she'd robbed a bank.

Laura sold her car for cash. Bought a new one using the name Delanie—again with cash.

After months of living in hotels, of cold calculation and the sheer will to *survive,* Laura's break with her old life was complete. By the summer of 2008 Laura Denton, murderer, no longer existed. She was now Delanie Anne Miller, with a clean record and a life to live. A family to build. Love to give. She would live quietly in some small town. Help others. Find happiness once again.

Laura's nightmares had finally ended. Delanie's dreams had just begun.

APRIL 2013

CHAPTER 35

Friday night after hearing my interview had hit CNN, I did not sleep. The next morning I couldn't get out of bed. I'd barely eaten since Clara's murder Wednesday evening. With little food and little rest, the blood in my veins felt like water. And I did not know how to get through the day.

Billy King's face hovered in my mind. I pictured him sitting in jail. Such a gentle young man. Little more than a kid, really. How could he ever stand up for himself against other inmates? Would authorities put him in a solitary cell for his own protection?

And he was facing *years* of this.

Meanwhile what was I doing? Certainly not pursuing justice for Billy and Clara. No, I was worrying about myself. Thoughts of calling off the engagement pounded me. I should tell Andy I couldn't go through with it right now. But he'd want to know why. And how long to wait? When would the threat of my being discovered end? At any time—a month from now, a year, five years—someone from my past could see me on a news video. If that someone was Tina, she wouldn't let it rest. She'd hunt me down just to ruin me.

I was supposed to be with Andy today. He'd called Friday night shortly after I talked to Cheryl. "Let's get out of town tomorrow, Del. Go for a long drive. Anything to leave Redbud for a while."

I didn't know how to say no, and I didn't want to say yes. I needed to get away, but the fear within me had risen like a rogue tide. Surely I would drown in it. My face was on *national TV*. Seemed like everyone in the California Bay Area watched CNN. And when one cable station picked up a local story, the others were sure to follow.

I told Andy about the CNN story, which he was not happy about. "Can you please call me back in the morning about going somewhere, Andy? I just can't think straight right now."

"Okay. Try to get some sleep."

Right.

True to his word, Andy called Saturday morning. I was still in bed. Not at all ready to talk to him. I tried to keep the anxiety from my tone as I answered.

"Good morning, lovely lady."

Andy's sweetness brought tears to my eyes. What was I doing to this man? "Hi."

"I just talked to my mother. She told me she called you last night. You didn't tell me."

Oh, great. "It ... wasn't a very pleasant conversation."

"So I gathered. I was appalled at what she said. I'm so sorry."

I clutched the bedcovers. "Guess she thought she was helping."

"She wasn't."

No.

Silence played out.

"I don't oppose my mother very often. Southern upbringing, you know. But I did ask her to please not talk to you that way again."

For Andy, that was a lot. He was very close to his mother. "Thank you."

Another pause.

"So, listen." Andy's tone lightened. "You ready to be picked up in an hour?"

I winced. "I'm still in bed."

"Well, get up. I'm taking you out of here. We'll pick a Kentucky back road and see where it goes. Stop at some little dive in a tiny town for lunch. We'll talk about you and me. Set a date for our wedding."

Our wedding. I couldn't think of it. How would I ever walk down the aisle, weighted as I was with all my lies?

"I'm not taking no for an answer, Del. You need to get out of town."

Andy was right. What would I do here if I didn't go? Hide when another reporter came to the door? Jump every time my cell rang? "Okay. I think I need more than an hour, though."

"Ninety minutes then. I'll see you at 9:45."

Somehow I managed to pull myself from bed. Dread hung over me, ran through me. My insides were on a constant low tremble. This could not continue. I would break apart.

In the shower I let hot water run over me, trying to clear my head. I told myself—unconvincingly—I would get through this. Some way. I'd lived through so much to get where I was today. Had fought long and hard. I couldn't give up now. People needed me. Andy. Billy. My "family" here.

I'd never seen justice done for my mother's death. How could I live with myself if I did not see it for Clara? And if I didn't pursue it, who would?

I pulled on jeans and a pair of blue flats. A blue top.

Colleen was in the kitchen, Nicole apparently still in bed. Pete was in his room as well. As I passed his room I could hear the drone of his voice recounting some story for his memoirs. Colleen and I had little to say to each other, deep in our thoughts. I forced down an egg and piece of toast. A mug of strong coffee pushed a little more resolve into me. I *had* to survive this, what other choice did I have?

Andy came to the door, dressed in jeans and a red Polo shirt. He looked wonderful. We walked outside to a beautiful, sunny day. It did not chase my sense of dread away. Andy opened my car door for me. I threw him a smile. "Where are we going?"

"Don't know yet. When we feel the urge to follow a road, we'll do it."

Andy pulled away from the curb and took side streets out of

Redbud, clearly avoiding downtown. Had he seen reporters there on his way over?

I didn't want to know the answer to that.

And then my dread became reality.

Andy asked me something, and to this day I can't remember what it was. Some casual question. One of those moments that should have been ordinary—were it not for the fact that it immediately preceded the rest of my very changed life.

From my purse my cell phone chimed. I picked it up to read the text, thinking it was Pete. Still, an inner voice said, *"Don't look at it now."* I hesitated, my finger hovering over the message icon. Then tapped it.

I did not recognize the number. But the message froze my limbs.

Look who I found. Laura Denton. --Tina.

CHAPTER 36

M y eyes glued to the words of the text. Inside me the shaking grew stronger. On some other plane I watched my finger turn off my phone. I placed the cell in my purse and eased back in my seat. A blizzard rammed my brain, my thoughts white and thick.

"Everything all right?" Andy glanced at me.

"Yes."

Was that my mouth moving?

My memory of the following hours is woven in haze.

Andy and I drove southeast on back roads, through Harrodsburg and Danville. Then east toward Richmond. We stopped in an old diner in Lancaster. The soup I ordered tasted like paste. I talked. I answered Andy's questions and even started conversations of my own. Somehow I held it together. But I felt outside my own body, as though I hovered at the ceiling and watched myself go through the motions.

At lunch I almost blurted out the truth. I simply could not exist like this any longer. Maybe Andy could help. Maybe he wouldn't hate me. But as always I held back. Andy was so honest. Had thought highly of me since the day we met. He would be devastated at my lies. Should I ruin his life just to ease my own mind? I'd lived under the burden of seeing no justice for my mother's death. Now it was slipping away for Clara. So much pain all around. I could not cause more. Not to the man who loved me so much.

We drove a wide circle, going north and through Lexington. There we stopped at a coffee shop for an afternoon latte. My mind was beyond numb. The cell phone weighted my purse like a time bomb. Had Tina sent more texts? What was she saying? What did she plan to do?

Lattes steaming, Andy and I perched at a high round table. He placed his hand over mine. "We should get married this summer. I don't want to wait too long. June maybe? July?"

So soon. The mere idea overwhelmed me. "I watched Clara and her mother plan her wedding. It takes months." And no doubt Andy's mother would want a huge, perfect ceremony. I cringed at the thought.

Andy rubbed my hand. "Yeah. And Redbud's not up for a big wedding this summer. Doesn't seem right. Maybe we should just go to Hawaii. Built-in honeymoon." He grinned.

The gesture couldn't cover his unspoken words. I knew he was worried about what townspeople would think. People who'd aligned against me because of my support for Billy would not forget what I had done. What if our wedding became a battleground for the much bigger issue of Billy's guilt—those who believed my cries of his innocence and so would attend the ceremony versus those who didn't?

I nodded. "Hawaii sounds like a great idea."

Maybe we could move there. Flee Redbud and never look back.

Until Tina found me again.

"Great!" Andy looked so happy. "Then there's little planning to do. So let's set it in June."

I winced. That would have been Clara's wedding month.

Andy gave me a sad smile. "I know. Not on that day. The following weekend, on the twenty-first."

And so, as terror encircled me, I set the date I'd dreamed of for years. The date that would begin my forever family.

Not until later would I realize June twenty-first is the longest day of the year.

Late Saturday afternoon I arrived home, exhausted and nerves humming. My cell was about to burn a hole through my purse. I headed straight for my room. Pete tried to ask me about my day, but I waved him off. "So sorry, I have a horrible headache. Need to go lie down."

I closed my door, threw my purse on the bed and yanked out the phone. For an eternal moment I held it in my sweaty hand. Part of me wanted to throw it off a cliff, never see what devastation lay inside.

With a wildly beating heart, I turned it on.

Five messages awaited me.

Been wondering where you went all these years, Laura. Then boom you're on TV. Major fail. Delanie Miller--real name Laura Denton, convicted in San Mateo, CA in 1995 of killing your mother.

Thirty minutes later: *Did you think I wouldn't find you? Delanie Miller--real name Laura Denton, convicted in San Mateo, CA in 1995 of killing your mother. Now the fun begins.*

One hour later: *You can't seem to stay away from murder, can you? Delanie Miller--real name Laura Denton, convicted in San Mateo, CA in 1995 of killing your mother.*

Next hour: *Don't think you can ignore me. Delanie Miller--real name Laura Denton, convicted in San Mateo, CA in 1995 of killing your mother. BTW, so sorry about Clara.*

And the next: *Your life as you know it is about to end. Delanie Miller--real name Laura Denton, convicted in San Mateo, CA in 1995 of killing your mother. Who's to blame for the death of Clara Crenshaw? YOU.*

Strangled noises bubbled up my throat. I stared at the last text. *I* was to blame for Clara's death? Did Tina really think I'd murdered Clara, just like I'd "killed" my own mother?

The cell phone slipped from my fingers. This was it. How Tina would destroy me and end up with all my mother's money. The fates, destiny, whatever you wanted to call it, had rammed together in her favor. She would call Police Chief Melcher, one cop to another, and tell him of my past. My conviction. How I was no doubt Clara's real killer.

Her accusation would sound so plausible. No matter that I had no motive to murder Clara. That I'd loved her and would never want to hurt her. Those truths hadn't helped me last time. Once again I'd "found" the body. Called 911. I'd made up the story about seeing a man in the Graysons' front yard. Just like I'd concocted the story about looking at dress catalogues for ten minutes on my front porch in California. My only point of conscience this time had been in trying to save innocent Billy. Who just happened to be in the neighborhood.

I fell on the bed and curled up on my side, trembling. My thoughts grayed and jumbled. For some time I couldn't focus on anything. Could only feel the jarring of my heart. Slowly, then, my brain began to grasp one pulsing question. What to do but sit and wait for Tina's inevitable move? I had no offense. I couldn't show anyone her texts, even if they turned threatening. Tina had been too clever to embed the truth of my past in every message.

From the floor, my cell phone chimed. The sound sent shock waves through me.

I curled in deeper, an arm over my face. My mind raced back to that first night in juvey eighteen years ago, just after my arrest. In one day the world had caved in around me. A black hole consumed my life for the next nine years.

Now the world was caving again.

This time, God, just kill me.

My phone lay silent. The rug around it seemed to crackle, pulling my torso over the edge of the bed, my fingers to the floor to pick it up.

I rolled onto my back, holding the cell in both hands. My lungs stopped moving.

Breathe, Laura, just breathe.

I hit the icon to read the message.

You'd better respond, Delanie Miller, aka Laura Denton, convicted in San Mateo, CA in 1995 of killing your mother.

The words blurred. I stared at the phone screen, wrenched by Tina's grip on me from three thousand miles away. Respond? What did she expect me to say?

I slammed the phone down on my bed. Stared at the ceiling. Picked up the phone again. Before I knew it my finger was tapping over the keys.

What do you want?

Within thirty seconds the cell rang. Tina's number. I stared at the digits, my veins freezing over.

After the third ring I answered. "What." My voice sounded defeated. Resigned. I hated that.

"Well, there's my girl."

Slowly, I sat up. "What do you want?"

"We need to talk in person."

"You expect me to come to *California*?"

"No need, dear Laura. I've made it easy for you. I'm in Redbud."

The walls of my bedroom closed in.

"Now here's what I want you to do."

Tina was here. *In my town.*

"You listening, Laura?"

"I … yes."

"On the west end of town there's a little out-of-the way place called Redbud Park. No one seems to use it. You know where I'm talking about?"

She could leave her work—just like that? And how did she get here so fast?

"*Laura.*"

"Yes. I know it."

"Good. There's a bench toward the back. Be there in one hour. We'll still have enough daylight. Come alone. Bring a laptop computer and your bank account statements and passwords."

I gripped the phone, my heart tumbling. She was going to drain me of all my money. I should have known.

"You got all that, Laura?"

"And what if I don't come?"

Tina laughed. "Then I make a phone call to your chief of police. Tell him who you really are. You wouldn't want that, now would you?"

I licked my lips. "You're telling me if I do everything you want, you'll leave me alone?"

"Of course." Such a sugar-coated answer. "Why would I want to make your life miserable?"

She was lying.

Or was she?

If Tina turned me in to Melcher after bribing me out of my money, I'd have no reason not to show him her texts. I could also show him my bank account activity as proof of what she'd done. She'd end up losing the money she'd just stolen from me.

Wouldn't she?

What was I not seeing?

"Laura." Tina's voice hardened. "I'm warning you—you'd better show up."

"I hear you."

"Good. Look forward to seeing you."

The line went dead.

CHAPTER 37

This was the last hour of the life I'd built.

After Tina's call, I slumped immobilized on my bed, mind fixed on that reality. I was the mouse, Tina the cat. Now I lay helpless in a trap—and there was absolutely nothing I could do.

Why had God allowed me the last few years of relative happiness, only to snatch everything away? Had I not been through enough?

It wasn't just the money. It was the fact that it came from my mother. The only thing I had left of her. Tina had already stripped away her jewelry. Far worse, I hadn't managed to see justice done for my mom's murder. Now I was going to allow her a second injustice. Everything her parents and grandparents had worked for would be taken from the family.

And I was to blame. I and my stupid, stupid choices.

Why had I ever thought I needed to assume a new identity? So what if Tina had hounded me wherever I moved? Maybe I would have had no friends, but at least the courts had awarded me my inheritance. She couldn't have taken that from me. Now I'd given her the perfect opportunity to take it all. No doubt she *would* turn me in to the police as soon as she got what she wanted, just for spite. She was a detective. She'd surely thought of many angles I couldn't see. Somehow she'd get away with my money.

Worse, I was going to lose Andy. My house. Pete, Colleen, and

Nicole. And I'd probably go to jail. Not just for my illegal identity. Maybe even for Clara's murder.

My head dropped into my hands. *God, I know I don't deserve it. But please help.*

Thoughts in my mind jumbled and rolled. I struggled to logic through details of Tina's call but could only dwell on the enormity of what was about to happen. The fallout of my own terrible decisions.

I could not believe it had come to this.

Then, out of the mental chaos a question resurfaced. How had Tina gotten here so soon after seeing the CNN news story?

At first I pushed the question away. What difference did it make? But the thought snagged in my brain. I tried to retrace the timeline but couldn't make it work.

Maybe the CNN story had run a time or two before Cheryl King saw it, and I just hadn't heard about it. Maybe … something. Had to be an explanation. Still …

I pushed off my bed. Started pacing the room. Another thought hit—so obvious once it rose through the fog. If I believed Tina would turn me in after forcing me to transfer her the money—why do it? The money was the only leverage I had.

Back and forth I paced, from my dresser on one side to bare wall on the other. I knew my mind was still too overwhelmed to think of everything. Surely I was missing key pieces of this puzzle. If only I had someone to talk to. But even now I could not admit my deceit to anyone.

When you live a lie for so long, it becomes a part of you. Like clothing first rough and scratchy, it eventually wears down, thins out. Sinks into your skin.

I checked the digital clock by my bed. Half an hour had passed. If I was going to meet Tina, I needed to start getting things together.

If.

I stopped my pacing. Sat back down on the bed. Gaze fixated on the carpet, I forced myself to think straight. I ran through various scenarios. Dared a few more prayers.

Time slipped away. With a jerk, I checked the clock again. Ten minutes left.

I knew what I had to do.

If I was going to lose everything, I'd at least go down fighting. The only way to do that was to meet with Tina face to face.

A strange feeling descended upon me, something akin to alert calmness. I rose and with purposeful movements gathered everything I needed.

Within minutes I was backing out of my garage.

CHAPTER 38

I took back streets across town toward the park where Tina awaited. Didn't want to go through downtown and risk being followed by reporters. Halfway to my destination, I was struck by an idea. A good sign. My mind was further clearing.

Pulling over to the curb, I made a phone call.

When I arrived at the park my nemesis was already there, seated on the bench. Same hard face and black, glossy hair. No one else was around. Some distance down the curb I spotted a white rental car. Had to be Tina's. I placed my phone in one of the inside pockets of the tote bag that held my computer and documents, and slid out of the driver's seat. Walked toward Tina, back straight.

"Laura Denton, how nice to see you again." The smile she gave me could have slit my throat.

I sat down beside her, placing the tote bag between my feet.

Tina glanced at it. "Looks like you brought what we need."

"Looks like it." My tone held a casual edge.

Tina's eyes shone. She shoved out her hand. "Let me see the bank statements."

My feet tightened around the bag. "How'd you get here from California so fast?"

"Give me the statements."

"Answer my question first."

"Let me *see* them." Her expression blackened.

"Fine. Want to salivate some more?" I leaned over and slipped the offshore bank statements from the bag—three in total. Handed them to her.

Tina grabbed them from me, her eyes flicking over each page. "Hah!" She slapped the papers down on her thighs. "There's still *millions* in here!"

My shoulder lifted. "I've been frugal."

Tina leaned back and studied me. For a moment I saw doubt flash in her eyes. Why was I not cowering before her?

Her lip curled. "Fire up the computer, Laura."

"I didn't kill my mother."

She rolled her eyes. "I am not going there."

"I didn't kill her."

"Good for you. Turn on the computer."

I made no move. Tina bent over toward the tote bag. I elbowed her away and pulled out the laptop. Set it on the bench between us.

Tina yanked open the cover and smacked the power button.

I watched the screen boot up. "You'll need the password."

"What is it?"

I picked up the computer and placed it on my lap. "On the way here I made a phone call."

Tina's jaw flexed. "Put in the password!"

How I enjoyed her desperation.

"I called the San Mateo Police Station. You know, where you used to be a detective?"

She shot me a dark look.

"Apparently you don't work there anymore. They wouldn't tell me why you left—or where you'd gone. Said they couldn't give out that information." I paused, deliberating whether to throw out some bait. "You know, the evasiveness you hear from an employer when someone's been fired?"

Tina's eyes narrowed—and I knew I'd hit home.

She tilted her head. "I can call this meeting off right now. Get in my car and drive to the police station."

"Go right ahead. Of course, then you won't get a penny of that money." I gestured toward the bank statements.

She smirked. "Think so? I know for a fact your name change can't be legal. Not with a felony on your record. Remember what the judge told you—the one who didn't even like his own decision? Keep your nose clean—or you could lose it all."

I flexed my shoulders. "Maybe. Even so, you'd have to fight for it, and that would take years in the courts. Meanwhile, seems you're out of a job."

"Oh, don't you think you know everything. Listen to me, *Laura*, you have no power here. Your life is in my hands."

Fear shot through me. I forced myself to return her stare. "*How* did you get here so soon?"

Her face crinkled in frustration. "What's it to you?"

"I think you lied to me."

"I don't care what you think."

"Why should I let you bribe me out of all my mother's inheritance when I can't believe you'll keep your end of the bargain?"

"I told you I'm not out to ruin you, Laura."

"Really? Then why did you track me down in Georgia? You had to have used resources at the San Mateo Police Station to do that. Did your boss know what you were doing? I was trying to build a new life. You hounded and harassed me just to tell my neighbors about my past."

Tina raised her eyebrows. "Oh, you mean tell them you *killed* your mother? Maybe they'd want to know."

"I *didn't* kill her."

Tina looked away and sighed. "I'm through with this." She threw the bank statements on the ground and stood. "Go home, Laura. Wait for the police to show up at your door. Once Melcher hears who you really are, what you've done, he'll look at you in a whole new light. In fact, you just might become his next best suspect for Clara's murder."

There it was. Her ultimate threat. My heart ground into a hard beat. "You know I didn't kill Clara."

She shrugged. "You killed your mother, why not kill your friend?"

"I did not kill my mother."

Tina heaved another sigh. "Round and round we go. And I gave you the perfect opportunity. Shame you're too stupid to take it. Goodbye, Laura." She turned and walked away.

I watched her go, pulse pounding. Counting her steps as I feigned indifference. *Turn around, Tina. Turn around!*

She didn't.

I broke into a sweat. This game of chicken was too much to take. Even if she did come back, what would I say? I still wasn't sure what I was doing. How to bargain with someone I could never trust?

Tina had covered half the distance to her rental car. My fingers curled into my palms. I could not let her drive away. So what if she took all the money? If there was the slightest chance she wouldn't call the police on me, it would be worth it. I wouldn't lose Andy. My life.

My lips parted to call her back. But before the words could form—Tina turned around.

I closed my mouth. Uncurled my fists. *Breathe, Laura, breathe.*

For a moment Tina merely glared. Despite the distance, I could feel her fury. It seethed across the park and over me, a miasma of the embittered years she'd spent suing me, then hunting me down.

As if a momentous decision overtook her, she stalked toward me.

Casually, I moved my computer back onto the bench. Leaned over to pick up the bank statements and slid them into my tote bag.

Hands folded in my lap, I watched Tina stomp across the distance between us. Surely she would see the pump of my heart through my blue top.

She carved to a stop before me, arms folded and legs apart. A cop stance. "You're going to wish you'd done this the easy way, Laura Denton."

As if it could get any harder.

"But you know"—Tina jabbed a finger toward me—"before I even came to Redbud something told me you'd play it stupid. And I was not about to let you keep my money from me. Not after all these years." A gluttonous smile spread across Tina's face. She tilted back her head and regarded me through narrowed eyes. "So I devised a plan. Just in case."

Fear trickled through me. Dealing with this woman was like trying to subdue a rabid dog.

Tina unfolded her arms and scratched beneath her chin. "You wondered how I got here so fast? You're right—I've *been* here. For over a week."

A *week*? A chill ran through me.

"Took me five long years of tracking you through bank records. But I finally found you."

Get a life, Tina. This woman was nothing short of crazy. "Bet it got you fired, too. You use police resources to do that?"

Smugness stretched Tina's mouth. "For the past week I watched you, Miss Laura. Watched the town. Learned things. Like the fact that you had a sweet little friend, Clara, who was about to have a wedding shower."

A hand clamped over my lungs and fisted.

"Seems everybody loved Clara. The town sweetheart. And then there was that lanky, gawky boy-man who had a crush on her. He and I had such nice talks."

Cold realization dawned. "You told him your name was Susan." Incredulity coated my tone.

But Billy had said the woman was blonde.

Tina's face creased in feigned disappointment. "Oh, did he tell on me? After I warned him not to."

"Why did you bother Billy?" My voice rose. "He's never done a thing to you."

Tina regarded me with supreme satisfaction. "Billy needed to be at a certain place on a certain night. I made sure he was there."

I frowned. Deep inside me the truth was beginning to gel. But I couldn't accept it. "On Brewer, you mean? When Clara was killed?"

Tina gazed around the park, as though remembering a fond event.

"Why?" My tone sharpened.

Tina's eyes locked onto mine. "One thing I couldn't have planned? *You* finding Clara's body. That was pure serendipity. A gift from the gods."

The vise in my chest tightened. One by one my limbs turned to lead. What was she *saying*? "You knew Clara was going to die?"

Tina spread her hands.

No. Impossible. Nothing she said could have made Billy do this. "You were there that night?" The words croaked. Suddenly I thought of the height of the shadowed figure I'd seen in the Graysons' yard. "Was it *you* standing by that bush?"

Another wicked smile from Tina.

But this made no sense. "Billy would not kill Clara, no matter what you told him."

Tina's eyebrows rose. She laughed. "Is *that* what you're thinking?"

I gawked at her, my mouth dry. If Billy didn't …

Understanding thudded in my chest. I drew my head back, sickness spreading to the core of me. "Are you telling me *you* killed Clara?" I pushed to my feet, almost tripping over the tote bag. "What are you *telling* me? *Why*?"

Tina shoved her forefinger in my face. "Don't act so sacrosanct, Miss Innocent. Don't you dare. This is *your* fault. If you hadn't run here and lied to the whole town about who you are, she wouldn't have had to die."

My jaw flapped. Words could not form in my throat.

"See what I mean, doing it the hard way? Now, thanks to your idiocy, Laura Denton, you get to live with the knowledge of what you caused. You'll forever have to look these people in the eye and *know*. And don't think you can run away from me to some other town. Because I'll find you again. And someone else close to you will die. Get it?" Tina's eyes turned black. "That money is mine. It's always been mine. And *I will not let you keep it from me another day!*"

My ankles shook. I felt myself sway. Tina was a *murderer*. As evil as she'd been, I'd never have thought it. Even now I couldn't believe it. For mere money, Clara had *died*?

"You—" My legs gave out. I sat down hard on the bench. Bent over, hands across my waist. "I'll never let you get away with this." The words squeezed from me.

Tina laughed. "Of course you will. Because you're going to transfer all the money in those accounts to me right now. Then I will walk out of here and never bother you again. You can keep your fake name and lying life. You can marry that man of yours. Sounds like he's got plenty of money anyway; you won't even miss what you've given me. You can have your happy ending, Delanie Miller."

Happy ending? "Billy's in jail for what *you* did!"

"Shame. No doubt he'll be convicted. We've seen it happen before, haven't we. But all the better for you this time. Case closed, life goes on. Mrs. Delanie Bradshaw, Redbud socialite. Has a nice ring, wouldn't you say?"

"No." My stomach roiled. "I … can't."

"Laura." Tina bent over me. "You have no choice."

This couldn't be true. If Tina committed this crime, she was right—*I* was to blame for Clara's death. And for Billy's arrest. Tina may have orchestrated it. But my lies, my wrong decisions had brought this evil woman here. How could I live with that?

I jerked up straight. "I *do* have a choice. I can go tell the police right now." I grabbed my laptop and started to rise.

Tina shoved me back down. "Tell them what? They'll never believe you, Laura. You have absolutely no proof. Especially after I tell Melcher who you are. Like I said, he may turn to *you* for the murder. Then you'll lose absolutely everything—for no reason. And I'll still go free."

The trembling had risen from my legs to my arms, my neck. I

thunked my laptop onto the bench. Stared at Tina. How could she *be* this way? How could anyone do this? I slumped back against the bench, my gaze raking the ground as if an answer lay hidden there. Surely God would show me something. Anything.

"We've seen it happen before, haven't we."

Tina's words pierced through my thoughts. I stilled, eyes fixed on a thick weed in the grass. The chaos in my brain turned milky. Trickled away.

"We've seen it happen before ..."

The comment bounced around in my head. Gathered momentum.

Memories flashed then, errant bits and phrases spotlighted into a new, horrifying picture:

My father in obvious misery the last time I'd spoken with him on the phone in CYA: *"I'll have to tell you everything."*

My attorney questioning him on the stand: *"When did you meet Miss Fulder?"* *"Two months after my wife was killed."* My father had looked down when he answered—because he was lying?

I'd been framed for my mother's death—by someone who obviously understood crime scene evidence.

My father driving around in his new red Porsche after my mother's inheritance—a car bound to attract the attention of a money-hungry woman.

Tina's constant rant, *"That money's mine. It's always been mine."*

My father's strange car accident, soon after our phone conversation.

No. *No.*

My insides deadened. I could not feel my heartbeat.

Slowly I raised my head. Tina's face swam before me. "You killed my mother."

Tina took a step back. Then drew up to her full height, chin high. "Think so?"

I wrapped my fingers around the edge of the bench. If I didn't steady myself I would slip to the ground, melt away like wax. "You made it look like me. You wanted my father to yourself. You wanted his money."

Tina's mouth twisted. "I *earned* that money. Then *you* go and take it away from me."

Acids drained down my throat. The world darkened. I gripped the bench harder and sucked in air. "My dad finally realized it was you, didn't he. He confronted you with it."

Tina smirked. "He was drinking too much those days."

Little wonder, once he put it all together. I couldn't begin to imagine my father's horror. "*You* sent his car over the edge of that cliff." A sob clogged my throat. "Didn't you!"

Tina placed two fingers against her jaw. She moved her head from side to side in an overt display of pity. "Laura. Dear." She sat beside me on the bench. I reared away from her. "Now you see the problem? There is nothing you can do about any of this. So why try? *No one* will believe you. The D.A. in California will always think you killed your mother. And Melcher's set on Billy. Leave it alone. Live your life."

Tears ran down my face. "When did you start seeing my father? Tell me that. *When?*"

Tina shrugged. "So he had an affair on your mother. Doesn't mean he didn't love her."

"*I love you. I loved your mother.*" My father's words in our last phone call.

"Now." Tina picked up my computer and set it back on my lap. "See there, it's gone to sleep. Wake it up. Time to finally let me have what I deserve." She curled one side of her mouth. "Maybe you'll send me an invitation to your wedding."

I swallowed hard. "You won't get away with this. You *can't.*"

She raised an eyebrow. "I already have."

"I'll stop it. Now."

"You'll stop nothing. You'll only lose everything you love. Andy. Your friends. Your freedom. At the very least you'll go to jail for assuming a false identity. But believe me, I'll push Melcher hard to pursue you for Clara's murder. Once the town finds out about you, you really think they won't find you guilty? Leave it *alone*."

My head shook. "No. I couldn't live with myself."

Tina laughed. "That won't change either way. Would you rather feel lousy about yourself as Mrs. Bradshaw—or in jail for the rest of your life?"

The thought of returning to jail, confined, cut off, again branded a murderer … I couldn't bear it.

Neither could I bear it for innocent Billy.

"Why didn't you kill *me*, Tina?" I bit off the words. At that moment I wished she had a gun. Just shoot me in the head. Finish it. "Why like this?"

She frowned, as though disappointed in me. "Too suspicious a trail, don't you think, when I'd suddenly "find" you and petition to be awarded the money?" Her face hardened. "Besides, you suffer far more this way."

Through tears I stared at the woman who had wrecked my life. I felt empty. Dead. Yes, I would suffer. Lose everything. But I had made enough bad decisions for one lifetime. What freedom had I gained, trapped by lies?

I closed the lid of my computer.

"What are you doing?" Tina grabbed my arm.

I shook her off. Slid the laptop into my tote bag and stood. Picked up the bag. Every movement felt precise. Weighted. "Claiming back my life." On one heel I turned and walked away.

"No!" I could hear Tina leap to her feet. "You're not going anywhere!"

I kept walking.

"Laura!"

My feet moved me. Away from my old life. Into my new one.

"*Laura!*"

Footsteps ran from behind. An arm whirled me around. "This won't work. And in the end I'll still get the money."

I gazed at her long and hard. Forcing her to see the resolve in my eyes. "Pity it'll take so many years. Wonder what you'll live on till then."

She grabbed for the tote bag. "Give it to me. I'll do it myself!"

I shoved the bag behind me. "The bank passwords aren't in there, Tina. They're in my head. And nothing you do, *nothing*, will make me give them to you now."

Chin up, I turned again and left Tina Fulder hurling curses at my back.

CHAPTER 39

From the park I headed straight toward Andy's house. Darkness covered my mind. There were so many realizations to grasp that I could handle none of them. I only drove, hands tight on the wheel, muscles clenched.

At Andy's house I picked up the tote bag. I did not want to leave its contents in my car. My legs felt like lead as I trudged up the sidewalk. Before I could ring the bell, he appeared at the door, concern on his face.

"What's happened?" He reached for me.

I fell against his chest.

He held me up, pulling me across the threshold. I started to cry. His touch, the feel of him—all would be gone. Andy took the tote bag from my hand and led me to his couch. We sank down on it. He put the bag on the floor.

I leaned against him and sobbed. By the time I quieted, my head pounded and my stomach cramped.

An odd resignation settled over me.

For my mom and dad. For Clara. For Billy.

"Andy, I'm so sorry." I pulled off my engagement ring and laid it on the coffee table.

He gaped at me.

I took both his hands in mine. Tried to speak twice before any more words would come. "I love you. So much that I didn't know how to tell you the truth. The more we fell in love, the more I was afraid to tell you."

Andy's eyes started to glisten.

"Now you need to know the truth first. You deserve that. Then I have to go to Chief Melcher." I took a deep breath and spoke the words that had so weighted me for the last five years. "My real name is not Delanie Miller. I was not born in Michigan, and my parents did not die together in a car accident when I was young." I swallowed. "My name is Laura Denton. I was born in California. When I was sixteen, I came home from school one day and found my mother murdered ..."

Once I began, it all tumbled out. My arrest. My trial and conviction. Losing my dad. Reuniting with him again in CYA only to lose him forever. Tina. The inheritance and lawsuit. My terrible decision to flee my tainted past.

Andy did not let go of me the entire time I spoke. He only held my hands tighter.

"Now Tina's found me. She's here in Redbud, trying to bribe me out of the money." My throat closed up. "Andy, she killed Clara. Because of *me*. And she killed my mother and father."

"*What*?" Andy drew back, unable to take it all in. When he could find his voice he pounded me for details, struggling to understand. How had this happened? How could it be? Was I *sure*? He got up and paced, running his hands through his hair. I knew how he felt. My boldfaced lies. The horrible truth about my parents. And the awful consequences I'd face in Redbud. It was too much to assimilate.

What to do when your world has scudded off its axis?

He sat down again beside me. His face looked hollow. "What can we take to the police?"

We.

I stared at him, not sure I'd heard right. I thought my head would split in two. My eyes moved from his face to the engagement ring, still on the table. Andy picked it up. "Why did you take it off, Del—?" He looked away, forehead creased. "I don't even know what to call you now."

My lips pressed together. I couldn't cry anymore. "You can't want me after this."

Andy opened his mouth. Closed it. He picked up my left hand and slid the ring back on my finger. Then he held me tightly. I could feel him shaking.

There was so much more to say. I knew, after he'd had time to think about all I'd done, how many times I'd lied to him, he might well change his mind. For now, we had other things to do.

Together we stood.

"I'll call Melcher. Let him know we're coming." Andy's voice sounded rough. In this, he could not protect me. I couldn't bear to see the stunned look in his eyes.

Before leaving the house we discussed the strategy we'd take with the chief of police. Readied our evidence. Andy's expression fell into one of grief-stricken but focused determination. "All right. Let's go."

We drove to the station in silence.

A not-so-friendly-looking Melcher led us to the back room where he'd first questioned me three nights and a lifetime ago. I carried my tote bag. My cell was still inside—with Tina's texts.

In the room, Melcher closed the door. "All right. What is it?"

I set my bag on the table. "Before I tell you the whole story, I'd like you to listen to something."

From an inside pocket of the tote bag, I pulled Pete's small voice-activated tape recorder. Clicked the *play* button.

"Laura Denton, how nice to see you again." Tina Fulder's sarcastic voice filled the room.

May 2014

CHAPTER 40

GUILTY IN CRENSHAW CASE

The Friday morning headline blared up at me from a sun-drenched sidewalk. I swept up the Lexington newspaper and returned to the house. My ankles trembled as I climbed the four steps to our wide front porch. I'd been in court to hear the verdict, of course. One of the most emotional moments of my life. Last night I had barely slept. Now, just seeing the word "guilty" in bold black letters rushed it all back.

In truth, over a year after Clara's death, my nerves were still easily frazzled.

"Pregnancy can do that," Andy's mother had informed me. "Once you're over the three-month mark, you'll feel better."

As if pregnancy should be the only reason. I was trying to forge a relationship with my mother-in-law. But so much of me she would never understand.

I entered the kitchen, smelling Andy's eggs and bacon. Made me queasy. I laid the paper before him on the kitchen table, my throat tight.

He read the headline and gave me a grim nod. "And she's not through yet. Next will be the California courts."

Tina would eventually be extradited to undergo two trials there— one for the murder of my mother and one for my father. She might even face the death penalty. I would attend those trials, staying with my wonderful Aunt Nicky and Uncle Ted. They'd already promised to watch our child while I was in court.

Andy studied my face. "You okay?" He reached for my hand. "It's over, Laura. She got what she deserved. I know you still have the trials for your parents, and your own situation. But at least this part is done. Allow yourself to rest in that."

"You're right." I tried to smile. How I wanted to rest and enjoy the life God had given me. A loving husband, a baby on the way. Everything I'd dreamed of. But guilt can be overpowering, an eclipse of the most brilliant sun. I knew God had forgiven me for the decisions that led to Clara's death. Now He would have to help me forgive myself.

As for some in Redbud, they had made it clear I would forever be blamed. The town was no longer a haven for me. Andy and I had chosen to settle in Lexington.

I squeezed my husband's fingers, then moved away to make a cup of tea. Coffee sat hard on my stomach these days.

My husband took a bite of his breakfast. "You're meeting with Wanning today at two, right? I'll be there."

"You don't have to come."

"I want to. Gotta keep that lawyer on his toes."

The process to overturn my own conviction was dragging through the California legal system. It would happen—a necessity before Tina could be tried for my mother's murder—but the hearings and filings seemed endless. For the innocent, justice turns slowly.

I threw the wet teabag in the compacter, struck for the millionth time at the irony I'd created. Even when my conviction was finally overturned, I would still have a felony on my record—one for which I alone was to blame. False Personation. I'd pleaded guilty and with the help of crack attorney Wanning had been given only probation. Better that than one to five years in the penitentiary.

At the table I took a drink of hot tea and shivered.

"Want to read this?" Andy pushed the newspaper toward me.

My eyes grazed the copy. By now I knew every minute detail of the case. My testimony—and the tape recording—had been key for the guilty verdict. I'd spent days on the stand. Tina's defense attorney had taken every opportunity to remind the jury I was a convicted killer and could not be believed. Cutting accusations, but a lame argument in the face of Tina's own words. Even though she hadn't explicitly admitted to the three murders on tape, her meaning had been more than clear.

Other evidence had also helped convict Tina. Her plane ticket to Kentucky. Her firing from the San Mateo police due to her "erratic" behavior. The phone texts to me. A blonde wig in Tina's hotel room, recognized by Billy King as the hair of "Susan."

Poor Billy had been terrified on the stand. He must have gone through a half dozen glasses of water. Shame-faced, he told of "Susan's" befriending him. Her whispered words of Clara Crenshaw's secret love for him. How Clara wanted to meet Billy on Brewer Street after her wedding shower. "Susan's" urgent call to Billy that fateful night after he got off work: "Come on foot—now."

Tina's plan to frame him for the crime had been so devious. So precise.

As for the details of my parents' murders, the California prosecutor would have to piece together a scenario of each and convince the juries. Once again, Tina would never admit her guilt.

Andy gestured with his chin toward the paper. "Does it say when the sentencing will be?"

"In a few weeks."

Tina would likely receive life behind bars.

I took another sip of tea. "After the meeting with Wanning today I'm going to visit Pete. Maybe stay until Colleen and Nicole get home."

The house where my old "family" lived still belonged to me. I'd promised Pete, Colleen, and Nicole they could live there as long as they wanted. They just had to maintain the place.

"You sure you're up to that?"

"I want to see them." Especially Pete, who had been my stoutest supporter. To this day he still called me Del-Belle.

"I know. It's just … Redbud."

I rubbed at a spot on the table. Andy had chosen me over his beloved hometown and the wishes of his parents. The thought made me want to cry.

My husband finished his breakfast and rose. "Thanks. I need to get to the office." He hugged me hard before he left.

I cleaned the dishes and wiped down the granite counters of my beautiful kitchen. Rewarmed my cup of tea in the microwave. From an end cabinet I pulled my Bible and sat back down at the table. Before my daily reading I prayed aloud the memorized verses from Psalm 25 I had learned to cling to in the past year.

"'Show me your ways, Lord, teach me your paths. Guide me in your truth and teach me, for you are God my Savior, and my hope is in you all day long. Remember, Lord, your great mercy and love, for they are from of old. Do not remember the sins of my youth and my rebellious ways. According to your love remember me.' Amen."

I opened my Bible and began to read.

In the end comes the beginning.

MY THANKS TO:

Attorney Rebecca Lee Matthias, for patiently answering my barrage of questions relating to California laws of inheritance. I could not have written the details of Laura's legal battle over her mother's estate without your help.

-- and --

Don Bechtold, for regaling me with stories from your thirty-four-year career as a locomotive engineer. Your experiences made my character Pete a very interesting fellow.